Music of the Unicorn

Gloria Conly

To Joe,
Without you there would be no book.
My love,
Glo

Acknowledgments

There is no way to thank everyone. If you know me then you are a part of this book. Woven into my words is something from each writing group, each reader, all my friends from all the years. Somewhere is an echo of each and every one of you.

To the horses I have spent my life with, the wise mares, the playful geldings, and the strong stallions, you are the dream and the teachers. After fifty years of living with you and learning from you, I still do not have the words to express truly what you are.

Music of the Unicorn

CHAPTER 1

Ellie's heart was thumping against her chest; her hands were moist inside her gloves. She was sitting on a large, well-muscled red gelding, named George. They were waiting their turn to enter the jumping arena. It was just a lesson but she wanted to have a good round.

Just a practice round, nothing to worry about, just breathe, her instructor's voice played in her head. It helped to steady her. She needed to focus on George, the horse she was riding. Instead, she had been thinking of the mare that appeared in those recurrent dreams she had been having. She brought herself back to the present and put her attention on the girl in the arena.

Nancy was just turning to the last fences, the combination, under the watchful eye of Jackie Long, the instructor and owner of Whispering Tree Farm. Ellie watched as the horse took the first fence effortlessly and went easily to the second fence, jumping it beautifully. "Okay, George, did you see that? That's what we're going to do." George flicked an ear in response, and Ellie reached down and patted his neck, taking a deep breath. If she completed this course of jumps in good form, Jackie had

1

told her, she could take George to the horse show in a couple of weeks. Ellie wanted to go to that horse show.

Nancy and her Thoroughbred mare, Kiss Me, cantered to a stop in front of Jackie who sat in a covered judge's stand. Jackie gave her a few instructions, and she nodded her head in assent. Then a smiling Nancy left the ring, waving a high five to Ellie for luck.

Ellie rode in at the trot, made a circle, took a deep breath and picked up the canter. She settled her seat deep and did a lead change right in the center of her figure of eight pattern. George was a gentle soul, always willing. *Okay, George, we're on*, she thought. She tightened her hands on the reins and headed for the first fence. She put George in a perfect position right toward the middle of the jump, and started counting her strides. "One, two—and suddenly the nerves were gone and it was just another lesson. She was doing what she knew how to do. She checked her body position, settled herself deep in the saddle and they took the first fence. She came down easily, remembered to breathe and then it was routine. All the practice and her two years of training were there in her muscles and she was riding without a conscious thought. It was a wonderful feeling. She was floating through the course in perfect harmony, with the horse under her.

With a radiant smile, Ellie pulled George to a stop in front of Jackie. She jumped down from his 16-hand height and patted his shining chestnut coat. Then she unclasped her helmet, letting her blonde hair blow around her face. She was a petite girl dwarfed by the handsome red horse. She had completed the course of fences, with one fence being a 3'6" wall jump. She knew that Jackie would think that she was ready for the show.

"Jackie, it was a good round, wasn't it? I felt together up there. I can go, can't I?" Ellie was still hesitant even though she knew she had a good round.

Jackie smiled back at her, "It was very good. I think you are definitely ready for the show coming up. You'll have to get your mother to sign a permission form. She should call me so that I can make the arrangements. Okay?" Jackie said.

Ellie frowned; her Mom could be difficult when it came to her involvement with horses and all the time Ellie spent at the farm. Thinking of her mother, Anne, took the smile off her face. Home and mother were not the same since the big 'D'.

"Right, I think that she'll be okay with it," she said, knowing it was not going to be easy to convince her Mom about the horse show. There was a chance that Anne would think of something to keep her from going.

As Ellie led George out of the jumping arena, Mary was coming in on the large pinto pony named Harlequin. "I saw part of your lesson. You guys looked together out there. Did she say yes?

Mary Johansen was Ellie's best friend. They went to the same school and did everything together. "Yes, she said yes. Now all I have to do is get Mom to agree. The lesson was easy. Now comes the hard work," Ellie said with a shrug. "Now, it's all up to Mom."

She decided to watch as Mary, rode the intermediate course. Mary looked good riding the fat Harlequin. He was patient and colorful with his brown and white spots, black tail flying. All the students loved him.

Jackie Long was a fine instructor, and both girls loved coming out for lessons. Twice a week their mothers took turns bringing them. Today it was Mary's Mom, Triana, who would be picking them up.

Back at the barn, she gave George a good grooming and put him in his stall, talking to him quietly. She began to tell him about her dream from the night before. She had once again dreamed of the red mare.

"You'd like her, George. She's so beautiful, not as big as you are, but quick and bold. Last night in my dream, we were flying around the meadow. I've never felt so free. She let me ride her, with no saddle, no bridle. What a feeling that was, and

I wasn't afraid of anything, but afterward—afterward, well, this sadness came over me. She's lonely, I think." As she spoke, an image formed of the dream mare in her head. She leaned into the big horse. The dreams always made her feel a bit sad and empty. They were so intense and seemed so real. "I'll not think about that now. I'm going to get to show you. You're the best." She gave him a hug. George rumbled a deep nicker that sounded like an 'uh huh'. It made Ellie laugh, and her sadness went away.

Ellie went over to help Mary with Harlequin. She and Mary chatted away about their rides. They were laughing when Triana picked them up.

Triana dropped her at her apartment complex's outer door. Then watched from the car as she opened the outer door with a key and went in, and then they drove away. Ellie walked up to her third floor apartment. She had lived in Chicago all her life, most of it in a large condo, with a courtyard. However, she and her mother had moved to this smaller apartment after her father had left them. Ellie hated this place. It was smaller, darker, and sadder. There were many things that had changed, her mother most of all. That had been three years ago when Ellie was nine.

The apartment was quiet and dark. This was the 'after' apartment, after he left, after her mother lost her smile, after they were alone. Yet, some things did not change. Her piano gleamed under the window with the top down. *I should practice more*, she thought, moving through the living room and into her bedroom.

Ellie threw her backpack on the bed; she had reading to do, but there was always reading to do. She and Mary went to Wilcrest Academy, a school for children with exceptional minds. Anne and Earl had chosen it for Ellie when she was three. The parents were both thrilled and scared when they had discovered that their precocious child, Ellie, was reading books and playing the piano. Their pediatrician had suggested the school after Anne had told him that Ellie was reading out loud to her, instead of the other way round. *A long time ago,* Ellie thought.

Somehow, the school, the divorce, her Mom's unhappiness were all mixed up with her differentness. Ellie felt she was the reason for her dad's absence. It did not matter how much her mother denied it.

She wished that she were just like all the other kids. Maybe then, her dad would have stayed with them and they would not be so alone. "Ellie is so serious," Dad's remembered voice played through her mind. "Why is she so serious? Not like other kids her age."

Anne had been supportive of all those things, but Ellie remembered hearing her mother and her father, Earl, arguing about the school and all the extra expense. Then one day Ellie came home from school and found her mother pale and withdrawn. She sat Ellie down in the living room, explained to her that her father was gone and he would not be coming back, at least not right away. He had gone to California to take a new job. Ellie had been nine that year.

That is when their life changed, Ellie often heard her mother cry in the night when she thought that Ellie was asleep. They moved to this smaller apartment and her mother had taken on a full time job. It was at that time that Ellie felt the laughter seep out of their lives.

Ellie pulled her thoughts away from that horrible year. Instead, she thought of the ride she just had, and the show she was going to be a part of, if only her Mom would agree.

She picked up the novel she was reading. It was a wonderful story about a girl and a horse, called *The Island of Horses,* found her place and tried to read, but the book did not hold her interest. Going over to the large windows in the living room, she looked out at Lake Michigan shimmering in the distance. The traffic moved steadily, car after car, on Lake Shore Dr. She had never lived anywhere except in the city, but the quiet country where horses stood under trees and ambled around in summer grass made the city seem frantic.

The riding lessons had been her Christmas present two years ago when she was ten; a surprise from her absent father. He had sold his first book and asked her what she wanted for Christmas. Her plea for a horse had left both parents shocked. After a hurried conversation by phone over this development, her father offered to fund riding lessons as an alternative to the horse. His new book was a hit and he was feeling generous.

He left Anne to explain about why owning a horse was impossible in an apartment, in the middle of a city. So on Christmas morning in a box with a beautiful Breyer horse model was a gift certificate for riding lessons. The brochure showed Whispering Tree Stable with its indoor and outdoor areas, and horses grazing in fields. Ellie was so surprised and excited.

On a cold winter morning in January, Ellie and Anne had driven out to arrange for the lessons. There they met Jackie Long at Whispering Tree Farm. They found her riding a huge brown horse in the indoor arena. She was a complete opposite of Anne. Anne was small, petite and blonde with huge blue eyes; Ellie would look much like her some day, having the same small frame and coloring. In contrast, Jackie was tall, with muscled arms and long dark hair, her brown eyes were kind, and she had a mouth that begged you to smile back at it. She jumped lightly down and led the horse over to them.

Ellie had to tilt her head way back to see the huge horse. She had never been that close to the real thing before, and when the beast reached out his head to snuffle her shoulder and nudge her with his nose, she stumbled back almost losing her balance, and her mother jumped too. Ellie had never seen her mother show any fear before, but the large horse was intimidating.

"Andrew, you stop that," Jackie moved him back a step, "You must be Ellie? This is Andrew; he doesn't realize how big he is. He really just wants to be friends."

She smiled down at the large blue eyes of the little blonde girl. "Just let me take him back to his stall and then I'll show you around." Jackie led the horse out of the arena and into the barn.

They followed Jackie into the stable area. The warmth inside felt good and the delicious smells of horses, leather, manure and grain wafted into Ellie's nose. In that moment, she felt a sense of safety and peace. Ellie stopped in the aisle, taking it all in, the huge heads with the kind dark eyes, ears forward, and the soft woofing sounds. The horses were almost all looking at her and in that moment she knew she belonged here, near these wonderful beings.

Ellie smiled at her ten-year-old self. She had come a long way from that day. She knew those faces by name now, and they were her friends. She knew which horse would go eagerly to a fence, and which one would make you work at it, knew about saddles and bridles, grooming and tacking up. She could ride a 3'6" fence. It was all so familiar.

Restless now in the silence of her home, with her mind skittering from one thing to another, Ellie walked back into her room and there on nightstand lay her journal, just where she had left it at three o'clock this morning. It was open to the latest entry, written by Ellie just after the dream woke her. Here was her reason for the unsettled nervousness. Every time she dreamed about the red mare, Ellie woke feeling empty, desolate, longing for something that had no name. She picked up her journal knowing those dreams filled the pages. Ellie sat down on the edge of the bed and began to read.

> *Bright sunlight painted the valley vivid with color. The small stream sparkling in the sun, and the birds chattering in the pine trees, made the scene seem real. The meadow shone with the green of lush, tall grass, the red mare stood in the middle, beautiful in the light, framed by tall mountains all around. Suddenly, the mare threw up her head, her ears*

forward and body tense. She whinnied, whirled around and started to trot through the grass. Then the perspective changed, I was seeing the meadow from her back. It was not a large meadow, maybe five or six acres, and had become well known to me, having been in all my dreams.

The red mare was moving under me as first we trotted, and then broke into a canter, gaining speed with the wind-blowing cool on my face. She flew over the ground, her hooves flying, and me laughing. Her ears were flicking back and forth and I was screaming encouragement to her. I had never been so free. Finally, we slowed to a trot and she stopped at the stream, I slipped off her warm back and she dropped her head to drink from the cold mountain water. I put my arms around her neck, I was so very happy.

These dreams were becoming more frequent, the bright red chestnut mare with a flaxen mane and tail, the meadow where the horse lived, blue sky, sun, lots of tall green grass, the little stream, with the high ragged mountains all around, always the same.

They had started about six months ago. At first, she had observed the red mare from a distance, but in each dream, she drew closer, and in last night's dream, she had actually been on the horse. She thought about the dream ride on the red mare and the ride today on George. She had ridden today with more confidence than ever. She wondered if the dream ride from last night had anything to do with that.

Sitting there on the edge of her bed, she glanced around her room. There by her window stood her easel set up with a new canvas. Now she knew what she was going to do; she was going to paint the dream horse. The red mare as she stood by the stream, in her dream from last night.

The image from the dream grew in her mind. *Yes, yes,* she thought, *I must paint the dream mare.* Striding over to the canvas, touching its white and empty space, Ellie could feel the picture she was going to paint, the picture in her mind demanding release. Now, full of energy she started to prepare the canvas, thinking about the colors she would need. In her hurry, she forgot to change out of her uniform; the urge to paint the scene from her dream was a force. *I must paint,* she thought, *I must capture the mare, that magnificent horse.* The room disappeared from around her and there was nothing but the canvas and the picture clamoring to be transferred to reality. She forgot everything else, her music, books, even food, everything else was gone from her mind. She focused on the image in her head. Paint the red dream horse, the glowing red dream horse.

Ellie started to block in the mare just as she had stood by the stream, her head up, ears forward, nostrils flared, her dappled red coat caught in the sunlight, gleaming gold. She worked steadily; absorbed, mixing colors for the glorious red of the mare. The image took shape beneath her hand; the mountains surrounding the valley, the deep grass, the cloudless blue sky, the little stream, and in the center was the red mare, reflecting the sun. Ellie, painting furiously, failed to hear her mother come into the room.

Anne looked in on her daughter, seeing her totally absorbed in her work. She stood there watching her child almost frantically brushing strokes on the canvas. Her uniform spattered with paint and her hands busy. A Schumann concerto was playing softly. The look of concentration on her face gave her mother pause. This look was not unfamiliar. Her daughter had an ability to become so absorbed in something that everything else disappeared. It was both an asset and a curse- this creative genius.

"Have you eaten anything?" Anne asked.

"What? Eaten—no I don't think so. I want to get this down. I really need to finish this. Have to finish this," Ellie looked up, frowning. She had a dab of paint on her cheek, giving her a poignant look.

Anne walked over to the easel and looked at the work in progress. *Good work*, she thought, fine *work*. *Maybe the best work Ellie has ever done*. The colors seemed to jump off the canvas and the horse looked ready to leap into motion. The room seemed charged with creativity. She stood gazing at the canvas.

Ellie was mixing paint at the table, having already forgotten her mother, totally absorbed in the world of the red mare. The Schumann concerto continued playing, adding emphases to the moment. Anne thought of the musician who had written the piece. The musician and composer had been obsessed with his work, too, and it had created many problems in his life.

Anne pondered this as she walked to the doorway and paused, watching her daughter. The twelve year old body just beginning to take on the characteristics of the woman she would become. Cold fingers of fear run through her. The weight of raising Ellie alone was the hardest thing she had ever undertaken, made even harder by that creative spark which was always driving her child.

CHAPTER 2

The finished painting stood on the easel in Ellie's room, it was her best work, and she planned to enter it in the Young Artists competition at the Art Institute. Mary had a sculpture that she was entering. This would be Ellie's first exhibit. Yet the dreams were always in her thoughts. They haunted her. She was glad to be going to the stable today. It was the place where she always felt safe. *I should be happy*, slipped into her thoughts; the painting was everything that she wanted it to be. It captured the essence of the dream mare, and her mother was letting her go to the horse show. *Yes, I should be happy so why am I uneasy*, Ellie sighed.

~~~~~~~

Ellie stood leaning on the fence watching the two horses on the other side. They were relaxing in the shade of a giant elm tree. Their tails were moving slowly side to side and they stood head to tail. The bright chestnut coat of George contrasted in a sun-dappled display against the dark brown of a gelding called Thundercup; Ellie watched the two gently knead the others

11

withers and swat flies with their tails. *If only I could be so tranquil*, she thought.

Ellie picked up the lead rope and climbed through the fence, "Okay, George, sorry to interrupt this mutual admiration society, but it's time for you to go to work. We've got a horse-show next week, remember?" Ellie snapped on the lead and started walking the big red horse to the gate. Thundercup tagged along and whinnied, as George walked through the gate and left him alone in the paddock. "Go eat grass; you're just lucky you don't have to work today."

Ellie slowly walked back to the barn, delighted that she was here for the whole day. She wished that Mary had been able to come too. It would have been fun to spend the day with her best friend and the horses. Jackie had invited Ellie out to help her with the lessons that day and Anne had agreed. *It's going to be the best summer ever,* Ellie thought.

She believed that her mother was being so agreeable because of the dreams she had been having. Well, she was worried about them too. "What do you think of my dreams, George?" she said as she tied him to the saddling post.

She patted him on the shoulder. Just then, an image came into her mind of the red mare standing in the high green grass. George turned his head and Ellie was sure he was looking directly into her eyes. He made a low sound that seemed comforting. "Well, thank you very much, old man. That certainly makes me feel better," Ellie smiled at him. "Let's go jump some fences."

Ellie had a wonderful day helping Jackie and the students. When her mother picked her up, she was a tired but happy girl.

"How was your day, luv?" Anne said.

"Good. George is such a wonderful horse. We had a perfect round on the course today. He made me look awesome. I can't wait to show him next week. Oh, and Jackie asked if I could come out on Wednesday afternoon for another lesson, then again early on Saturday to get everything ready for the show."

"This is taking a lot of time, Ellie; I hope it doesn't interfere with school," Anne looked at her with questioning eyes.

"I won't let it, Mom. It's just that I want to do this so much. The horses are so—as if they are a part of me. Can you understand that?"

"No I can't, Ellie. I understand that you are passionate and that in some way you feel connected to the horses, but I don't know how or why, no. I've no idea how you can become so close to a horse, or any animal. I grew up in the city. I've never been around animals. We didn't even have a fish aquarium in our home. So all I can do is believe you when you say it. I'm only concerned that this passion of yours will interfere with your school work," she smiled at her daughter, but the frown lines on her forehead told Ellie a different story.

"I won't let it, Mom. I'm not going to let anything slide, I promise," Ellie said.

Anne drove along the familiar route toward home and let her mind wander to her worry list, calling Ellie's dad, she wanted to talk to him about Ellie's dreams. *What would he think about these recurring nightmares?* In truth, they were not nightmares, but they unsettled Ellie. Ellie was different since they had begun. She was often distracted and then the painting. It was beautiful, but troubling. That was no dream on the wall, that was a painting of a real horse. She should call the therapist they had seen during that first awful year after Earl had left them. Call the therapist and call Earl, she decided.

Anne hated the thought of calling Earl. Not only did she need to tell him about Ellie's dreams but also she still had to resolve Ellie's summer plans. She wondered how she was going to explain to her ex-husband that his daughter did not want to visit him. She would rather stay home and ride horses. So many complications and such limited time. She sighed, bringing her attention back to her driving. Chicago traffic required your full attention; there was no time to daydream.

When they got home, she asked Ellie about setting up an appointment with Dr. Jen, the therapist. "I think it might be a good thing to see her and discuss these recurring dreams of yours," Anne said.

"It's okay with me, Mom," Ellie said. "I know you're worried about them. It's fine if we go."

"Then I'll call and make an appointment. I also need to call your dad and see if we can change that vacation so you can do the summer camp," Anne said

"Oh, that's wonderful. I really do want to do that. It's too bad that the camp and Sandra's vacation plans are at the same time. I wish that they had asked me about the dates. It's like I don't have a life and can just drop everything and go," Ellie had let her voice rise just a little.

"Well, your dad is a pretty busy man, you know. He probably thinks that you have more time than he does. You did try to do this on your own, didn't you? Did you email either one of them about the conflict?"

"Yes, several times. Once to Sandra and then twice to Dad, but she only said that the reservations were made and couldn't be changed. Then she suggested that I talk to my Dad. So far he's not answered me," Ellie said.

"Well I'm sure they will try to work something out," said Anne. "What shall we have for dinner? You must be starved after all that exercise," Anne smiled at her daughter.

"I had a late lunch with Jackie and some of the students. So, anything is okay with me. You know, Mom, sometimes I think that George understands when I talk to him. I was grooming him today and I told him about my dreams of the red mare, it was the strangest thing. A picture formed in my mind of the red mare. Then George pressed his nose against the top of my head and then made a whuffle noise."

Ellie looked at her mother. "Don't think I'm being silly but it seemed he knew what I was talking about and was trying to comfort me in so way."

"Well, I don't know about horses, but there are a lot of people who think their dogs and cats understand what they are saying. So, it can't be so strange that a horse would understand. Maybe, you just have a good rapport with him," Anne said.

"I've talked to Mary about this, too. She says sometimes one or another of the horses responds to her in a similar fashion, so maybe I'm not totally wrong." Ellie said.

CHAPTER 3

Mary and Ellie trudged from the large six horse trailer back toward the bunkhouse just as the sun set. The last item on their list was loaded. They were tired but excited to be spending the night at the farm with the other four girls going to the show in the morning. This was a rare thing. Both mothers were protective and the girls had not spent much time away from home without supervision.

"I'm exhausted. I didn't understand just how much work it took to get ready. I bet we've made twenty trips to the trailer already and I still have to make sure that my show clothes are packed," Ellie said. "I don't know what I would have done without you, Mary."

"Those new clothes are really awesome. You look like a professional in them, in that black velvet hat, black coat, and high boots. I can't wait until I can show. This is a learning experience for me, because at the next show, I'm going to ride, too," Mary replied.

"Well, I think we'll sleep tonight even though I didn't think I would, because I'm so nervous. I'll be glad to get this first show over with. George is an old hand at this; I know that we'll be fine," Ellie said, "but I have preshow nerves." The girls walked hand in hand back to the bunkhouse. The four other girls were there. No one wanted to get up at 3am to drive out, so everyone slept over. Ellie and Mary were there because neither mother wanted to have to get up at that hour either. They would be coming directly to the show grounds in the morning at a civilized hour.

Joyce and Nancy owned their own horses and had been showing forever. Missy and Amy were students who would ride two of Jackie's horses, but they were old hands. Ellie was the novice. All four were being so helpful and both Ellie and Mary were appreciative. Making her debut into the show arena would have been daunting without their support.

Ellie and Mary were having a blast. They had been watching Joyce and Nancy come out for lessons on their own horses for over a year. Joyce's big warm-blood gelding named Centaur was rumored to have cost a lot of money. He was a beautiful horse and both girls were a bit envious. Joyce was older, sixteen this year, a pretty teenager who had proven to be a very nice girl. She was sweet, kind and helpful. Mary and Ellie were enjoying getting to know her better. Joyce was an excellent rider and had been riding most of her life. She told them that the horse was her mother's compensation for never spending any time with her.

Nancy was quiet and not as outgoing, she was serious with none of the bubbly personality of Joyce but they were good friends. Nancy's mare, Kiss Me, was a Thoroughbred, flighty, temperamental and difficult, but an excellent jumper. Nancy and Joyce had both won many classes and usually placed high in the ribbons at shows. Ellie felt happy to have them there as reinforcement.

The other two girls, Amy and Missy were just a little older than Ellie and Mary. They had been taking lessons for several years, and were old-timers. Jackie was letting the girls show two of her young horses to give girls and horses some show experience.

Jackie was in the bunkhouse delivering a large pizza with pepperoni, sausage and extra cheese for their dinner. Ellie was in heaven, not only an overnight, but pizza as well.

"You guys got here just in time. I want you all to eat, go over your preshow list, and check everything off. The only thing I want to load in the morning is the horses. Everyone understand?" Jackie was speaking in a stern tone of voice but she was smiling. "Also, get to bed; 4:00am comes early, any questions?"

Mouths full of pizza everyone nodded a 'yes'. They were too tired to stay up late, and they would be sure that everything was checked off.

"Okay then, I'll see you in the morning," Jackie left them to their pizza and soda party.

"Straws for the shower, short straw first," Nancy said.

Amy drew short straw and everyone began to finish their projects preparing to settle in for the night. Ellie went over her preshow list and dutifully checked everything off, right down to hair clips and comb.

When they all turned off the lights, it was just after 8:00pm, tired Ellie soon fell asleep; thinking of the dream mare, however, not George, the real horse.

The alarm went off in the bunkhouse; groans arose all around the room. Ellie was the first to brave the cold and jump out of bed. "Come on, you sleepy heads. The horse show is waiting. Get up, up, up."

Joyce stuck her nose out from under her sleeping bag, "Go away, novice, I'm sure the alarm clock is wrong, I only just closed my eyes. It can't be morning already."

"Well, if anyone thinks 4:00am is morning then they're nuts, right. I think it's still the middle of the night. No one who gets up at this hour is sane. I hate horse shows," Nancy grumbled, dragging herself out of her warm bed. "Brrrr, it's cold in here even if it is spring." She hurried over to the wall heater and turned it on full blast.

Ellie and Mary were trying to dress, hopping around to keep warm. They hastened to the heater and pulled on jeans and shirts. "Last one to the barn's a rotten egg," Mary shouted as she and Ellie grabbed jackets and ran out the door.

"Oh youth," Joyce yelled after them, "thy name is Ellie."

"We forgot to brush our teeth. We'll have to go back," Mary stopped her mad dash. They slowly retraced their steps and reentered the bunkhouse.

"You guys forget something?" Nancy asked with a smile.

"Well, only to brush our teeth, wash our faces. A few things like that. I don't want George to be scared of me," Ellie said.

"We weren't going to ride with you two unless you came back in. Hygiene is a good thing, especially after that smelly pizza last night." Missy was laughing.

"OK, OK, just let us be," Mary said, "We'll make ourselves presentable. I promise."

Twenty minutes later, they were all standing in front of their respective horses stalls waiting for the horse trailer to come.

Jackie, a veteran in dealing with jittery students and her less jittery horses, had the horses in the trailer and the girls in the van in no time. They were all ready to be on their way with the girls laughing and talking.

The girls chatted away as Jackie carefully followed the big horse trailer. Joyce, being the most seasoned rider in the group, told show ring stories both good and bad. Ellie was hanging on every word. They stopped at a restaurant about half way to the show arena for breakfast, but Ellie was too excited to eat very much.

"Nancy, did Kiss have anything to say to you about how she was going to perform today?" Joyce asked. "You guys know that Kiss talks to her on a regular basis, don't you?" she said to the rest of the group.

The table went quiet, as Nancy looked up annoyed. "I really do think she talks to me! I don't know why you think that's so funny," she retorted. "Sometimes I'm sorry I told you."

"You think your horse talks to you?" Ellie asked quietly.

"Well, I don't know, not in words exactly—just like, maybe a picture or something comes into my mind when I'm with her. It's hard to explain, because it isn't words, not like we're talking or anything like that. Just, oh, I don't think I can explain it," Nancy went quiet.

Ellie spoke then, "I sometimes feel that George is communicating with me. I talk to him like he's another person, and sometimes he just—seems to understand," she said lamely. She looked around at the other girls, thinking that maybe she should not have said anything.

Jackie the practical diplomat spoke up, "Horses are really empathic or sensitive, and they pick up the feelings or emotions of people easily. I can see where you might think they are communicating. Anyway, eat up; we have to get back on the road."

Ellie remained quiet all the way to the show. She was thinking about what Nancy had said. She felt that sometimes George tried to comfort her or that sometimes the pictures in her mind were coming from him. Finally, Mary, who was sitting next to her, reached out and took her hand. "It's okay; see other people think their horses talk to them, too."

When they arrived at the show grounds, the trailer was parked in front of their stalls. Ted, Jackie's farm manager was putting straw in the five stalls. The girls helped unload the horses and arrange the saddles and other tack in the extra stall *it all looks so neat and orderly,* Ellie thought.

Ellie's first class was scheduled to begin at ten o'clock and the second one supposedly at two in the afternoon, so she had plenty of time to get ready. She stood on the mounting block braiding George's mane with Mary handing her the rubber bands. She already had her breeches on under her coveralls. There would be lots of time, as it was early. She put the final touches on her horse's mane, "Mary, how does he look?"

"He looks like he's been to the hair dresser. These are the best braids we've done. I think Jackie will approve. Let's go see if we are good to go," Mary said.

Jackie believed that all students had to get their own horse ready, even for the show ring, if you rode, you groomed. Ellie and Mary had been practicing braiding for a couple of weeks, much to the regret of George, who was patient, but not particularly excited about getting his mane braided.

However, this morning he was standing quietly, and seemed to be calm and collected. "It's his way of telling me everything will be fine," Ellie said. "I think it's neat about Nancy saying her horse talks to her," she looked down at Mary inquisitively.

"I don't know. I think maybe some people are more attuned to certain animals, like maybe for her it's her horse, or for someone else, it's their dog or cat, or whatever," Mary said.

"Have you ever thought that Harlequin was giving you support or understanding you?" Ellie asked.

"Well I don't really talk to him, but sometimes it feels like he knows when I'm upset, or not feeling well. I don't know. My mother says that girls like horses more than boys do. That horses give girls a feeling of power or something," she looked up at Ellie, "It makes me feel uncomfortable somehow. I've never been as involved as you are. Like wanting my own horse and having those dreams. I would be so scared if I had those ongoing dreams as you do. It's weird. Don't you think?"

"I'm not scared of the dreams, but I do feel like I've been singled out or something. At first, I thought it was just strange, but now I don't know. It's as if something is about to happen, something I'll be a part of. Then I've always felt different,

21

somehow. Well, you know. We aren't like other kids. Not really."

"Yeah, I know. All the kids at our school are different in some way or another. It's more than just being able to learn more quickly." Mary answered with a frown.

"We are different; we don't see things the way normal kids do. You know it, and I know it. All the kids at school know it. I think we'd all like to be just—normal," she jumped down. "All done here. My fingers are about to fall off. Let's get an okay from Jackie and see what we should do next. I think I'm getting nervous," Ellie said.

Jackie approved the straight braids looking like little dread locks running down George's shining red neck. "Fine job, girls, now let's just leave George in his stall cross tied and go over to the jumping arena. It's covered so we'll be in the shade, but it's going to be hot this afternoon."

They clipped the sidelines on George and walked with Jackie to the warm-up arena. Several horses and riders were already moving around. Some were trotting or cantering, others were jumping over low fences, and others were trotting a row of caveletti set along one rail. It looked like controlled chaos out there.

"You should bring George in here about twenty minutes before you need to go into the ring. I'll tell you when to do that, spend five minutes on the rail at the trot, and then two minutes at the canter then a couple of flying changes through the center. Wait for me to take the warm up jumps. Got all that?" Jackie asked.

Ellie repeated the instructions, and they walked over to the covered show area where fences were being set up. It was exactly 9:00am. In an hour, she would be in that arena with George. She looked at the space and the jumps, not very different from the arena at the farm. She felt the first of the stomach jitters she always got before she had to give a talk or perform in some way. This was not so much different from that.

Jackie wouldn't have let me compete if I weren't ready, she was rationalizing, she realized. Ellie smiled to herself.

Suddenly, the thought came into her head. *Just relax,* came a calming presence, *it will be fine.* She felt her stomach relax and the anxiety leave her body. *Well, if that's not George then who is it?* She did not share any of that with Mary as they walked back to the barn.

"I would say 'break a leg', but I don't think it's appropriate for a horse show," Mary said as she gave Ellie a leg up. "You'll be just fine. I'll wait outside the arena to take George for you after you win the class, okay?"

It was 9:45am and the announcer had called her class number to be ready at the warm up arena. Jackie's instructions played in her head as she walked George down the aisle to the ring. There were nine other girls in the class and she was going in fourth. It was a novice jumping course, similar to the one she had been working on at the farm. The other girls and horses were shining in the sun as they moved around the arena. It was already hot and somewhat humid.

Ellie saw Mary walking down to watch. She hoped that her mother and Triana had arrived. She walked George around the arena and then following Jackie's orders did the trot and then the canter. George seemed at ease, with his ears flicking back and forth, taking no notice of the other riders. The first two numbers were called to the main arena. The class was on. Ellie realized that she was not nervous.

Then Jackie was there giving instructions just like at home. "I watched the first rider, Ellie. It's an easy course. There is only the one combination that gave her any trouble. When you make the turn on the far side to the in-and-out, make the turn wide and give George enough room to come to the fence perfectly centered, then count your strides and he will land just right to the second fence. You'll be fine; this is an easy course for George. Oh, and don't forget to breathe! Good luck and smile, we're having fun," with that Jackie turned and headed back to the in-gate.

Ellie watched the girl in front of her do the course, at the fourth fence the horse dropped a hind leg and slightly hit the bar. It wobbled but stayed up, and at the combination, the rider cut in and caused her horse to hit the first rail hard, it fell causing her to have one fault. She saw what Jackie had meant about the combination, but if you made the turn wider, you could come up to the first fence right in the middle, just where Jackie had told her to put George.

The gate swung open and George started forward. She settled herself deep in the saddle and they were off. She centered her mind and pictured each fence as she rode to it, over it and on to the next. Suddenly the combination was there. Circle wide, circle wide, come to the center of the first fence, and sit deep. We are up! We are over, collect him, one, two three strides, up, over.

"We did it George, we did it. I think we're clean." She leaned forward and patted him on the neck. She looked to the gate and Jackie was giving her a high five and a big smile. It was just as Jackie had said. They had been perfect. Anne and Triana waved and smiled as she left the arena. She had no faults and no time faults. She did not know where she would place, but she was mighty pleased with herself and with George. He had taken all the fences easily and then gave a little buck once, as if to say, "Well, how about me!" she had laughed with pleasure.

Jackie stood just outside the gate. "You did good, Ellie. Couldn't have done it better myself."

"Yeah, wasn't he wonderful?" she was still laughing as she jumped down and threw her arms around the big red horse's neck.

"You wonderful guy, you." Mary laughed and took the reins to lead him off; he needed to keep moving.

"Just walk him, to keep him loose. I don't know if they will need to reset the course, yet," Jackie said, turning back to watch the next rider. Ellie stood beside her and watched as the novice rider in the ring worked her way around the course. She had one rail down early, and at the in and out she lost her cool, and caused her horse to take down a rail with a left hind foot. "Oh, too bad," Ellie commiserated with the hapless rider. "That will keep her out of the ribbons for sure."

As the horse and rider left the out gate, the girl gave a hard pull on the reins, bringing the horse to a stop; he threw up his head, and the girl in a fit of temper hit him hard with the whip in her left hand. The horse swirled and trying to get away from her hands started to back up. She hit him again this time on the rump and he went straight up in the air on his hind legs. The girl screamed as she slid off and a woman cried, "Jean, darling," and came running over.

"I told you he was dangerous!" the girl cried. "He made me lose this class!" The girl was sitting in the dirt in front of the gate.

Jackie and Ellie were watching in horror. Then, Jackie ran over and grabbed the reins of the frightened horse.

The woman, obviously the girl's mother, threw her arms around the girl. "Oh darling, are you alright?" she glared at Jackie and Ellie, but continued to hold her daughter. "Where is Julio? He's never around when we need him." A man in riding breeches headed toward them at a run.

"What happened, Jean? Did you fall? Are you hurt" He glanced at Jackie who was holding the reins of the horse, now standing quietly.

"Yes, I fell off and he made me lose this class and then he reared up and threw me. I could have been killed!" the child screamed, with tears streaming down her face.

He looked at Jackie and shrugged his shoulders slightly. "I'm sure everything will be alright, Ms. Gruder. I was with

Natalie who is going in next. I'm here now. You're not hurt are you?"

"No, she's not hurt. No thanks to you. We'll talk at the barn, Julio." The woman stalked away, with the girl in tow, leaving the man to take the horse from Jackie.

"What happened?" he asked as he took the reins from Jackie.

"She took her frustration out on the horse. She hit him hard and then tried to correct with her hands." Jackie said. "Spoiled brat is what I'd call her. She was at fault over that last fence."

"I know. She can be a handful. She'll want to get rid of the horse. It's never her fault; she just goes from horse to horse. It's sad."

"Yeah, sad for the horses, you mean." Jackie said.

Ellie had walked up to the front of the horse and was stroking him on the shoulder. She laid her head on his shoulder and rubbed her forehead on his satiny coat. "I'm sorry, guy. I know you weren't to blame. It's just too bad," she turned and walked with Jackie back to the barn.

Jackie took Ellie by the hand. "We have to get back to George, Ellie." Her body showed her irritation, as she quickly walked away. "It's sad what people do to horses. Sometimes I just want to treat them the way they treat their horses. I wonder how she would have liked it if we hit her with the crop and pulled a piece of iron through her mouth!"

"He seemed so sad," Ellie, responded.

"Who, the trainer," Jackie asked.

"No, the poor horse," Ellie said.

Jackie turned and looked at her, "The horse?"

"Yes, he felt so sad. Like he wanted to make her see how much he had tried for her. Oh, I don't know, maybe I'm over reacting," Ellie walked on looking for Mary and George.

Later, Jackie threw Ellie up on George and she trotted into the arena with five other riders, she was pleased, she and

George placed fourth in her first class. George seemed very pleased, too.

The horse show became a hurry up, and long wait, day. Hot and humid made it more tiring, with dust clinging to perspiring bodies, everyone felt it. It was so hot in the afternoon that they put the fans on the horses to keep them cool. Black coats became steam jackets and the girls were soaking in their boots.

Anne and Triana came back to the barn after her class to admire her ribbon. In her second class of the afternoon she had lost her way and missed a fence, but over all she was pleased with her first day of showing.

They returned home put the horses out in the pastures, for an evening of green grass. Everyone was feeling happy. There were six ribbons. Two blue, one each for Joyce and Nancy and two red seconds, for Amy and Missy, her green fourth and a yellow fifth that Amy received in a maiden class. Jackie was well pleased with the girls. She gave them all a hug as they were leaving for the night.

"Well, was it all you thought it would be, Ellie?" Anne asked as they were driving home.

"Yes, it really was fun, but a lot of work. I'm tired and ever so dirty. I want a bath and bed," Ellie felt like she would fall asleep in the car.

"For sure a bath first, we were only watching and we're sweaty and dusty," Triana said.

"I'm hoping to ride in the next show. I can't let Ellie have all this fun," Mary said dryly.

"If fun is what you call it," Mary's very fair-skinned Mom responded. "I think I got some sun, even with the hat and sun screen."

The horse show had been a success. Now the summer was upon them. Ellie hoped for more time to be at the farm. Her perfect world would be living on a farm just like Whispering

Tree, riding wonderful horses, just like the red mare, or maybe George.

She could never imagine that such a dream could become a reality...

CHAPTER 4

Two months later, Ellie and her mother were celebrating at Arturo's Pizza Parlor with Mary, Triana and Jackie. Ellie ran her hand over the crystal free-form trophy that was sitting in a place of honor on the table. They were all celebrating her first place win with her painting of the red mare. The Art Institute competition for young artists was an impressive show. Both she and Mary had entered the competition. The painting had just won first place and Mary's sculpture of an old woman's hands had gotten an Honorable Mention.

The Chicago Tribune and Sun-Times had interviewed her. The photographer had taken a picture of her standing by her painting, holding her trophy. The two judges said the painting showed wonderful technique and maturity for such a young woman.

Triana and Anne were so happy for them that after the showing they had come here to celebrate. Ellie and Mary thought Arturo's pizza was the best thing in the world, but their mothers did not let them eat it often, so it was a real treat.

Ellie was glad that her mother, Triana Johansen, and Jackie Long were becoming friends, it made things so nice that she and Mary were best friends and now her Mom had friends, too. After the divorce, Anne seemed to withdraw from everything but her work. She had centered her life around her daughter and her husband. His friends had been hers. When he left, there was an abyss of loneliness. It was nice to see her laughing and joking with the other two women. They were having a good time, the women were celebrating with a glass of wine and were laughing and talking, while Mary and Ellie were eating pizza and drinking soda.

"I think that Ellie's picture will be in the paper this weekend," Anne was saying. "Did they get a picture of Mary, too?"

"They got one of the sculpture but not of Mary," Triana said. "The girls did so well."

"You know that someone even offered to buy Ellie's painting. I was shocked," Anne looked over at Triana," I can't believe it."

"Really? Would you sell it?" Triana asked.

"I don't know if she would or not. It would be up to Ellie. I'm going to call her dad and let him know how well she did. He never understood about the art work," Anne frowned, "or anything else regarding—," she stopped, looking guilty. She never talked about her ex-husband in front of Ellie. The two others nodded in response. Triana certainly knew about exs, having one of her own. Jackie never talked about relationships.

"When you call him, ask him about changing the date of my trip to California," Ellie said. Both girls had stopped talking between themselves and were listening to the conversation going on around them.

"It seems that Sandra started planning that trip just after the winter holiday, but they should have asked you whether it worked for you," Anne said.

"Sandra? Triana raised her sculpted eyebrows, looking at Anne with worried eyes.

"Sandra Robertson is twenty eight and has been living with Earl for about six months. I think this one might be serious," Anne said.

"Well, that will probably change things," Triana said.

Anne knew what Triana and Mary had gone through. Triana's ex husband had several live-ins before he married a much younger woman, who promptly produced three new children. Mary's father had a completely new family to deal with, which left him little time for Mary.

Earl had hardly been around Ellie since the divorce. He had come back to the city a few times, but always seemed in a hurry to leave. Then last year he had sent a ticket for Ellie to come out and spend a week with him in California. Ellie had not had a very good time. She told Anne that he had been very busy with speaking dates and book signings, so his girl friend Sandra had been the one with whom she spent most of her time. This was just one of the reasons that she did not want to go on a trip to Hawaii with them. She needed her mother's help in getting them to understand that she wanted to spend the summer with Jackie and the horses. That she had plans of her own. She would really prefer not to go at all. Especially since her dad was now living with Sandra.

Anne changed the subject of the conversation. She would not discuss her ex-husband in front of Ellie. "Well, I'll see what I can do, luv. I need to call him, anyway. I'm sure that he will want to know about your big win."

They laughed their way through the pizza. Ellie was buzzing with energy, so staying up late was not a problem. Tomorrow was Sunday and she could sleep in. Fun times with friends were rare in their household. She and her mother had a good time celebrating the day. It was one to remember. When it was over, everyone gave hugs and said good night.

Sadly, she remembered times when her dad lived with them. Her mother had been much different then, bubbly and smiling most of the time. She sighed as she got into bed for the night, perhaps tonight the dream of the red mare would come. It had been a long time. Her eyes closed and she thought of the horse she would someday own. She let pictures form and play against her eyelids. A dappled gray, a bay or black, but not the red mare and she wondered why. *I dream of her all the time and yet I can't picture myself owning her*, she thought.

Slowly sleep overcame her and when Anne looked in on her a little later, she was sound asleep.

Ellie was in the valley of the red mare but the stream had become a huge river and she was walking toward it with some reluctance. It was definitely pulling her. She moved forward slowly with difficulty, as if she was walking in deep sand. The air around her was viscous and it was hard to breathe. The water dragged her forward.

Her mind screamed at her, "I can't go into that water". Something forced her forward anyway. Step by step without stopping, her feet moved into the river, the water rising around her. She thought that it would be cold, but as it rose about her body, it was like being in a warm bath. Slowly she moved deeper and deeper. The bottom was smooth on her bare feet. The panic was subsiding, she felt herself relaxing and just before the water covered her, she looked to the far bank and saw the red mare standing there shining in the sun. Standing by her side was a beautiful baby foal, not white or red but a rainbow of shimmer, a palette of colors. She was seeing this through a prism of water. The tiny head was so perfect, beautifully chiseled, but just in the middle of its forehead was a small bulge. Then the water claimed her.

"I can't swim, I'll drown," she was panicking again.

"Drift, drift with me," the voice was inside her and with it came acceptance. Suddenly she felt very calm, that is when the river took her. She and it were one, there was no need to breathe she had become the water. The sensation maintained her and somewhere inside her, she knew it was only a dream, but different somehow. Now there was no longer the red mare, no time to think about the foal she had seen on the bank, just the water that was her and she it, with a feeling of sameness.

She became part of something that was not a human thing. She was the water now, but even thoughts were different here. She could feel herself split and move around the stones, they were not in her way. In this fluid state, she became free in this oneness, this ability to be.

Ellie had no sense of time here but after a while she became aware of musical tones that were as much her as the water was her. Like the water, the music resonated within her, through her, and took a place in her mind. Wonderful music that she knew was as much a part of her as she was a part of the river. She thought, "I must remember it. This song is the song of beauty and life. I must remember it."

She began thinking in some strange way. The music was making unusual things happen. There were visions here for her to see and they played like movie clips before her; a large horse like unicorn with a golden horn shimmered in the water and the music seemed to be coming from him. There were songs she needed to sing, her eyes and mind were seeing colors and life forms pulsing with the beat of the music.

She did not feel time just the music, pictures, colors, playing around her. How long this went on she did not know. There did not seem to be time here, just being.

Then came a movement, the harmony became disharmony. She felt more than heard a huge disruption, heat and chaos. Some monstrous force tossed her and sent her tumbling about in the water. A very powerful surge was making everything move and disintegrate. The big creature was whirling upside down, right side up, swirling away from her and in her mind came the thought, "Remember the music, the music, the music!"

She no longer flowed and the discordance was so horrible, so violent that she lost her oneness with the water. She became aware that she needed air, needed to breathe. She needed to breathe now. She screamed and struggled. Her arms and legs flailing, she began to fight her way up out of the water. The water was no longer her element.

Desperately she floundered around, all sense of being one with the water gone. She frantically fought her way up, "I must reach the surface, I must breathe."

"Remember the music, remember the music," was all she heard as she rose.

"Ellie, Ellie, What is happening to you? Wake up, luv. Oh, please wake up. You're having a nightmare."

Ellie came awake in her mother's arms. Anne was holding her tightly and rocking her gently. Looking up into her mother's face, she felt the tears streaming down her face.

"The music. I must remember the music," Ellie said.

"What music? What are you talking about? You've been struggling for quite a while I thought you were strangling. I'm so glad you woke up. Tell me what you were dreaming."

Ellie looked at her mother, but could not speak. She clung to her and cried. Finally, she got her sobs under control and lay quietly in her mother's arms.

Anne was stroking her hair and rocking her gently.

"Are you fully awake now?" Anne said.

"I —I think so. The music was so beautiful. I must remember how beautiful it was. I must remember how it went."

"If it was a nightmare, how could it be so wonderful and the music beautiful, I don't understand," Anne was still holding her, face lined with worry. "Do you want to tell me about it?"

"Maybe, but I need to think about this. I want to write it in my journal. I want to remember the music. I want to write it in my journal. I want to remember the music," Ellie was trying to sit up.

"Were you being attacked? You were really thrashing around and making these horrible noises, like you were trying to catch your breath or something."

"It was a dream, not like the other dreams, but the red mare was there and the stream became a huge river or ocean or something," Ellie was trying to make sense of what had just happened to her.

"And oh Mom, she had the most wonderful baby foal standing by her side. I was seeing them through the water; the colors were like prisms, wonderful and strange. But, the dream was not about them. I was hearing this music, but not just hearing it, I was being it, tones so clear and harmony so perfect, it was wonderful and I was the water too. Then something awful happened, horrible force and noise. I was thrown over and over, and I couldn't breathe."

Ellie looked at her mother and knew that what she was saying was making her mother more anxious. Stammering to a stop, she sat quiet in her mother's arms. How could she explain something that she did not understand?

Anne looked down and said, "I know it's hard, luv. I know. Dreams are not reality. When you try to make sense of them the

35

thoughts get all confused, how about a cup of hot chocolate? The warm milk should make you calmer. How about it?"

"Maybe, yes that would be good, hot chocolate." The thought of warmth and her mother being with her made the dream less scary.

"I'll make some then," her mother said.

Ellie could tell her mother was very upset. She did not want to worry her, but she could not control her dreams, could she? The dream had been scary after the—whatever happened to her in the river. Then there had been the red mare and a baby. What was that all about? She was trying hard to remember but already the dream was taking on an unreal quality.

She reached into her nightstand and took out the latest journal. She needed to get the images and feeling down now, before they were gone. In addition, she needed to try to remember the music and get that down too. She could feel the notes in her mind. The combinations and harmonies were still there. *Good*, she thought, *I'll be able to duplicate some of it, anyway.*

"What time is it?" she asked when her mother came in carrying a tray with steaming cups and some cookies, too.

"About 4:00am," Anne replied. "Do you want to talk about the dream?"

"No, I can't yet. It was very strange."

"Not the horse one this time?"

"Well, sorta, but not the same. It was more about me this time. Although I saw, the mare with a foal, but this dream was about me and something terrible that happened. I don't know I'll have to think about it more."

They drank their chocolate and ate cookies. Anne had noticed the journal open to a new page and Ellie's writing had filled about half a page. She could tell that Ellie wanted to get back to it.

"Try to get back to sleep, luv. The dream will wait and you need to sleep. She gathered up the tray and cups and went to the door. "Shall I leave the door open?"

"No, that's okay. I'll just finish this and go back to sleep, Mom. It'll be alright now."

Ellie was an accomplished pianist. She had been playing since she was two or three, so she knew music and composition. She hummed the music to herself and tried to write it down. She could not get the harmonies but she would remember how they sounded in her head. Tomorrow when she was at school, she would be able to organize the notes she had written in her journal, and try to put the music reverberating in her head into some type of order.

Turning out the light she heard again the music in her mind. It was beautiful.

CHAPTER 5

Ellie sat at her computer downloading pictures from the camera that Mary's mother had taken at the horse show on Sunday. She intended to send some to her dad, hoping that pictures would help him see how much fun she was having and why she did not want to go to California in June. Maybe it would help him understand that being at the farm and helping with the day camp was something that she wanted to do.

It could be so difficult. Adults could not conceive that their children might have plans of their own. She did not want to go to Hawaii anyway. He would just spend all his time with Sandra and it made Ellie uncomfortable. *Why, oh, why couldn't parents understand?*

She found a good picture of George and her going over the wall jump. It was quite impressive, almost a front view, and it showed her concentrating on the next fence and George with his knees tucked up nicely to his chest in perfect form. *Oh you darling you*, she thought. She attached the picture to her email and carefully re-read her argument for staying in Chicago took a breath and hit send. The email was off to her father.

Jackie had all the rider's rounds on video and they were going to meet at the farm to critique them. The girls were going to go over their rides with Jackie on Saturday after lessons. Her mother and Triana were picking them up to take them out to dinner after. It was going to be so much fun.

Today Mom was picking her up after school to take her to the therapist they had seen after the divorce. They had gone twice a week for quite a while. Ellie had been ten then. She liked Dr. Jen. Ellie remembered that Dr. Jen had recommended they start the journals. Dr. Jen had told her mother that the journals would be a good idea for both of them. Ellie wondered if her mother still wrote in her journal. She remembered the day they had gone to the bookstore and picked out the lined notebooks. She had picked out one with horses on the cover and different pictures of horses throughout. She could not remember the color of her mother's journal.

She still heard her mother crying in the night, but it was much less than that first awful year. Actually, Ellie had heard her only last week. She knew that her mother was worried about her having those repetitive dreams and the nightmare one had really scared her.

She was having a snack in the kitchen when her mother came home.

"Hi, luv, are you about ready to go?" Anne asked as she put down her briefcase.

"Yeah, just having a pb&j, want one?" Ellie asked.

"No, but thanks, we should probably get going. Did you check the messages on the phone? Your father was going to call me back."

"No, I just got home myself. The el was late." Ellie said.

She heard her mother go into her bedroom, just as the phone started to ring. Ellie quickly went into her room and gently lifted up her extension. Holding her breath, she eavesdropped on the conversation her mother was having with her father.

"Thanks for calling me back, Earl." Anne had said.

"Is something wrong with Ellie?" Earl asked.

"No. Well not really." Anne stammered. "But I wanted to talk to you about, well about her dreams. She's been having nightmares about a horse. The dreams are repetitive and they are all about the same horse, she's painting the horse over and over, compulsively. I'm really worried about her. Also, she's really upset about her trip to California. She doesn't want to go. They've asked her to be an assistant at the stable this summer and she is so excited about it. I'm so worried about the dreams that I've made an appointment with that therapist I took her to, when you — well when she was ten."

"Don't lay a guilt trip on me, Anne. I had to go. It wasn't you or Ellie-it was me. I was stifled there. Look what I've done since I left. The books, the success —"

Anne broke into his monologue, "Earl this is about Ellie, not about you. Please, I need your help, here. I'm not sure how to handle this." Ellie could hear her Mom's voice get whiny; she knew how much her Mom hated these phone calls.

"Ellie's having dreams and you're worried about her. She doesn't want to come to California this summer, and you are backing her up in that, too. What do you want me to do, Anne? I'm three thousand miles away. Just take her to the therapist, and I'll let her stay in Chicago and not make her come to Hawaii with us. Will that make it better?" Earl's voice had risen.

Ellie put the phone back on the hook in her room and let the tears roll down her cheeks. She was the cause of all this upset. Why, had she not just said that she would go to Hawaii? Why was she having dreams, and upsetting her mother. No matter what her mother said, or the therapist said, she knew she was the cause of her father leaving them. It was her fault that her mother cried in the night and that her father was living in California. She turned on the CD player in her room so her mother would not hear her crying.

Ten minutes later Ellie had washed her face and changed into jeans and a new top. She checked her face in the mirror and found that her eyes were not puffy, but just a little red. She tried a smile and called to her mother.

"Who was on the phone, Mom, was it Dad?" Ellie tried hard to put some enthusiasm in her voice.

"Yes Ellie it was your father. The good news is he's going to let you out of the trip to Hawaii." Anne voice sounded strained. "Are you ready? We need to leave. Thank heaven I can drive to the clinic, they have off street parking."

"Oh, I really appreciate you helping me out on that. He was pretty adamant in his email. I didn't think he was going to change his mind."

"Well, he's concerned about your dreams, just as I am." Anne said.

Ellie did not let on that she knew about the conversation. She just went over and gave her mother a hug. "Thanks ever so, anyway."

When they got to the clinic she remembered the waiting room, but somehow it felt smaller, and she felt like a different person. Now coming in at twelve, well almost thirteen, she felt in control and more grown up. There had been many changes in her life since those visits when she was ten.

Ellie thought that Dr. Jen, like the waiting room, had not changed much in those two years, she was still slim and smiling.

"Ellie, how nice to see you, you are quite the young lady now. I saw a picture of you in the Sun. Congratulations on your painting. The review was very complimentary." Dr Jen said. "Why don't you and Anne sit down and tell me something about why you are here." She indicated two upholstered chairs in front of her desk. The colors were the same as before, deep rose, and shades of pink and green.

Ellie and Anne sat down facing the desk. Ellie was holding the latest journal in her hands. Anne was the first to speak.

41

"I am really concerned about Ellie, she is having dreams and last week she had a nightmare one. They are all connected and seem to be about the same subject." Anne came to stop. She turned to face Ellie.

"I brought the journals with me, Dr. Jen. They have all the dreams in them." Ellie spoke up.

"And how do you feel about the dreams? Why don't you tell me something about them?" Dr Jen asked.

Ellie looked up at Dr. Jen. "They are all about one horse, well all except the last one. I've written them all down. The horse is always in the same place, a valley surrounded by high cliffs. It is a beautiful place with a stream running through it. The grass is high and the horse seems to be all alone. At first, I would watch her as she ate or drank. I felt that she knew I was there. Later I would be with her, we'd walk together, and then the last ones I was riding her. It was wonderful to be on her," her voice was soft as she talked about the horse. "Then I got the idea to paint my dreams of her. That picture that won the prize is of her."

Dr. Jen then asked, "All the dreams are the same. Do they seem like a movie?"

"No, not a movie, it's like I'm really there. I feel the air, smell the grass; it feels like I'm really touching her. When I have the dreams, I'm there, it's real, the night I rode her I was really riding. I was bareback with no bridle, no saddle, just the horse with nothing else. She just did what ever I wanted her to do. It was wonderful."

Anne then spoke up, "Tell her about the last one, Ellie."

Ellie looked up, "Well, this last one was very different from the others. It was about me. Oh, I saw the mare and the valley, but where before the mare and I were together, this time I was alone, drawn into the stream, which wasn't really a stream anymore. The mare stood on the bank and she had a foal, a baby horse by her side, they watched as I went into the water, became the water, then something happened. I don't know, I had become the water and music washed over me and I became that too. It got jumbled, but I remember that I was able to breathe in the water, it was me, and the music was me too. Then there was something like an explosion and I was separate again. I couldn't breathe and the water was strangling me. Then Mom woke me up.

"I felt like I had to remember the music. I wrote it down. It was so beautiful, more like harmonies but nothing I'd ever heard before, and just before I woke up, I thought I saw something white like a horse but not really. Like a prism of color in the form of a—you're not going to believe this but it was like a picture I'd seen of a tapestry, you know the one with the unicorn in it? The white creature looked like—like a unicorn." Ellie looked first at Dr. Jen then at her mother.

Anne was looking at her, "You didn't tell me that. You told me about the music and things, but not a unicorn?"

"I didn't tell anyone, I didn't even write it in the journal. I just was so compelled to write down the music that it slipped my mind. Just this moment, telling Dr. Jen did I remember the unicorn, if that's what it was. But, the colors of it I remember now. How could I have forgotten the colors?" She seemed in a reverie.

Dr. Jen sat quietly, she was thinking about what she had heard. The room was quiet. "Well, those are certainly some dreams you're having, Ellie. Of course, dreams are a part of our sleeping self. Some therapists think dreams are a way for the subconscious to communicate with the conscious mind. Dreams are the subconscious trying to reach our awareness. I don't think that I agree with that theory, but then I'm not going to discount it either. Obviously, these dreams are happening in sequence and always about the same thing. They must mean something to you. Do they make you sad? Happy? How do you feel after you have one?"

"I'm usually sad, or maybe lonely, after. I feel restless, as if I'm missing something. I want to go out to the stable and be with the horses. When I'm there, I think everything is good again, or when I'm painting. Then I feel like the mare is with me. Not like at night, but she is there in my mind with me. It's almost as if I can hear her or something. It's really difficult to put into words, Dr. Jen," Ellie looked pained, she was trying so hard to clarify herself.

"You're doing ever so well, Ellie. You have a good way of describing yourself." Dr. Jen said.

"I want to talk to your mother for a few moments alone, if you don't mind, Ellie. Will you wait outside?"

Ellie stood up took her mother's hand and held it to her cheek, "Do you want the journals? All the dreams are written down chronologically if you want to read them."

"No, not now, those are your journals, they are not meant for others to read. Have you been keeping them since you were here last?"

"Well, I used to write in them when I was upset or just wanted to remember something. But now they are mostly about the dreams, although sometimes I write about, well other things." Ellie looked down.

"Yes well, they're yours, you keep them. Let me talk to your mother for a few minutes. Okay?"

"Yes fine, I'll wait in the lobby." Ellie went out the door.

Anne watched her almost adult daughter leave. Ellie was growing up so fast now. "What do you think?" she asked.

"To tell you the truth, I don't know." Dr Jen answered. "Dreams can be –well, we don't know, I'm not a student of Jung, you know. I believe in helping problems with talk and drugs if indicated. I don't see that Ellie is having an episode of depression or mental instability-she seems mentally stable. These children, these kids that are gifted as Ellie is, they don't fit the norms, so I can't say that you don't have a problem, but truthfully I don't think there is anything to worry about. She's writing down what the dreams are about. They don't seem to be intruding on her real life. She's doing well at school? She has friends? Nothing that you think is out of the ordinary with her?" Dr. Jen looked at Anne.

"No, although she paints the horse obsessively. But then, when she explores something, it's with her whole being. So, I guess that's pretty normal for her. When she was playing the piano, it was constant. When she listens to music, it's in depth. She seems to need to be totally immersed in whatever she's doing." Anne stopped talking.

"Well, Anne, I'll do a little research on dreams and see if someone has come up with anything on repetitive dreams etc. In the meantime, I'd just do what you've been doing, support her and love her, that works in most cases. If you want I'll continue to see you guys once a week or more if you think necessary?"

"I think I want to keep coming on a regular basis, for moral support if nothing else," Anne laughed.

"Fine. Once a week okay?" Dr. Jen was up walking Anne to the door. "Call if you need me, please. I'm here for you and Ellie."

"That makes me feel –not so alone with this. Thank you so much," Anne said.

Ellie looked up from her book as her mother came out. "Are you ready, Mom?"

"Yes, I'll just make an appointment for next week." Anne went to the receptionist and the girl handed her a card.

"Thank you," she took the card and put it in her purse. "We'll see you next week."

They were silent as they went to the car. When they were driving out of the lot Ellie asked her mother what Dr. Jen had said after she left.

"She was just reassuring me that you were fine. She doesn't think there is anything too unusual about your dreams. Although she said she'd check to see if there was any documentation in the field about that type of dream." Anne said.

"I think the mare is real," Ellie said. "I think she is trying to get me to find her."

"What? You didn't tell Dr. Jen that."

"No, but how could I have. Dreams are dreams, but this is something else. I don't want to upset you, but there is something about that horse and I that—Oh I don't know."

"Anyway, we have an appointment next week. I think I need support with this, I need someone to talk to." Anne laughed as they made their way home.

Neither one mentioned the unicorn in the nightmare dream.

Anne had laughed when Ellie said she thought the horse was real, but she was concerned that Ellie had said it. It was the first time that Ellie had been so open about what she thought the dreams meant. She hoped that Dr. Jen could come up with some plausible data on those types of dreams.

Ellie wondered why she had suddenly remembered the unicorn image in her nightmare dream. She had not written it down, nor had she thought about the unicorn at all. Just today, it had come to her. Now, the memory was strong and clear in her mind, of a unicorn, a creature of myths and dreams. She remembered the prism like colors, pearlescent shades of white. He had appeared with the music. The music had been coming from him. He had pulsed with it. He was the one saying, "remember the music." She had remembered the music, just not the creature responsible for the music.

She had read about unicorns but never that they were associated with music. She could not wait to get home to look them up on line. She would cross-reference them with music to see if there was a relationship.

Talking to Dr. Jen had given her more insight into the dreams. She now realized that she thought the horse in the dreams, the red mare, was real. She now thought that the music in the last dream was important. Something was happening to her and it was real. These dreams were more than just dreams. Somehow, she, the mare, and the music were related. Things were going to change and she was involved.

CHAPTER 6

Anne was quiet when they got home. It was only Thursday so there was one more day of work and school. She sighed as she started to prepare dinner. Ellie had gone directly to her room. Hopefully, she was doing her homework. The school kept the students very busy. There was always reading, reports, math; the work was way above anything that Anne had any knowledge of. The math in particular was already at a theoretical level that left her shaking her head. Ellie excelled in math, as she could have excelled in music, but she had been concentrating on painting this last year. She seemed to get deeply involved in something for a year or two and then suddenly switch to something else. The one thing that she had never pursued intensely was writing. She wrote well enough, but she thought of it as a tool to express her interests in other things.

Anne attended the parents meetings and read all the studies that were done on these exceptional kids. She was lucky that the school had been right here in Chicago, some parents had uprooted their families just so their children could attend Wilcrest, there was no doubt that dealing with these exceptionally bright kids created many challenges. Always in the back of their minds was the fear that their kids would become over-stressed by the strain put on them, mostly self-imposed, or slip into mental illness. There were stories of these brilliant children falling into psychosis. She was glad that Ellie had the horses to help keep her grounded. At least she had been glad that Ellie had the horses at the stable but these dreams were so upsetting.

She called Ellie in to dinner, just a chicken salad and a baked potato, nothing fancy. They had ice cream for dessert. Ellie stayed quiet and immediately went back to her room. The computer was on, Anne saw, as she went into her room to shower and get ready for tomorrow.

After her shower, Anne wanted to do her own research in repetitive dreams. Even though Dr. Jen did not seem to be concerned, she was. She turned on the computer and typed in repetitive dreams.

There was Jung with his consciousness, unconsciousness, myths and dreams but that did not seem to apply. There was a lot of data on repetitive dreams. They seemed to be quite common. She read several articles from psychologists, and psychiatrists. The consensus seemed to be that these dreams were common and probably had something to do with some personal problems either of long standing or, if late occurring, from the stress of something happening in one's life. There was only one that went into the issue of dreams as a predictive tool, or a warning of something about to happen. There did seem to be some evidence that in some instances dreams had been a tool for predicting future events, but the article warned that although there was evidence to support this there had never been any real in-depth work on predictive dreams.

Anne felt reassured after her search. It was nice to know that repetitive dreams were common and that many people had them. So maybe Ellie was just dealing with some stress in this way and it would all resolve itself.

She went in and found Ellie's light out, the computer on standby and Ellie herself asleep. She stood in the doorway looking at her daughter. In sleep, Ellie looked young and defenseless. Anne sighed as she checked the apartment and went to bed herself.

Anne's alarm went off about a moment after she set it and she turned it off angrily against the sleep she wanted to continue. Another day, she thought as she climbed out of bed and headed for the kitchen. Her morning coffee was making noise in the pot as Ellie came out of her room.

"No dreams?" Anne asked.

"No dreams," Ellie said. "I slept really well. How about you?"

"Yes, me too, how will your day shape up? Anything happening that I should know?" Anne asked. "I looked at the calendar and there doesn't seem to be anything going on this weekend. So, we have a weekend with nothing to do! Wonderful."

"We were so busy with the horse show stuff. I guess we didn't have time to plan anything. A weekend with nothing to do will be a treat. Although I have a riding lesson Saturday morning and then we are all meeting with Jackie to look at the videos of the horse show. That should be fun. It'll only be the regular time, and I think that Triana's taking us out this weekend so that lets you off the hook. You should look in the paper and see if there's something going on that you would like to see. I think I've taken up all your time for this horse show stuff. It's time you did something for yourself," Ellie was putting her dishes in the dishwasher. She looked at her mother, smiling she said, "You're not the only one who can worry, you know."

"Well thank you for being concerned. I might just do that," Anne said. "We need to leave in 10. You ready?"

"Just have to brush my teeth and grab my backpack," Ellie said.

CHAPTER 7

Ellie shut the door to the apartment and went into her room; she put her backpack down and returned to the foyer. She looked through the mail that she had brought up from the mailbox on the landing. In the middle of the pile of junk mail and bills was a white envelope with her dad's familiar writing on it. It was addressed to her.

Tearing open the envelope, she started to read. She did not often get mail from her father, usually an email or a phone call; even those were rare. She finished reading the letter. Then laid it carefully on the table, and smoothed it flat. She danced around the kitchen, and went back and read the letter again. It had not changed. The page was still there with her father's writing, saying the same thing it had said before. Her dad was buying her a horse. She was going to have her very own horse. Ellie was having trouble getting her mind around the news.

Dear Ellie,

I'm writing this to tell you that you don't have to come out for your vacation. Your mom has told me that you would rather go to camp, and since I've just signed a new book deal I'll be extremely busy this summer. I'll try to come up to Chicago for a couple of weekends so that we can have some time together.

The new book deal was a surprise, but I have to go get busy on it right away. I would like to give you something that you will love and be able to spend a lot of time with. I know how much you like horses, and your mother has told me how much you enjoy your lessons. Therefore, I've decided to let you have your own horse. I've written a separate letter for your mother to arrange for the financial end of it. I hope that this will give you lots of pleasure and fun for the summer and the coming years. I will call you later in the week to wish you a Happy Birthday and you can tell me all your plans about the horse.

Love you,

Dad

Ellie read the short letter again; she still could not believe it. Jumping up and down with excitement, she was laughing, even though the tears were falling. She could not hold this news to herself, she needed to share it. Clutching the letter to her chest, she grabbed her cell phone and speed-dialed Mary. "Pick up, pick up."

"Ellie, what's going on? Mary said.

"Mary, you're just not going to believe this. Dad wrote me a letter, and he's buying me a horse for my birthday! My very own horse! What could be better than that?" Ellie asked.

"Oh, My God! You're right I can't believe it! Wow. What a lucky girl. I wish I — Oh you know. My dad doesn't even —. Anyway, I'm so happy for you. What horse are you going to get?" Mary asked.

"I don't have a clue. It's just not anything I ever thought about. I didn't think I would get my own horse until I was grown and on my own." Ellie responded.

"What is your mother going to say?" Mary's voice had gotten quiet.

"I've not really thought about it. I don't know what she is going to do. I can't think that she wouldn't let me have a horse. No, she wouldn't do that. Her refusal in the past has been that it was not financially possible. But now Dad has said he will pay for it and everything." Ellie had lost some of her enthusiasm with the reality of her mother's reaction to this.

"Well, Mom will be home soon, and I need to start dinner it's my night to cook." Mary said. "Email me later or call, whatever. I'm so happy for you. You having a horse will be the next best thing to having one of my own," Mary said as she hung up.

Ellie's conversation with Mary had made her think of what her mother would do. Anne had never really understood Ellie's obsession with horses. How would she deal with Ellie having one of her own? Just getting her to agree on a horse show had been an effort. How would she respond to Ellie owning her own horse? She got up, took the letter to the kitchen and laid it open on the table so her mother would see it first thing when she got home.

Maybe she should do what Mary did when she wanted something and thought her mother might not want to agree. She would start dinner. She looked at the clock-5:15, she had about forty-five minutes. She opened the refrigerator to see if her mother had gotten anything out of the freezer for dinner. There was a package of chicken breasts defrosting. She thought about what her mother would do with them, something simple, probably. She turned on the oven and got started.

Ellie did not cook often but she had watched her mother a lot and she had made salads, veggies and stuff. She felt cooking chicken would be easy. In twenty minutes, she had the chicken in the oven and a small salad made. Ellie was happy with what she had accomplished; she should do more cooking and take some of the work off her mother. Ever since her dad had left, Anne had been working full time, leaving her little time for herself. Ellie decided right then to be of more help to her mother.

She went back to her room, but she was restless, unable to focus on anything. Thoughts of horses were playing scenes in her brain. *My own horse, my very own horse*. Tears rolled down her cheeks. *What would it look like? Would it look like the dream horse, the red chestnut mare? No, not like that, like George, maybe. It could be a warm blood, one of those large imports from Europe. They were the new craze in jumping and dressage. One of those would be neat.* Ellie was not very tall and Jackie would probably say a horse that large was not suitable for a short rider. Jackie would know just what to get for her.

Just at 6:15, she heard her mother's key in the lock. Anne was home. "Hey Ellie, it smells good in here, what are you doing?"

"I thought I'd start dinner, Mom. Mary shamed me into it. She cooks every other night for Triana." Ellie smiled.

"That's nice, thanks. I'll just go change then." Anne said.

"Well, we got, well I got a letter from Dad today, it's on the kitchen table I think you should read it right away, Mom."

"Can't it wait a few minutes?"

"I'd really rather you looked at it right now. Please?"

"What is he up to now, I wonder? You look absolutely joyous." Anne had suddenly taken a good look at her daughter. "Whatever has he done?"

She walked quickly into the kitchen and Ellie followed and stood in the doorway watching as her mother read the spread out letter. She saw the color leave her mother's face. "What in the world made him do this?" Anne said. "Why would he write you something like this without even letting me know first?"

53

Anne picked up the letter and read it again; angry spots of color had come into her cheeks. "How could he do this?"

Ellie stood watching and holding her breath, she knew that Anne was very angry. Maybe Anne would be so angry that she would not get to own a horse after all. She had an idea that her father had written to her first in order to stop Anne from saying no. Sometimes the games that adults played were beyond her comprehension but this time she could see her father sending the letter to her, circumventing Anne's objections.

"This is just like him, you know." Anne said. She sighed, and firmly closed her mouth.

Ellie knew that her mother would not say anything else. She knew that it was just another time that her dad had manipulated her mom. It was a good ploy though. Her mom probably could not say no after her dad had agreed to buy and finance the horse, since her objection had always been money.

Ellie felt bad for her mother. She knew that it was unfair the way her father had done this, but she could not help being happy about the horse. She had mixed feelings because she knew her mother did so much for her and that letting her have a horse was just one more thing that Anne would have to deal with, always for Ellie, everything is always all for Ellie. Still she was so happy.

Anne had looked for the letter that Earl said he had sent to her regarding the financial part of buying and keeping a horse, but it had not come with the letter to Ellie. Anne had gone into her room, changed out of her work clothes and came in as Ellie was setting the kitchen table.

"Almost ready, Mom, I've never cooked chicken before, would you look at it a see if it's done?

"Sure luv, it looks delicious. I appreciate the effort." Anne smiled.

After they had eaten mostly in silence, Anne said, "You really want this, don't you?"

"More than anything, it's a dream come true. But I know that it's going to cause you a lot more work." Ellie replied earnestly.

"Mostly I'm concerned that you'll fall behind in your studies. They expect so much from you there." Anne said.

"No more than I expect from myself." Ellie said quietly.

"Oh, I know how focused you are, luv. I didn't mean that. It's just that you drive yourself so hard and the addition of a horse will just give you more to do." Anne looked at her daughter anxiously.

"Oh Mom, it will be so, so — a horse of my own. It will be just wonderful," Ellie was glowing.

Anne knew in that moment that she would give in. Ellie would have her horse. She did not know what they were getting into but she could never say no to that look of joy on her daughter's face.

CHAPTER 8

Jackie Long was explaining to Anne on the phone the complexities of horse buying. "You see we have to first find the right horse. This alone will take a lot of time. Then after it's found, there are things like vet checks, x-rays, things like that, before the horse will belong to Ellie."

"So first we have to find the horse, then it has to be healthy, and then we buy it?" Anne asked.

"Yes, that's about it."

"Well, I guess we'll find one out there somewhere. How do I go about looking?" Anne sounded weary.

"The good news is I look. You just keep your weekends clear." Jackie said.

"There are always more horses for sale than there are buyers. I'll put the word out and you'll be inundated. We can weed a lot of them out just by looking at videos, but there will certainly be some traveling involved," Jackie said cheerfully.

"Just keep my weekends free, huh. Gosh, I don't have anything else to do, now do I?" Anne laughed.

The horse hunting had begun.

Three weeks later Ellie found herself sitting on a large chestnut gelding. She looked around the course and decided how she would ride the fences. She had done two practice jumps and was now circling the arena at the canter. The fences were set at 3 feet, she took the horse to the first fence and he pricked his ears and took it beautifully. He seemed to enjoy the jumping and went easily to the next fence. She experimented with letting him have more rein and he still went forward at a steady pace. She brought him back and he adjusted. He was a lovely horse. Ellie could not fault him. She finished the course and saw Jackie standing in the middle of the ring, watching.

"Well Ellie, what do you think?" she asked.

"He seems really responsive, but —," Ellie answered. What was his name again? Oh yes, his name was Grand Rojo. What a name.

The owner-trainer said they just called him Red. He was an impressive horse, at just under seventeen hands. He had two white socks on his back legs and one right fore sock, and a star on his forehead. Still as beautiful as he was, she did not feel that empathy that she felt with George at home, and certainly not the rapport she felt with the red mare in her dreams. "I just don't know. He's really tall, maybe I feel intimidated on him, or something." Ellie carefully lowered herself to the ground.

"Beautiful horse, just not the one for you, huh kiddo?" Jackie gave her a knowing look. "Okay, well that's the last one today. How many have we looked at so far?" she asked.

"I know I'm being silly, it's just that I — I don't know, I want it to be the perfect horse." Ellie patted the gelding on the neck and led him to the gate. Her mother was waiting in the barn aisle.

"He looked beautiful, Ellie. What's wrong with him?" Anne wanted to know, as Ellie led the horse back inside.

"He's just a little too tall, I feel intimidated riding him," Ellie said.

Anne gave a sigh, "Okay, then, we should thank the man, and get going I'd like to get home before I have to go to work, and you have to go to school." Her voice was irritable in spite of the smile she was wearing.

They had a two-hour ride back to Chicago, and it was already four. Ellie looked at her mother and knew just how hard this was for her. They had been looking at horses all around the area for the last three weekends and each trip taking longer as they got further from home. They had looked at two other horses today, and even Jackie had not been able to fault this one. Ellie could tell that she had thought he was perfect, yet Ellie knew that although this was a good horse, he was not her horse.

Jackie was out of prospects that were within driving distance so they decided to give it up until another good prospect turned up. Jackie said that there were always new horses coming on the market, and it would not be long.

Anne and Ellie dropped Jackie off at the farm and Jackie made a point of asking Anne to give her a call the next day. "I have a couple of things to talk to you about," she said. Anne sighed and said, "Okay, I'll call from work." They drove home in silence.

Ellie spent the time in the car thinking what Jackie wanted to talk to Anne about, although she knew what it was. Jackie was going to tell her mother that Ellie would not be able to settle on any horse but the dream mare. *Is that true?* she asked herself. Could she be comparing all the horses that they had seen to the red mare of her dreams? *Maybe, maybe I am. How will I ever find a real horse?* she thought.

When they got home, knowing she needed to try to explain herself, she said, "I know I'm being picky and I know this is really hard on you, but getting the right horse is just the hardest thing for me. I want it to be perfect. I need to feel a connection with the horse I choose. It's not easy to find. I'm trying, and I appreciate that you are spending all this time with me, doing something you neither like nor understand. I'm sorry if I seem to be ungrateful. I do understand how you feel," Ellie knew that this was not the best way to describe what she was feeling, but it was the best she could do.

Anne looked at her, "I'm glad we're taking some time off. I'm tired, and if you don't mind, I'm going to get ready for work tomorrow and go to bed. Have you got all your work done? Are you ready for school and everything?" Anne asked.

"There's not too much to do right now. I've been working mostly in the music department," Ellie said.

"The music department?" Anne asked surprised.

"Well, after the nightmare or whatever it was, I decided to try to get the music I heard in the dream down on the recorder. I'm finding it difficult. Sometimes the music is so clear that I can't wait to get it down, and then I do, and when I try to play it or reproduce it, it just doesn't sound right," Ellie said.

"I didn't know you were working on music again," Anne said.

"Well, only for this, the music seemed really important in the dream, like painting the red mare was important, only maybe more so. I feel compelled to get the music written down. It's like a beautiful symphony playing repeatedly in my brain. At night when I'm sleeping it's so clear, but when I try to pin it down, it gets all muddled." Ellie had not been going to tell her mother that she was working on music, but it had slipped out. Now she knew that her mother would start to worry again. She just could not do anything right anymore.

CHAPTER 9

*T*he tones were vibrating through her body. Was she still asleep? She wondered, perhaps not. She tried to open her eyes, but maybe they were open, it was just black, the black of an unlit cave deep in the earth. It was the vibration or sound that she was hearing or feeling. She had been thinking about the music from her nightmare dream when she went to sleep. Thoughts were running through her head, but the music and vibration, whatever it was became the only element in that blackness.

Vibration and music resonated in her very cells. Like an ocean wave, they moved through her. She tried to remove herself from the wave of sound, but found she was locked inside it.

Then in the blackness, she started to see colors, faint at first. Since total blackness was so scary, she began to focus on the colors. They were growing closer and became more distinct, pulsing rhythmically. There were seven distinct spheres of *different colors. She tried to decide what the spheres were, but was unable figure out what they were or meant. Beautiful, they swirled to the beat of sound. Ellie watched them. Then she was in them, moving through each one slowly. There was a distinct tone to each vibration and sound; she heard the tone from the sphere she was drifting through and the tones of the others, a harmony so pure that she was awed. It was music beyond music. It was silence and noise, harmony and disharmony, it was vibration, it was sound. They hung in the blackness pulsing with something that was beyond music. It was elemental and her body knew it.*

When she felt that she was going to explode, she began to slide away from the spheres, back into the blackness, yet the sound, beat, music was still a part of her. Her artist self wanted to keep the vision of the Seven Spheres of color and sound in her mind. If only she could make a painting that pulsed with music, was her fleeting thought.

The blackness was back. "Am I ever going to wake up?" Again, she tried to move her body, but was still in the paralysis of sleep. The sleep journey was not yet over and then she was back in the valley of the red mare. The red mare had whinnied when she became aware of Ellie. However, to Ellie it was like coming home and her breathing slowed. At last, the paralysis gave way and she moved into the warmth of the mare. She let the red mare nuzzle her shoulder and then slipped her arms around the familiar red neck.

"I've been to a strange place," Ellie said. "Music and color, strange things to be dreaming about." The mare nuzzled her as if to give her

comfort. *The familiarity of the red mare and the valley calmed her.*

Suddenly the mare grew tense under her hand. "What's wrong?" Ellie asked. The mare whinnied and moved away from Ellie. The mare had never done that before. Ellie became aware of another presence in the valley. A glowing ephemeral being appeared about midway in the meadow and music was pulsing inside her again. Ellie knew what he was now, a unicorn.

He was magnificent; the sun glinted off his pure white coat and his gilded horn shone gold. The creature was like the mare in many ways, but more, much more. Ellie had seen a stallion once going down a lane, led by a man. The stallion was pure power, hooves hardly touching the ground as he moved alongside the insignificant man. The unicorn had that presence, too, but he was blinding in his beauty.

A thought formed in her mind, music, color, vibration, the pulsing spheres, they were pure magic. In the nightmare dream, he had told her to remember the music. This time he was the music. He moved to the middle of the meadow and the mare moved toward him. Ellie stood where she was, watching.

"They're dancing," she thought as the two swirled around each other. The mare seemed totally focused on the unicorn, and Ellie was a bystander to a dance older than time.

Ellie felt the music and the magic of the moment. She thought of the Seven Spheres bright in the blackness, and the music became the colors, the two creatures became the music, colors, and a part of the spheres, bright in the elements of combining.

Ellie did not know how long the dance in the meadow lasted. When she became aware again the mare was alone, the unicorn was gone. The mare called once to the emptiness, then looked back at Ellie standing alone by the stream. Her head low she returned to Ellie, and girl and horse stood together by the stream.

When Ellie woke up the next morning, she did not immediately reach for her journal to record her latest dream. It was early morning. The sun was just rising over the lake, and she stood at her window thinking, not about the red mare, but about the unicorn. Like the nightmare dream of becoming the water, in this dream she had somehow become the music. What was the unicorn trying to show her? She stood there watching the sunrise and tried to recall everything that was in the dream. The total blackness, the rise of the colored musical spheres, like the music she had been trying to recreate, the colors of the spheres would be almost impossible to duplicate.

Finally, she went back to her journal lying by the bed. She reread the nightmare dream. She knew that last night, she had watched the mating of the red mare to the unicorn. From her reading, she knew that although unicorns were in mythology worldwide, they were not real creatures. Yet unicorns, like dragons, were found in literature around the globe.

Ellie went through her journals looking at the reoccurring dreams about a unicorn and a red mare. In the nightmare dream, the unicorn told her to remember the music; in this one, she was seeing spheres that were color, vibration, and music. She sighed, picked up her pen and moved to the next page of her journal. She thought for a moment then started to record this latest and strangest of all her dreams.

She reread her latest dream. Satisfied that she had written it as clearly as she could remember, she closed the journal and went over to her computer. Somewhere in her memory, there was something about musical spheres. She typed in "musical spheres" and the computer dutifully filled her screen with source information. There it was. Pythagoras was where she had read about the spheres. Pythagoras had written about a theory in mathematics and something about harmony and music, something like that. He and his followers thought that vibration and music were the threads that made the universe.

It was getting late and Ellie needed to get ready for school. She would continue that line of research with Dr. Gregory. He would probably think she was crazy, and who knew, maybe she was.

~~~~~~

Phelistia

Her head low over the Sacred Pool, Phelistia leaned forward. She could feel the planet core's pulse running through her body. There in the pool the scene played out before her disbelieving eyes. "What are you doing," she whispered to herself. She did not believe what was happening in the small valley. The vivid red creature was much like herself, but there were many differences. Whatever this creature was, Phelistia knew that what was about to happen could not be. Phellsome was about to commit a crime of such import that it could never be forgiven.

"Don't do this thing. Please brother, don't do this thing," she was pleading with the image in the Pool. The twin bond was very strong and distance was not a deterrent, nor was the shield that her errant brother was using could keep her from his mind. In moments like these, they were as close to one as was possible between two separate beings.

She knew that he could hear her and feel her emotions as if they were his. She knew that he could feel the fear, anger and sadness, consuming her this moment in time. There were questions with no answers. They had never been apart, and now she was feeling betrayed. They had consulted with and worked with one another in complete trust. Now, suddenly, without explanation he was breaking a law that had never been broken. He was tainting the bloodline, on this planet that had somehow lost the harmony of the universe.

"How can you do such a thing," she cried.

"Sister, this has to be. You will understand. I promise. Now, you have to leave my thoughts. You must go. This has to be, no matter the consequences. This has to be. Please trust me."

He was gone. What was happening would be a reality. "There was going to be a—a, a what?" *She shuddered as she realized what most would believe.* "It would be, an abomination."

CHAPTER 10

Ellie went directly to Dr. Gregory's office after assembly, but it was empty. She left a note asking for some time later, saying she would be in the music room most of the day, and would come whenever he might be able to see her. Once in the music room, she found her folder of notes on the nightmare music and sat down at the piano.

The music flowed from her brain, out through her fingers and on to the keyboard. It was good, but it was not what she had heard from her dream. Now the newest dream music was intruding into the old, frustrating her even more. It was not a jumble exactly, but not clear either. Her mind was on the spheres and the colors. *All artistic work is connected*, she thought, *math, music, painting, color. All connected with our emotions and feelings.*

She let her fingers move over the keys, her eyes closed, as she thought of the spheres. Each sphere she remembered had vibrated with swirling colors moving inside it, with a definite pattern. The vibrations had sounded like a tap on a crystal glass or those musical bowls, leaving a resonating sound in her head. Once she had heard an instrument made of crystal. It was played by wetting the hands and touching spinning crystal bowls. She had forgotten the name of the instrument, but now it seemed that the music from the spheres was somewhat like it.

At that moment the music was in her mind, her fingers took on a life of their own. Music flowed from her hands. Yes, yes, this is what it was. She was rejoicing in it. "I've got it at last," she said aloud, as the tears ran down her cheeks. She did not know how long she played, but it was as if the unicorn were there showing her hands what to play. Then he and the music were gone just as suddenly as they had come. Ellie's cheeks were wet from the tears. She sat very still, afraid to move.

"Ellie, Ellie are you okay?" a deep voice said.

She jumped and screamed. Startled, she looked up to see Mr. Gregory standing just inside the room. "I'm sorry, Mr. Gregory, I just didn't know anyone was here. You scared me," Ellie said.

"I'm sorry too, Ellie, I didn't mean to scare you. What were you playing? It's not a piece that I know, but it's absolutely stunning," he said. "Is it new?"

"It's just something I've been working on," she stammered. "It's been running around in my head for a while, and I've been trying to get it down on paper."

"Well, it's certainly going to be something when you finally get it. In fact, I think you should show it to Ms. Hansen. I think she'd like to hear it."

"Yes, thank you, I'll do that," Ellie got up and smiled. Ms. Hansen was the music director at Wilcrest.

"You wanted to see me?" Dr. Gregory said.

"Yes, I've some questions about something. Have you got a few minutes?" Ellie asked

"Yes, of course. Let's go to my office. Have you had a change of heart and want to get serious about math?" he laughed, but Ellie could tell he was somewhat hopeful.

"Well, maybe, but something has come to my attention, and I was hoping that you could help me with it." They were walking down the hall toward his office.

"Anything that I can do," he said.

Ellie was trying to think of what to say. The music had disrupted her thinking. She could not just say, "Oh, Dr. Gregory, by the way, there's this unicorn in my head and he's showing me spheres in the universe somewhere, they're really pretty and they are making the most wonderful music." That certainly was not going to help. Perhaps she could just say that she had come across Pythagoras in her research and had some interest in his theories about music and the Seven Spheres and she was wondering if he could give her some direction on those theories. It sounded lame, but the truth would definitely not work.

"Now what can I do for you?" he said kindly, as he pointed to a chair in front of his desk.

"I've come across something about Pythagorean theory and I was wondering if you could point me in the right direction for research," she said.

"Pythagoras, the Greek mathematician?" Dr. Gregory asked.

"Yes, that would be the one," she tried to look just interested.

"Well, that's an interesting request. I suppose I could find some books on the subject. You know there is no way of knowing how much was his work, or the work of his followers," Dr. Gregory said.

"I know; I did a little research on line, but I needed something more in depth. Has there been anything recent on those theorems?" Ellie looked up earnestly.

"I'll tell you what. I'll look in some journals and see what, if anything is happening. I don't think there's anything recent, but you never know. Vibrations are getting a fresh look now with this new physics work. Very exciting."

"Also, anything about the Seven Spheres. That would be helpful." Ellie said.

"The spheres?" he seemed dubious.

"Yes, the spheres," she said.

"Okay, let me have a day or two and I'll see what I can come up with. There may not be anything very new. These theories date back before almost everything," he smiled.

Ellie thanked him and left. She walked back to the music room and sat at the piano letting her fingers roam over the keys. The music she had played earlier had not been hers. It was as if the unicorn from her dream had taken over her mind and hands and played the music through her. This was the first time that any of her night dreams had interfered with her day life. It was scary, in that she had lost control of her own actions. What would her mother think about that? More so, what was she going to think about it?

Mary found Ellie in the music room at the computer running a software program that recorded the notes and filled out sheet music. She waited until Ellie had completed a page.

"Hey, I've been looking all over for you. I expected you to be in the art room this afternoon. How's the horse hunting going?"

"Not very well, we've exhausted everything within driving distance. Mom is not happy. I wish you could have been there yesterday. We saw the perfect horse, but I just couldn't relate. I think Jackie was disappointed that I didn't like him," Ellie said.

"Why didn't you like him? If he was so well trained, you should have been happy. What happened?" Mary asked.

"I just don't know. We have looked at so many. They all had good things about them but none of them felt like the right horse for me. I don't know. I'm just confused," Ellie admitted.

"Do you think the dream mare has anything to do with it?" Mary asked. "You paint her all the time and you dream about her too.

"I know that's what Mom thinks and maybe Jackie, too. It was obvious yesterday. That horse was perfect, except that he didn't talk to me. But, I couldn't say that to anyone, now could I?" Ellie smiled.

"Well, you said it to me," Mary responded.

"Of course, I said it to you. How could I not? You're my best friend. We tell each other everything, don't we?" Ellie looked at her friend.

"Yes, I think we do. We're lucky to have each other. Everyone here is so — so into their own thing. It's hard to make close friendships," Mary said. She reached out and took Ellie's hand, squeezing it gently.

"So tell me what you were doing with Dr. Gregory. He's not the best looking teacher in the school, you know."

Ellie laughed, "Well, now, I don't know about that, he's pretty cute, in a professor kinda way."

Both girls laughed. There were many boys in the school, but very few were what they would call handsome. "Actually, I was asking him for some information on Pythagoras and the Seven Spheres. I was hoping there was some research out there that would give me some ideas on celestial harmony," Ellie said.

"Celestial harmony? You never cease to amaze me. What brought that about, as if you don't have enough on your mind right now? Does it have something to do with the music you're trying to write?" Mary asked.

"Well yes, in a way it does, but mostly it has to do with a dream I had the other night," Ellie said.

"What, another dream? One you haven't told me about?" Mary asked.

Ellie looked at her friend. *I need someone to talk to*, she decided, and before she could change her mind, she began to speak.

"Okay, sit down and let me tell you about it," and with a sigh Ellie started to relate the dream about the unicorn, music, and spheres.

CHAPTER 11

Horse hunting was proving to be time consuming and difficult. Nothing had suited Ellie. Anne was beginning to tire of all the searching. They had looked at many horses and most of them had looked beautiful to Anne. Still Ellie could not find just the right horse. Her father's check had been generous and money was not going to be a problem, but there was something wrong with every horse they looked at.

Anne was getting anxious about Ellie's inability to make up her mind. She was thinking that the dream horse was standing in the way of finding a real horse. Ellie kept saying the right horse just had not been found, that one was out there somewhere. However, after the last horse they had looked at, Jackie told Anne that she would continue searching, but she would not be able to find a better horse than the gelding, which Ellie had turned down. Anne knew that Jackie was implying that Ellie was looking for the dream horse, too.

Since there was nothing left to see now, she was free for the weekend. What a treat. This was the last weekend before Ellie's school was out for the summer. Anne was tired. It had been Earl's idea to buy Ellie a horse. Yet as usual, he was

73

leaving the looking and buying to her. She should have refused to spend her time looking for one. He did not have a real job taking eight hours a day out of his life, as she did. He did not have the daily care of their child. Being a single parent was just so hard. She smiled at herself and thought, *Get over it, you have a beautiful, thoughtful, lovely daughter. You wouldn't trade that for all the free time in the world.*

For the first time in a month, they were not racing off to look at a horse. *Maybe they had looked at all the horses in the world,* Anne thought. Thinking of a whole weekend with nothing to do, she hummed softly to herself and decided to take a long soak in the tub.

The next morning, Ellie was looking through the newspaper trying to find a movie that she wanted to see. She was discouraged over her inability to find THE HORSE, and had just decided there was nothing that she wanted to do today and as school was out next week, most of her work was finished. Maybe she would call Mary and see if they could find something to do together, when an advertisement caught her attention. She read the ad and then read it again. It was about an auction of BLM horses in a neighboring small town that served as a bedroom community to Chicago. The horses were being auctioned this afternoon. She flew across the room to her mother.

"Mom, look at this," she was waving the newspaper under her mother's nose. "They are having an auction of BLM horses in Crystal Lake, can we go? Please, can we go?"

"What's a BLM horse?" Anne asked, cautiously.

"The Bureau of Land Management is responsible for keeping the wild horse population under control. They round up many wild horses and offer them for sale to qualified buyers. Otherwise, the wild horses would starve because they don't have enough land to graze on," Ellie's eyes were big and she was clearly excited. "Also, they're right here, close to town. Well, pretty close to town. They're going to auction some off this afternoon. Oh Mom, can we go? Please, please, I'd love to see real wild horses! Oh please? We could call Mary and Triana. We could go for a drive. It would be so much fun. It would." Ellie was pleading.

Anne looked at her daughter, animated and charming. How could she refuse? It was just so good to see her looking happy. She sighed as she thought about her day of doing nothing. She knew she would give in and spend another day looking at horses.

"Okay, you call Mary, and see if they'd like to go. We're not; I repeat NOT, going to buy a wild horse. You understand that, don't you?"

"No, of course not, Mom, I just want to see them. They must be beautiful. Don't you think?"

"I suppose so," Anne said, as she got up and took her coffee cup to the kitchen.

Ellie grabbed the phone and called Mary. "Crystal Lake is only about an hour north. No, we've never been there, but it should be fun. It'll be fun to see the wild horses. It's so nice out, and a drive will be wonderful. Don't you think?" Ellie ran out of breath.

"I'll talk to mother; she was just going to stay home today and rest. But, I'll call you right back." Mary said.

Anne was looking on the computer for directions, thinking about the details of a lunch and drive time. Things that Moms thought of and daughters took for granted. She sighed, and thought that it probably would be a good day to go for a drive.

Knowing her mother was giving up her lazy day for yet another horse adventure, Ellie was careful to be helpful. She filled the cooler with ice and put in some water and snacks. Mary had managed to get her mother to agree to come, so Anne and Ellie stopped by and picked them up and they were on their way.

They finally got out of the congested city traffic and the roads became uncrowded. Triana and Anne sat together in the front seat chatting about Anne's trials of horse hunting. Ellie and Mary in the back were laughing and chattering away about the horses that Ellie had ridden on her buying expeditions.

"And they all look the same to me," Anne said.

"I'd no idea that finding a horse was so difficult," responded Triana.

"Nor did I. I just wish Earl had to do the shopping. He probably thinks you go to the mall and hand them your credit card!"

Both Mary and Ellie laughed at that. They were now discussing their plans for the summer because now that Ellie would have her own horse, it was going to be much more exciting. They planned to spend all their time at the stable with Ellie's new horse. If that is, they found a horse.

"This is such pretty country," Triana said. "It'd be nice to live out here and get out of downtown."

"I don't know about that," Anne said, "with the girls at school and all the other classes, I don't think either of us could move. Maybe when they get to college full time, there will be less stress."

"Well that might be next year. Mary and Ellie will be taking classes at Chicago University, this year and will probably be going there full time next year," Triana said.

"Time is flying by, college is the next step, and they are so young," Anne said.

They reached the auction yard in about an hour. When they arrived and opened the car doors, the day proved to be hot and dusty after the air-conditioned car. In the back behind the large auction building were two big corrals with dust swirling around.

"Well, we're certainly here," Anne said.

"Let's walk around to the back and take a look. There seem to be lots of horses out there," Mary said.

"The paper said about seventy five in all," Ellie replied.

Leaving their mothers to lock the car and look for shade, the girls walked quickly around to the corrals. Many people were watching as the horses moved about in the pens. There were horses in all colors, even palominos with their flaxen manes and tails. Ellie was surprised to see so many pinto horses here. Most were brown and white with large spots, but two or three were splashed with color like paint thrown on canvas. All of the horses seemed skittish and the heat shimmered over the corrals.

Anne and Triana followed staying well away from the fence. Mary and Ellie went right up to see the spectacle. Most of the horses were small, with tangled manes and a look of pure terror in their eyes. They were very different from the large, well-fed horses that Mary and Ellie were used to.

Ellie thought they looked sad and scared. "Poor things, they look so scared."

"You'd be scared too, if you had been running free and then been caught and suddenly transported to a place with fences and people," Mary said.

"Yes, but if they don't relocate them, the mustangs will overpopulate and destroy their range land. They could starve to death and the overcrowding destroys the vegetation. Already the ranches want to take it all for their cattle," Ellie replied. "It's a really big problem. There doesn't seem to be a good solution."

"I guess, but it's sad to see them like this."

Ellie was standing at the fence watching the horses mill around in the corral, but she was thinking of the red mare trotting across the meadow. She remembered the mountains all around the little valley and the stream running through it. Why had the mare been all alone? Horses liked to be together. Her red mare did not look like these horses. She was bigger, probably fifteen hands or more. Ellie knew this because she had dreamed of leaning against the mare's side and putting her arms around her neck.

Mary said, "They're back with humans after hundreds of years running free. I read that some of them are pure Spanish Barb horses, lost by the Conquistadors. Isn't that something?"

"From the Arabian desert, brought by the Moors to Spain, across the Atlantic to the Americas," Ellie said, "what a long journey."

"Girls, we're going to go inside and sit down. They'll be starting the sale in about thirty minutes," Anne said. "You two stay together and come find us. It's too hot and dusty out here."

"Okay, Mom, we just want to look at the other corral. Then we'll come in," Ellie said.

Ellie and Mary walked toward the second corral. "It's really fun to see them," said Mary.

"Yeah, just think, these are the horses that the Indians rode, that the cowboys rode," Ellie said.

"They're tough little guys, no doubt about it."

At that moment, Ellie felt something like a blow to the head. She staggered, and caught Mary's hand. "Wait, something's wrong." She looked around to find the bright day dimmed and the air thick and hot. She could not move. Nothing was moving, everything and everyone had stopped. Mary was holding her hand but was frozen, with a startled look on her face. Then a picture formed in Ellie's mind of the red mare.

Get me out of here, came whole into her mind. Ellie suddenly felt nauseated and disoriented. Mary's mouth was moving but no sound was coming through.

Get me out of here, resounded in her head. The voice was so loud she thought her head might split open. Her body felt like she was swimming in a lake of mud and standing here holding Mary's hand at the same time. What was happening to her? Something was in her head talking, and again, the picture of the red mare formed.

You are here, I feel you, come get me out! Ellie felt like throwing up. It was so strange, what was going on in her head. She was with Mary at the corral, and yet inside her head, she was seeing the red mare and hearing the mare's voice. It was disorienting.

"Are you alright?" Mary asked as Ellie fought to bring order of the chaos of words and thoughts forming inside her head. Mary was looking at her with concern.

"No — I mean maybe. I don't know," Ellie stammered.

'Let's go find our mothers. You don't look so good."

"I'll be okay. I just need to catch my breath for a minute. All right?"

Ellie was getting herself together. It was okay as long as the voice and pictures stayed out of her head.

"We need to look around some. I think there are more horses here somewhere," Ellie said.

"I don't know where they'd be," Mary replied.

"I don't either, but—listen, I think one just spoke to me," Ellie decided to be honest with what had happened to her. She did not know what Mary would do, but she had to share some of this with someone and Mary was still holding her hand.

"What, what did you say? A horse talked to you. How? I mean what—what did it say?" Now, Mary looked white and unbelieving.

"It was the red mare, the one I paint all the time. First, I had a picture of her in my mind, and then, it was as if I was looking out at what she saw! All at the same time, she spoke words in my head. She said, 'Get me out of here.' I know it sounds strange but it's really happening, and when she's in my head, I feel nauseated and sick. It's really weird." Ellie looked like she might cry.

Mary was still holding her hand and looking scared. "Ellie, I know you are obsessed with the dreams and that red horse. Could you be hallucinating or something?"

"I don't think so. This was real, I know what I heard, and I know what I saw."

"Let's go get your mother. Maybe she will be able to help. You should sit down; get a drink, or something. I don't like this," Mary was pleading with Ellie and trying to lead her toward the door of the auction hall.

"No, no I'm okay I just need to —" that thought was lost as the voice and pictures returned to her mind. *Come get me out of here,* screamed in Ellie's head.

"Just shut up! I can't think with you doing that! Just shut up." Ellie said it aloud and Mary became even more scared.

"Ellie, please come on. You're scaring me, please come inside and sit down." Mary was pulling on her arm and trying to drag her toward the safety of the building. She knew she could find Anne there and get help.

"Mary, the voice is back, and I've got to find the mare. I can't think with her in my head, but she's here and I need to find her. You go and get Mom, and tell her what's happening. I'm going to look around in the back. The picture in my head showed me a dark place, maybe a stall of some kind. Okay? Please-" she trailed off and looked at Mary, "I think that the mare is in some kind of trouble. She needs me."

Mary looked scared and worried, but after a moment, she agreed. "Okay, but don't you do anything foolish until I get our mothers. Okay? Please don't do anything, don't DO anything, okay?"

"No, I'll just go looking in the back for something that looks like the picture in my head, I'll be careful. But, I need to go. Now." Ellie walked off with a purposeful stride.

Mary watched her for a moment, then turned and ran for the wide doors that led to the inside, where she was beginning to hear the sound of an auctioneer. The sale had begun.

Ellie went around the building. There was a large covered area with lanes laid out to move stock from the holding pens to the sale arena. The riders were beginning to move the frantic horses into the lane and out of the large holding pens where Ellie had been watching them. She moved along the side of the pens and found her way to the back where there were several large, covered stock trucks. *This had to be the way the horses were brought in*, she thought.

She wondered about how frightened these poor horses were. This was an awful start for their new lives. How many of them would be able to make the adjustment and lead productive lives in this new environment.

Now, you should talk to me. I'm looking for you, where are you? Ellie thought these words and tried to project them. It was new to her and she was not sure of how to communicate with the horse. By now, the crowd of people had gone into the building for the auction. She was all alone in the back.

Please talk to me, I'm looking for you and I don't know how I'm going to find you. Ellie was still not talking aloud.

She was looking for stalls or something, but saw nothing but the trucks. The mare had not spoken to her again. "Talk to me, I can't find you!" this time she spoke the words aloud but softly.

I don't want to hurt you. I make you sick. This time the voice was soft and there were no pictures to confuse her. Ellie was still able to walk and stay in her own space.

"That's better, the voice needs to be quieter and then I'll able to function around it somehow," Ellie spoke back. "Can you tell me where you are?"

Let me show you in pictures. I don't have the words. Slowly the picture formed in Ellie's mind. She was more prepared for it now and didn't feel quite so ill, although the pictures in her head still caused her to feel dizzy. It was a stall with straw on the floor. Two board rails served as a gate. It wasn't very large, but there was room for a horse to lie down if necessary.

"I don't see any type of barn back here. Are you with any other horses?"

No, I'm all alone; they took me out of the other place." The mare was trying hard now to be quiet with her pictures and her voice. Ellie was beginning to understand that the pictures were from the mare's perspective.

I don't have words for where I am. All I can do is show you pictures. Pictures are easier for me; the mare seemed apologetic. *I've been trying to find you for a long time.*

You were trying to find me? Ellie was walking through the parked trailers looking for some kind of stall. She saw that the very last truck had a trailer with a ramp that led up into it. That looked promising and anyway it was the last trailer, so she decided to go up the ramp and see what was inside.

I've been calling you for a long time. Finally, he showed me how to get to you.

He, who is he? Ellie was walking up the ramp, but the interior was dark and she could not see inside. She would have to go all the way up and into the trailer.

Phellsome showed me how to get out of the valley, the mare said.

What is a-a-Phelleso, what?

A picture of the large white unicorn from Ellie's dreams formed in her mind. If he was real, the red mare was real. All the dreams could be real. In a weird way, this made sense to her.

His name is Phellsome, he's a — I don't have a name for what he is. He's a — again the picture came fully formed.

Ellie had stopped just at the top of the ramp. She concentrated on the image. *We call them unicorns. They aren't supposed to be real*, Ellie said.

Unicorns. Yes, well his name is Phellsome. Come on in; you are right outside. I'm waiting for you, the mare said.

Ellie came out of her reverie about unicorns and stepped into the trailer. It was dark but there was enough light that she could see. Someone had made a small stall just like the one she had seen in her head. In the center, with ears forward, stood the most beautiful horse Ellie had ever seen, at least ever seen in real life. She had seen her many times in her dreams.

You're real. You're not a dream; you're even more beautiful than my picture of you. Ellie had stopped just outside the two boards that made a gate to the stall.

Of course, I'm real. Why wouldn't I be real? The mare was standing there talking to her just as a person would be, except no words were being said.

But, I thought you were only a dream. I paint you and think about you, but I didn't dare believe that you were real. What should I call you?

My name is Dream, of course, and I'm real enough. But I want you to get me out of here, the horse repeated her complaint.

Ellie threw the boards down from the stall and ran to the mare. The mare nickered low in her throat and reached out her head, just like in the dreams. Ellie sobbed, throwing her arms around the horse's neck. She felt the warm body and the smell she knew so well. She had found her horse. The tears rolled down her cheeks and the strangled sobs racked her chest. She clung to her horse, *you just don't know how I've wanted to do this; you just don't know.*

Yes, I do know. I know because I've been trying to get to you for over a year, the mare said.

It was at this moment that Ellie saw that the mare was disproportionately large in the middle. *Why you're — you're going to have a baby! You're in foal, when will it be born?*

Soon I think, but you really don't know about that until it is time, the mare said complacently.

That's going to be a complication for sure. I'm not sure how my mother is going to take my finding you, much less you plus a baby. How will we explain that? Ellie was still hugging the horse, rubbing her neck and clinging to her. She did not want to think about her mother, and her mother's vehement opposition to buying one of these mustang horses.

CHAPTER 12

Mary raced into the building looking for her Mom and Anne. She was frantic. There were many people in bleachers on both sides of the small arena; the air was cooler inside, as the building was air-conditioned. She stopped and looked anxiously around. Then, slowly started to walk toward the ring where a young pinto horse was standing, looking wild-eyed at the crowd. How was ever she going to find her mother?

Then Mary heard her mother call her name. There on the left hand side of the arena at the foot of the bleaches stood her mother and Anne. With a sigh of relief, she ran over to them.

"Where is Ellie?" Anne asked, looking around, confused.

"She's," it occurred to Mary that the she would have trouble explaining just what had happened to Ellie. "Oh, Anne, you need to come right away. Ellie thinks she's found the red mare."

"What? Where is she? What are you saying? Ellie has found a what? A red mare? What red mare?" Anne reached out and grabbed Mary's arm.

"Mary, what are you talking about? Where is Ellie?" Triana said.

"Yes, where is Ellie? You should be together." Anne was looking around as if Ellie would come walking into the building.

"I'm trying to tell you. You need to come with me, Ellie and I were looking at the corrals of horses and suddenly she started acting strange. She told me the red mare, the one in her dreams, was here, and wanted Ellie to come and get her. Ellie started off to the back of the building. She told me to come and get you." Mary took Anne's hand and pulled her toward the door. "You need to come with me, now. I'm scared."

"Oh my, Mary, You just left her alone?" Triana said.

"Mom, I couldn't help it. She told me the mare was calling her, for me to come find you. She was confused and white. I thought she would faint or throw up or something. Then she just walked away," Mary said with tears in her eyes.

Anne looked at the crying girl. "It's okay, Mary. We'll just go with you and find her. It's not your fault, I'm sure everything will be alright," she said, but she did not believe that. She did not believe that at all.

She released Mary's hand and started for the door, with Mary and Triana bringing up the rear, looking confused.

"She went around the end of the building," Mary said, as they walked out into the heat of the early afternoon. "She said the horse was talking to her or something."

Anne was walking quickly toward the rear. Triana had Mary's hand. Both women were wearing worried frowns.

They reached the back of the building and saw a line of truck trailers. "Mary, where did she go?" Anne said.

"I don't know I ran inside to find you. We probably need to look in all the trailers," Mary said.

They peered into the first trailer only to find it empty and went on down the line. Anne was almost running. When they got to the last one, she ran up the ramp, stopping just inside the door. Mary and Triana were standing at the bottom looking up. When Anne neither spoke nor turned, Triana called up to her. "Anne, Anne is she in there?"

Anne turned and motioned for them to come up the ramp. She had the forethought to put her finger to her lips in the quiet sign. They came up to stand beside her.

There in front of them in the dim light of the trailer was a red horse in a small stall with the floor covered in straw. Standing with her arms around the horse's neck was Ellie, tears running down her cheeks. She seemed to be talking softly. The mare would nuzzle her and blow in her hair as if answering her.

Anne stood watching for a few moments and then quietly called her daughter's name "Ellie, Ellie, are you okay? I want you to back away from the horse, now. Can you come out of the stall and come here?"

It took a while for her voice to make any impression on the girl, but finally Ellie, still holding on to the horse, turned slightly and looked at her mother. "She's here, Mom. Dream is here. We've found each other. It's my dream horse, just look at her and you'll see." Ellie had a strange look on her face, but a tremulous smile played around her mouth.

Anne walked a little closer to the pair. "I want you to come out of there. I'm afraid you'll be hurt. We don't know anything about that horse, Ellie. It can't possibly be the dream horse. Please turn her loose and come out now."

"Oh Mom, look at her. Of course, she's the dream horse, and she talked to me. We have to take her home, can't you see. Just look at her." Ellie had not moved away from the horse, her arms were still around her.

Anne was moving slowly forward trying not to panic. "Ellie, I need you to listen to me. I want you to come out of that stall, please. We can talk more when you are out here with me. Even if it is the dream horse, you will have to come out of there. I don't want anything to happen to you."

"Mom, this is Dream, she would never hurt me. We know each other very well. We've known each other since the first night I dreamed of her."

"Ellie, if you say you know her. If you say you talk to her, I believe you. Okay? Look at me; I want you to come out of there. I need to feel that you are safe. Then we will talk about what to do. Please, please turn her loose and come out here, so we can talk. You are making me so afraid for you," Anne was standing close, with her hand outstretched.

Ellie looked at her mother and saw that she was white with tears running down her cheeks. She knew then how this was affecting her mother, and that Anne was truly afraid for her.

Ellie had not thought about how this would look to someone else. Her mother was scared. "Okay, Mom. I'll come out now. Just give me a second. I need to explain what I'm doing to Dream." *That'll scare her even more.*

Anne stepped back a slow step. She watched as her daughter laid her forehead against the red neck and closed her eyes. It seemed forever, but finally Ellie lifted her head, stroked the mare's neck and backed out of the stall. She replaced the two boards to close the gate, and walked to her mother. "Thank you for believing me, Mom," she said.

The moment Ellie was safely out of harm's way, Anne felt the anger rise swift, up through her body. She wanted to grab her daughter, shake her, scream at her. How dare she put herself in such danger? *How could she do this to me? I love her so much.* She drew a deep breath and then another. Slowly, she wrapped her arms around this almost woman, but always her child and the two clung to each other.

"Can you leave the horse until we can figure this out?" Anne asked.

"I don't know, Mom. Maybe; let me go ask her," Ellie looked up at her mother. "Do you believe me that I can talk to the horse?"

"Ellie, I want to believe you, I do. Right now, I don't know what to believe. This horse certainly looks like the horse that you painted. But now isn't the time for all this. Now we need to figure out what to do. Have you forgotten Mary and Triana?"

At that, Ellie looked beyond her mother to Mary and Triana standing just inside the trailer door. It had not occurred to her what they might be thinking.

She turned back to her mother. "I'll just be a second, okay?" She walked back to the stall, but did not go in. She stood very still and concentrated on the mare, *I'll have to leave you for a while, will that be all right?*

I'll be here, waiting. You will take me with you? The mare was speaking directly in her mind.

We have to figure out how we're going to get you out of here and how to take you home, Ellie answered.

Ellie reached in and gave the horse a soft touch on the nose then turned and went to the ramp. "Let's go down. We need to find out how to buy the horse and how we're going to get her home. Mom, you'll help me, won't you?"

"Of course, Ellie, we'll figure this out." She sighed as she took her daughter's hand, and with Mary and Triana following, they walked down the ramp.

When they got to the bottom, Triana suggested they go to the food stand and get something to drink, and to think about what they were going to do.

"That's a good idea, Triana. We need to settle down. Something cold will be just the thing." Anne said, looking gratefully at her friend.

They all walked to the front of the building, ordering cold drinks and some chips from a kiosk. Ellie was suddenly so thirsty she drank half of her drink in one big gulp.

"Hey Ellie slow down, you'll throw up, if you don't watch out," Mary said.

"I'm really thirsty; I think I need a bottle of water, too."

Triana looked at Anne and then Ellie, "Mary and I will go get the cooler; I think you two need a few minutes alone. Since we're here, I think we'd like to see how this auction works, so take as long as you like. We'll take the cooler to the sale ring. You'll be able to find us there in the bleachers."

Anne looked over at Triana. "What a good friend you are. I'm so grateful you two are here. You can't know how much I mean that." She reached over and squeezed Triana's hand.

Triana squeezed back. "We're here for both of you. We've become very close to you both, haven't we, Mary?"

"Yes we have. You know how I feel, Ellie. You're my very best friend," Mary said.

Ellie looked at her mother, then at Mary and Triana. Here was her base. These three would always be there for her. They might not always agree with her, but they would always listen to her and support her. Tears formed in her eyes as she got up and hugged first Mary and then Triana. "Thank you both for everything."

Triana and Mary walked away toward the car. Anne and Ellie watched them go. "Now what are we going to do?" Anne asked.

"I don't know for sure. I do know that I've found the mare from my dreams. I know that she can communicate with me somehow. I don't know how it is happening, just that it is," Ellie looked up at her mother. "I also know that she wants me to take her home. It's like all the dreams have been leading up to this moment. I think that our coming here wasn't a coincidence, but was somehow planned, so that the mare and I would be together."

Anne did not want to think about what Ellie was telling her. She did not want to think about any of that. There was too much mystery. Too much that required acceptance, too much faith in something she did not or could not understand. Something that would require her to believe things that just could not be, talking horses, dreams that were real, a daughter who insisted she was doing these things. Anne shook her head to clear it. Mother and daughter stared at each other, both white and trembling slightly. At that moment, they looked very much alike, with their blonde hair and petite features.

Then Anne spoke, ignoring the implications of Ellie's reasoning, "Okay, if this is the horse you want then we'll try to buy her. I don't know why she's in that trailer out of sight, but I'm sure someone does. We have to find out if she is a wild horse or what. Then we can figure out how to buy her and transport her back to the stable."

"I think that Jackie will be able to come pick her up with the trailer. It's only about an hour or so away," Ellie said.

"Okay, then that leaves us with finding out who owns her," Anne said, feeling better, now that they had a plan. "Let's go to the sales office. Someone there will surely know about her."

They got up still holding their drinks. "Okay, first, we'll find out if she's a BLM horse, and if so, can we buy her. Then we'll call Jackie to see if she will be able to come with the trailer and pick her up."

Anne and Ellie went searching for the sales office. They were directed to a table set up in the back of the sales area. Once there they waited in a line of people who were waiting to pay for the horses they had successfully bid on in the sales area.

They reached the front of the line in about ten minutes. Ellie was getting scared. 'What ifs' were running through her mind *What if we can't buy Dream? What if she's already been sold? What if someone else owns her?*

Of course, I'll go home with you. Don't worry so much. It will all be all right. He wouldn't let it go wrong. We need to be together. It's meant to be.

Ellie wanted to believe the horse, she really did, but she knew a lot more about how her world worked than Dream did. Things did not always work just because it was right or should happen. Sometimes things went wrong. In fact, many times things did not work the way they were supposed to. Ellie just hoped that this time they would not. Maybe the unicorn could make things go right. Maybe he was out there watching. He did have an interest in the mare. She was carrying his foal. This was not the time to think about that. Ellie was not even sure that her mother knew the mare was pregnant. She should have told her, but things had been happening much too fast. She did not have time to consider the consequences of what they were doing. She just knew that she and Dream had to be together. All her dreams led to this moment.

The clerk at the counter was calling them. "Do you have your horse's number?" she asked.

"Uh um, no, actually we were trying to inquire about a horse that's not in the sale. We want to know about a red mare that's in a stall in one of the trailers. Is there someone that can tell us about that horse?" Anne asked.

"A horse that's not in the sale, I don't think there are any horses that won't go through the sale," the clerk said.

"Yes, there is a horse that's in the back in a trailer. That's the horse we want to ask about," Anne said. "Perhaps, we could speak to the manager? Someone that is in charge of the horses?"

"That would be Mr. Edwards," the woman said. She looked around and called to a man in a uniform. "Joe, would you get someone to find Mr. Edwards?" Then, she turned back to Anne and Ellie. "If you'll wait over there, Joe will try to find Mr. Edwards. He would be the only one who could help you." She directed them to a bench on the side of the wall. They went over and sat down.

Ellie took the time to try to call Jackie. She knew that Jackie would have to call them back, as she was sure to be giving lessons. Ellie just hoped that she would get the message soon. The machine picked up, and Jackie's voice came over the cell phone, "Hi, you've reached Whispering Tree Stable, please leave a message, and I'll get back to you as soon as possible."

"Hey Jackie, this is Ellie; can you call me back, ASAP? It's important. I think I've found my horse. Call my cell phone. Thanks."

She watched as a man with an outdoor weathered look, wearing jeans and an open necked western shirt, came over. She and her mother stood up.

"Mr. Edwards, and you are?" he asked.

"Mrs. Miller, Anne Miller, and this is my daughter, Ellie. Thank you for seeing us. We need to inquire about a horse you have in the back. A red mare in the last trailer? Is she a BLM horse?"

"Mr. Edwards frowned. He thought he had seen this type before. Mother and daughter dressed up and from the city. They had no idea about owning a horse, much less a wild horse. Yet, there was something about them. The mother and daughter looked vulnerable, particularly the mother. "All the horses that are for sale will go through the ring. They are all for sale."

"No, this horse is in the back, in a trailer. There's been a stall set up in there and she's in the stall. That's the horse we want to know about," Ellie said.

"My daughter saw her in there and wants to buy her. She thinks she looks like a," she paused, a stuttering pause, as she thought about how to phrase the rest of the request. "If you know anything about this horse, please tell us. We can pay whatever you ask." Anne knew her voice sounded pleading, but she did not know how to make him understand. Dare she tell him her daughter had a picture hanging on the wall of their living room of this horse—this horse, who had called her daughter to her by some means and now they had to buy her because the horse wanted it? She did not think so.

Mr. Edwards looked confused, "You want to buy a horse that's not in the arena and not on the sales list?"

"Yes, my daughter found her in the back, in a trailer with a stall set up. We are very interested in that particular horse. Is it possible that she is a BLM horse that for some reason has been taken out of the sale?"

"If we have some that are not on the sales list, John will know. Sometimes one is injured and has to be taken out. Let me just check with him, and I'll get an answer for you. Okay? You just wait here. I'll be back soon." With that he left by a back door and Ellie and Anne were left standing on the sidelines. There seemed to be nothing to do but wait.

CHAPTER 13

All Ellie wanted was to be with her horse. However, she knew that she had to wait with her mother. There would be a good outcome to this. If the mare had gotten this far, then it was all going to work out. She just had to trust the unicorn. They were supposed to be a myth but if Dream was real, he was real. He was responsible for the dreams. She could not worry about that now. Now she needed only to trust, in her horse and in a unicorn. Her mother's cell phone rang, breaking into her thoughts. Ellie sat listening to her mother's side of the conversation.

"Oh, hi, Jackie. Yes, Ellie called. I know. She has found a horse. Well, it's not the horse we've been looking for. She thinks it's the horse in the picture, the dream horse."

"Yes, I know what I said, the horse looks very much like the picture she painted. The horse appears to be in good shape."

"No, we've not bought her yet. We believe she belongs to the BLM, but maybe not. The officer in charge of the auction is out trying to find out about her, but—"

"Yes we intend to buy her if at all possible. Ellie is adamant. She wants that horse. "

"Well, we would like you to bring the trailer and come pick her up. Is that possible? Today would be best."

"You can?"

"Yes, we're at the BLM auction at Crystal Lake."

"Yes, we intend to buy her." Anne's voice firmed as she said that.

"Thank you, yes we'll be waiting." Anne put the cell phone back in her pocket and looked over at Ellie.

"It will be alright, Ellie. Jackie will be here in a couple of hours to pick her up." She smiled at her daughter, "It will be alright." This last sounded as if she were trying to convince herself.

They sat and waited for what seemed a long time. Ellie's face was white and strained. Anne was silent. Anne held Ellie's hand and from time to time squeezed it. There was nothing to say so they just sat and waited.

It took about thirty minutes before Mr. Edwards returned. He had some papers in his hand and was smiling as he came up to them. "Well, took a little while to find John, but I've gotten to the bottom of this. The good news is that the mare is a BLM horse and I think we can arrange the sale. That is, if you meet the requirements and have the money to pay for her. The difficulty is that she is very much in foal. Neither John nor his helper has any idea how she was put in this load. Normally, she would have been vaccinated and turned back into the wild. But somehow here she is and John put her in the trailer to protect her from injury. He was going to tell me about her as soon as the sale is over."

Anne frowned, "In foal, you mean she's going to have a baby? Oh, oh, dear. Ellie did you know that?"

"Well yes, Mom, it's pretty obvious, and she told—" she stuttered to a stop, looked anxiously at Mr. Edwards, and then continued, "Yes Mom, she will have the foal very soon, but not too soon. We have time to get her home, maybe even a couple of weeks."

"But Ellie, then you'll have two horses. What are we going to do with two horses? I don't think we can keep two, and I've not cleared that with Jackie. She may not allow a mare and baby to stay there. Shall I call her back and ask her?"

"She won't care, Mom. It will be alright, I think." She looked up at Mr. Edwards. "It will be alright to take her, won't it?"

"Well, it will be alright with us. In fact, it will save us a lot of work if we can leave her here, but if your mother doesn't think you can keep a foal, then we can make other arrangements for her."

"They have pasture at the farm, and Dream and her baby can stay there, Mom. I have to have Dream I just have to. It will all work out. Please, oh please, say yes."

"Well, if Jackie says it's okay, then I guess. Promise me you'll listen to Jackie and do as she says. This is a real complication, and it'll be a lot of work," Anne was still frowning.

Mr. Edwards spoke up, "Ellie, a foal is a lot of work and a big responsibility Are you sure that you want to take this on? You can't ride a mare that has a new foal. Sometimes they are very protective of their babies and can cause trouble, especially a wild one. She might be dangerous."

"I do understand the problems, but Jackie Long is an experienced horsewoman and she will help me, I know she will. Dream will never hurt me, never. I know she won't." Ellie looked up at the officer and two large tears ran down her cheeks. "She will never hurt me."

Anne stood next to Ellie looking scared at what Mr. Edwards had said.

Her daughter, hugging a wild horse, claiming she could communicate with it, and it looked exactly like the horse in the painting. Now she finds out the mare is pregnant and about to deliver a foal. This was getting very complicated. She could not be sure what to do. However, she clearly would have to purchase the horse. She did not know what Ellie would do if she was separated from the mare.

She spoke, "Mr. Edwards, can we please purchase her? I know there will be difficulties but you can see how committed Ellie is. I just don't see any other solution. Ms. Long is very experienced and she will help us in any way she can, I'm sure."

"Well, I don't see why not. Ms. Miller. It will certainly help us out. There is not much call for a wild, pregnant mare this close to foaling. I'm not sure what we would have done with her. Let's get started on the paperwork, shall we?" he smiled down at the uncertain woman. She was very attractive, he realized. Where had that thought come from? It startled him and he frowned.

Anne picked up on the frown, thinking it had something to do with Ellie. "Oh, I'm sure we will be okay. Ellie will take good care of the horse. Ellie's father said that he will be responsible for the expense, so that's not a problem." Her voice tightened as she spoke.

Well, attractive or not there was a Mr. Miller. Get a life, Allen, Mr. Edwards thought to himself. *Get a life, man.*

Ellie and Anne walked with him to a desk in a corner of the office. It was piled high with papers. They sat in the two chairs he pulled up for them. He took the seat behind the desk. He handed an application of purchase to Anne, and said, "Please fill this out. The stipulation of purchase is that you must retain ownership for one year. When the foal is born it will be yours to do with as you please."

Ellie looked up at him, "You mean that we will own the foal without any conditions?"

"That's right. It will be yours to do with as you please," He looked at the young girl. She looked very much like her mother, blonde and petite. "Have you been riding long?"

"About two years and I've wanted a horse all my life. I've been dreaming about this mare for quite a while." Ellie said.

"This mare?" he said.

"Yes, this mare. Dream is her name," she said, "I've got a picture of her at home that I've painted from my dreams."

Anne looked up from the form she was filling out. "Ellie, please. Let's not bore Mr. Edwards, shall we?" There was warning in her voice.

"No, I'd like to hear more about this, Ellie. Please go on," Allen Edwards said.

Ellie took her mother's hint that she not tell the man any more about her obsession with the mare. "Oh, I mean I've been painted the horse of my dreams. My father, who lives in California, has finally agreed to let me have a horse. So, we've been looking. It's so exciting to find one that looks so much like my dream horse."

Allen Edwards was so relieved to hear that Anne's husband lived in California, which probably meant that they were divorced, or at least not living together, that he did not even hear Ellie's explanation.

By this time, Anne was handing him the form neatly filled out and reaching for her purse to write the check for the mare. "How do I make out the check?"

"Just BLM, will do." He clipped the check to the paper work and smiled at Anne. "When will your trailer arrive?"

"She should be on her way; it takes about an hour to get here." Anne smiled up at Mr. Edwards. She should have felt strange and scared, but somehow the tall officer made her feel like everything would turn out okay.

"Very good then, I'll have Margaret give you a bill of sale. Please let me know when the trailer arrives. I'll come out and help you load your new horse." He smiled at Anne and gave Ellie a pat on the shoulder.

"Thank you," Anne responded with a smile of her own.

CHAPTER 14

I t was amazing to Jackie what people would do. Anne and Ellie were buying a wild horse. Horses were unpredictable, but people were even more unpredictable. That made her smile to herself.

Yet, in the conversation, Anne had seemed upset. What were they thinking? There was no way a mustang horse would work out for Ellie. Anne had told her Ellie had found a horse that looked just like her painting. That was weird. How could it be? Of course, many horses looked alike. That had to be it.

Jackie pulled into the auction yard. There was a lot of activity. She stopped and looked around. She did not see any sign of them. She rang Anne's cell phone. Anne picked up on the first ring. "Anne, I'm here, where are you? Okay, I'm on my way to the back, last trailer. I can't wait to see this fabulous horse."

As she turned into the back of the yard, she saw Anne and Ellie with some others at the bottom of a ramp by the last trailer. Pulling up beside the large van, she climbed out and was met by both Anne and Ellie. They looked excited and tired. Mary and her mother were standing a little to the side with a tall man dressed in jeans and a western style shirt. He had dark, crisp hair and looked capable and in charge.

"We're so glad you're here." Ellie cried. "Wait 'til you see her. She's so beautiful."

Anne was more circumspect, "Well, we've got a surprise for you. The horse is about to have a foal. It will probably be born in the next week or two. I hope that's all right? Ellie is adamant and I just can't say no." She looked like she might start to cry.

Jackie was even more mystified now. Not only were they buying a wild horse, but they were buying a pregnant one. Well, there was nothing for it. She would just have to find a place for the horse and hope that everything was going to be okay. Ellie had always been reserved and grown up for her age. Now she looked so young and happy.

"Where is she? Can you lead her? I hope she's not so wild we'll have trouble getting her home. It wouldn't be good for her to hurt herself." She had thrown in some lead ropes, a long rope and a halter.

The official looking man spoke up, "I have help if you need it. I don't know how much handling she's had. But I think that Ellie has been in with her?" He looked questioningly at Anne.

"Yes, yes she has. She seemed to have no trouble with her," Anne said.

"Jackie, this is Mr. Edwards, he's in charge of this auction and has been kind enough to make it possible for us to purchase the horse."

"Mr. Edwards, this is Jackie Long, Ellie's riding instructor. Jackie's the owner-manager of the farm where we'll be keeping the mare," she smiled at them both.

"I don't think that she'll be a problem. I'll go in with her and see if she'll lead out." Ellie said.

Jackie's truck and trailer were right up close to the ramp. She opened up the rear doors and with the help of Mr. Edwards or Allen, as he asked her to call him, got her trailer doors open. Then they turned their attention to the long ramp with wooden ridges running across it so that a horse going in or out would not slip. Ellie was already at the top of the ramp waiting. Jackie came up and handed her a halter with a long lead rope attached. There in a make shift stall arrangement stood a red mare very much in foal. She stared at the rather round mare, Ellie had been right. This horse was an exact duplicate of the picture Ellie painted, right down to the hind sock that had a crooked streak of chestnut running to the hoof and the slightly off center star in the middle of her forehead. She could certainly see how Ellie had gotten excited over her. The mare did not look much like the typical wild horses she had seen, but she had not seen many. This was a beautiful horse.

Ellie went slowly into the stall, removing the makeshift gate. Speaking softly, she approached the mare. By this time, both Anne and Mr. Edwards had joined Jackie.

"Shouldn't someone help her?" Anne said, looking strained and white.

"Probably better to let her see if she can get the halter on by herself, too many people may make the horse more upset." Allen Edwards said.

Ellie put her hand on the mare's neck, speaking so softly to her no one could make out what she was saying. The mare was looking very alert with her ears flicking back and forth. "I'm just going to put the halter on your head. It buckles on this side. I need to do this to get you out of here, Dream." The mare tossed her head and backed into the rear wall. Ellie went with her. "Let me do this now, it won't hurt and it's necessary to get you out of here and home. We're together now. Everything will be alright." She continued to talk and stroke the neck of the mare. Not once had the mare offered to strike, bite, or anything that might endanger the girl.

Jackie and Allen stood looking at the girl and the horse. It was obvious to both of them that the mare was acting as if she and the girl had a relationship. She was not behaving as a scared, skittish, wild horse would. Jackie looked up at Allen and whispered. "I don't believe what I'm seeing. How can this be happening?"

"This is really interesting. Do you think that maybe the mare is a lost domestic horse?" Allen whispered back to Jackie.

"Well maybe, but this child has been dreaming of a red mare for over a year and she has a painting that she did of a horse that looks just like this one hanging in her living room. This horse is identical to that painting. I've seen the picture. Ellie painted it from her dreams about six months ago," Jackie responded.

Allen looked down at the riding instructor, "Really, she has a painting of this horse?"

"Well she has a painting of a horse that looks very similar to this one. And she's been dreaming about her for a long time," Jackie said.

"No kidding, that's strange," he responded.

"No kidding."

Anne looked over at the two whispering. "There's nothing wrong is there?" she asked.

"No, everything is going so well it's almost not believable," Jackie said.

At that moment, Ellie looked over at them and asked them to walk down the ramp to the ground. "I think everything will be okay, but you should wait at the bottom of the ramp, while I lead her down."

Ellie started forward and the mare followed her out of the makeshift stall. She hesitated at the ramp and then with a word of encouragement from Ellie, walked down to the ground. She paused at the back of Jackie's trailer, and then went quickly into the dark interior. With all eyes watching her, Ellie attached the lead rope to one of the ties. She stood next to the mare.

"Well done, Ellie," Jackie said. "That was amazing." She walked around to the side of the trailer and opened the escape door, while Allen Edwards slowly started to close the trailer doors.

"I told you she'd be fine. She knows me, I think from my dreams," Ellie was acting as if nothing unusual had happened. It did not occur to her that she just put a wild mustang in a trailer without any help.

"That was remarkable," Allen Edwards said. "I've never seen anything like it. She's obviously been handled before. Somehow, she managed to get loose with the wild ones. She is branded with a BLM number, however."

Anne gave Ellie a hug. It was as if the horse had been going into trailers all her life. She was standing in there not making any fuss.

"Well," Allen said to them all. "That was anticlimactic. I don't think you'll have any trouble. She's acting just fine. Anne, I would love to come to the farm to see how the mare is settling in. Just to see how you are all doing. This has been rather unusual. Would it be all right if I called you to make an appointment to come out? We are supposed to check out the facilities where our BLM horses are taken after the sale, anyway."

Anne looked surprised but after a moment said, "Yes, yes that would be fine. I'm sure that all will go well, but if you want to check, just call me. You have our house number and my cell number on the application."

"Well then, good luck. It was nice meeting you all," and with a smile at the group he turned to go. "I've got to get back to work; we still have a lot to do. Have a safe trip."

A chorus of "Thanks," and "Goodbyes," followed him as he made his way back into the building.

"Well, shall we get going?" Jackie asked. "I've still got the barn to see to when I get back.

"Can I ride with you, Jackie," Ellie said. "I want to stay close to Dream, in case there's a problem?"

Jackie looked over, "Okay, Anne?"

Anne thought for a moment then said, "Sure that's fine, maybe Mary would like to ride with you too?"

"Sure both girls can ride with me and you and Triana can follow. That'll be good," Jackie answered. Ellie got into the front seat with Jackie and Mary settled in the back.

With everyone settled in, they left the arena area and started the drive to Whispering Tree. Jackie drove carefully, in deference to the mare's advanced pregnancy.

"You should have a vet out as quickly as possible to make sure she is in good shape for foaling. I can call her for you tomorrow, if you like. She will want to give her a vaccination and for that, you will need to be there, as I don't think the horse will respond well to anyone else. Would you like me to call her in the morning?"

"Yes, please call her in the morning and I'll be out as early as I can."

Jackie was curious about the horse but hesitated to bring it up. Finally, she said, "Okay, are you going to tell me how you found that horse?"

Ellie looked at her, "Well, I'm not sure you will believe me," she took a deep breath, looked back at Mary. "It's hard to explain, isn't it, Mary?" Mary just nodded her head.

"Try me," Jackie said.

"All right, maybe if I tell you about it, I can make myself believe it," and she started talking. She told Jackie about the voice in her head, the horse calling to her, and how the mare had insisted that she had been searching for her a long time. When she finished talking, she realized how hard it would be for someone to believe her; dreams, talking horses, her painting identical to the horse in the trailer, if someone told her that, would she be able to believe it?

Jackie listened without interruption. When Ellie finished her story, she was unable to think of anything to say. She had heard strange stories about horses and people before, but this one was the most mysterious. Finally, she said, "Well, I've seen the painting, and that horse looks just like it. I don't know how it happened, but your Dream is in my trailer. She's real, so it has to be true."

Ellie had left out any mention of the unicorn. *You don't even know the half of it,* she thought. "Thank you, that means a lot to me," she said.

"And Dream will be her name?" Jackie said with a smile that broke the tension.

"Yes, Dream will be her name. It's appropriate, don't you think," Ellie was smiling back at her.

"Very appropriate," these were the first words that Mary had spoken in a while.

"Oh yes, very appropriate," Jackie said and all three laughed. The laughter seemed to make them all feel better.

"We'll put her in that large stall on the end. It has a run to the outside so it should work out well. We'll need to re-bed it with straw, in case she should foal. Shavings won't do for that," Jackie said.

When they arrived Ellie went into the trailer to make sure that Dream understood what was about to happen, then walked her around for a few minutes while the stall was being prepared. "This is Whispering Tree Farm, you'll like it here. Jackie is wonderful and will be able to help us. There is lots of green grass and warm stalls for the winter," she told the mare, speaking in a low audible voice. She did not want to speak with her mind or use pictures. That was too new. When the stall was ready, she led Dream in and stayed for about twenty minutes.

By this time, Anne and Triana had arrived. The drive back to the farm had settled them down. They were somewhat rested and cooled off. Anne seemed to have come to terms with the day. Triana and Anne had talked all the way about the strange and alarming day. Anne was scared and bewildered over what had happened. Triana was supportive, but had no explanations to offer. In both of their minds rested the fact that the horse in the trailer looked just like the horse in the painting. There was just no reasonable explanation, none at all.

Jackie took Anne into the office, "You'll need to come out in the morning. We need to get the vet out here to examine Dream. I want to know what kind of shape she's in. The foal looks imminent, but mares are deceiving, so we don't know. We can fill out the boarding contract and all that tomorrow. I imagine that you are exhausted. Go home, sleep if you can. It is going to be fine. You can count on me to help Ellie. Try to rest, Anne."

"Bless you, Jackie. I can't thank you enough. It's just like I've fallen off a ship, with no life jacket, and going down for the third time," Anne said.

"Well, tomorrow is another day. Sleep, if there is any reason to call you, I will. Go home," with that Jackie gave her a hug and pushed her out the door.

Mary dragged Ellie out of Dream's stall and everyone got in the car to go home. They were all tired, hungry and still excited. Anne wanted food, a shower and bed. Triana said exactly the same thing. Mary would be spending the night with Ellie, so that she could go out with them to the farm in the morning.

When they arrived at the Johansen apartment, Triana kissed her daughter goodbye, hugged Ellie, and told Anne to call her if she needed anything. They watched her go inside the door and drove away. On the way home, Anne asked Ellie to call for take-out at a Chinese Restaurant they all liked.

Anne went immediately to the bathroom for a shower. The water soothed her somewhat and when the food arrived, she was ready to eat. No one seemed to want to talk much and everyone went to bed early.

It was late when Ellie, seeing the light under her mother's door, knocked gently, "Are you up?" she asked.

"Yes, just reading, come on in." Anne said.

Ellie came over to the bed and sat down. "I wanted to thank you for Dream. I know that what happened today is strange. It was for me too. But, I know that this horse and I are supposed to be together. I know it."

"Ellie, understand that I will always love you and support you. I'm not sure what to believe about the horse. I realize that you think you are talking with it, but I can't comprehend how that could happen. I want to believe you, I really do, but what you are telling me, is almost beyond belief." Anne looked up at her daughter and took her hand. "I often worry about you, you know I do. People with your special gifts are fragile in some ways; no one fully understands how your brain works. Why you can do the wonderful things that you can do. Do you realize how very special you are?" Anne looked at her daughter, then reached over and hugged her close.

"That's just it, Mom. I don't want to be special. I want to be a normal girl. I want what all girls want, friends, parties, fun, a normal life. I can't even get a horse in a normal way. No, I have to have dreams, nightmares, unicorns, hopping around in my head. My horse has to find me at an auction. I thought that buying a horse would be a good experience. Yet here we are with an occurrence that is unbelievable."

"Well, the good thing is that you did find her, don't you think?" Anne answered.

"Yes, I am glad that we found each other. She's the special one. What a beauty she is," Ellie said.

"Okay, then. Go to bed. Get some sleep. Jackie guaranteed that she would take care of Dream, and that all would be well, at least overnight. So go to bed."

"Okay, but I really did want you to know how much I appreciate you. To me you're the one that is so special," Ellie kissed her mother on the cheek and smiled at her. "See you in the morning. Love you."

Ellie went back to her room; Mary was sleeping soundly in the pulled-out trundle bed. Ellie eased herself on to her bed, stretched out, and sighed. Her mind went to Dream. She found that she could feel the mare settled and sleeping in her stall, but it took her a long time to fall asleep.

CHAPTER 15

Ellie woke early, it seemed that she had just put her head down and closed her eyes, but she could see the sun shining in through the window. There was a fleeting thought that there had been a dream, but she did not remember it and had slept soundly. Mary was still sleeping and Ellie did not want to wake her. Quietly she eased herself out of bed and silently left the room. Moving to the kitchen, she made some hot chocolate and sat at the kitchen table.

What kind of changes would the responsibility of a horse make for her and her mother? There would be more trips to the stable. How often would she get to go? Ellie wanted to go right now. She wanted to be with her horse as much as possible. Then, there was Mary and Triana. Triana drove them out every other lesson day. That would help. Maybe she could go by public transport.

Ellie let herself drift with thoughts of her horse. What did this mean? All those dreams, the pictures she had painted. Taking her cup, she walked into the living room and looked at the large painting she had done of Dream The vision of the white unicorn and Dream dancing the mating dance flitted

109

through her mind. As did the nightmare, in which Dream and a foal had watched her go into the water. Could it be that the small glowing filly standing at Dream's side was the unicorn's foal? Had she seen the foal that Dream was carrying? The father of this foal had to be the unicorn.

Are you awake?

Ellie, deep in reverie, was so startled that she spilled her chocolate. "Oh —what are you doing?"

Talking to you. Are you awake?

Dream's voice was in Ellie's head. The disorientation came and with it the nausea. Ellie looked with dismay at the spilled chocolate on the rug. She hoped that it would come out. She would certainly have to try before her mother got up.

What will come out?

"Oh you scared me and I spilled the chocolate on the rug, not a good thing to have happen. My mother will kill me if I can't get it out." Ellie was speaking aloud; she had to stop talking aloud. She would have to learn to form the words in her head.

Pictures work too.

"What? Pictures?"

Yes if you form a picture, I can see it just as well. I feel what you are feeling, I know your thoughts and I can see what you are seeing — but I don't know the words to use, my knowledge of words is limited. Communicating will get easier for us, I think.

You know what I'm feeling? Could I lie to you? Ellie was now speaking just inside her head.

Dream could speak into her mind in English, but she was also saying that emotions, feelings, and thoughts, were equally open to her. Ellie would absolutely have to think about this.

What's that? Dream asked. *I don't understand "lie."*

Lying is when someone says something that isn't true, Ellie said

Why would you want to do that? Dream asked.

110

Ellie thought about it. Why would someone lie? She saw how difficult it was going to be to explain some things. This relationship with a being that could read her mind would require some adjustments.

I guess that wouldn't be a good idea, Dream, she said.

Well, I should think not.

Yes, well how are you this morning? We are coming out after everyone wakes up. I'm bringing my friend Mary with me. You saw Mary yesterday, remember?

You should come right away! I want you to be with me.

Well, I will come as soon as I can. I want you to tell me about the unicorn, Phell—whatever. Is he the father of your foal? I dreamed that he was. Can this be true?

Yes, it's true. It's necessary. As you and I are necessary, The foal is necessary. You have a lot to learn and I can't teach you, but Phellsome will continue to teach you. You and I, we are necessary.

I am trying to understand and you're right I— do have so much to learn. Yet right now, all I want is to be with you. That I understand. Now I have things to do. Eat your breakfast. I'll be out as soon as I can.

Mary wandered in to the living room just as Ellie was heading for the kitchen to get some cleaner to work on the rug. "I spilled the chocolate. Now I've got to try to clean it up before Mom gets up."

"I'll help you. Is there more of that chocolate? I feel like I've not eaten in a year. We did eat yesterday, didn't we?"

"Yes, we did but it was a really long day. I barely slept last night I was so excited," Ellie said. "There's instant cocoa and the milk is in the frig. One minute in the microwave."

"I'll make myself a cup and then help you with the floor," Mary replied.

"Mary, Dream has been talking to me this morning. That's why I spilled the chocolate. I'm not used to her just appearing in my mind. I wonder if I'll get used to it?"

Mary was standing at the microwave with a cup in her hand. She looked over at Ellie, "I can't even imagine how that would feel. I sometimes think that I understand something one of the horses is thinking but in no way is it words or pictures. I get more of a feeling, an emotion or something."

"I'm not sure that I like it. It's hard to have another something inside your head. She can read my thoughts. It feels like an invasion. I'll have to start watching what I think. It would be a totally different world if people could understand each other's thoughts," Ellie looked at Mary. "It's as if I wouldn't be able to think something. We'd have to be as careful with our thoughts as we are with our words. I wonder how that would be —," she sighed.

"Maybe there's a way to block out some of your thoughts," Mary said. "You know, something you could do to keep things private. I would hate to have someone inside my head hearing all my thoughts. Even if you mean well, you don't always think good things."

"Well, I hope that I can come up with something; otherwise, I'm going to lose it." Ellie went to the cupboard; got the scrub brush and a spray can of spot remover. She went back into the living room, got down on her knees and started working on the brown stain. "I hope this comes out," she said, scrubbing with both hands.

"When are we going out to see Dream? I really didn't get a good look at her yesterday; it was such a hectic time."

"Well, it can't be too soon to suit Dream. She's anxious for me to come out to her."

"She's not about to have the baby, is she?" Mary asked.

"No, at least she didn't mention it. Do you know how weird this is? The horse didn't say anything about the baby."

"Well, with time I'm sure you'll get used to it." Mary said. "Just think how much fun this is. A horse of your own and not just any horse, but the dream horse," she laughed and reached down to give Ellie a hug. "You are so lucky, you know that?"

"Maybe, but right now I'm excited and afraid," Ellie's voice was tremulous.

After repeated scrubbings, the stain in the carpet was gone. Mary and Ellie fixed Anne some coffee, anxious to get going.

Anne heard them giggling, *I might as well get up*, she thought. She had not had much sleep, anyway. Yesterday had been exhausting, and a night thinking what this horse would mean had not helped. She had a vague headache. Hopefully, a shower and some of the coffee she smelled would get her through the day.

Ellie was impatient about how slow everyone seemed to be moving. All she wanted was to get to her horse. This was going to be hard, her horse in one place and she in another. Finally, everyone was ready. Ellie and Mary were in the back seat, sitting quietly now that they were on their way.

"You're very quiet, Ellie," Anne said when they were about half way there. "What are you thinking about?"

"Well, I was just wondering about Dream and the new baby, Mom," Ellie said.

"How is that?"

"Well, like how much time it will take. All the driving and stuff like that."

"It's going to require some planning, for sure."

"It's good that school is almost out. I'll have most of the summer to be with her. Mary and I can spend a lot more time out there."

"My Mom will help with the driving, and maybe there's a bus or something," Mary said.

"We'll deal with one thing at a time. That's all we can do right now," Anne frowned. She had been thinking about it too. It was going to be difficult; her job required her full attention, but she knew she could do a lot of it at home on her computer. Maybe they would let her work from home.

Ellie would want to go out to the stable every day. She would have to work something out. Trying to balance work and spending quality time with her daughter was so hard. Sometimes, the stress just got to her. She was so tired of it all. She was always making compromises with her time. There was never enough for her job and for Ellie. At times like these, she almost hated Earl for going off to find himself and leaving her with all the responsibility of their child. It was not Ellie's fault, but it was not hers either. She turned and glanced back at her daughter.

Ellie watched her mother as the conflicting emotions chased themselves across her face. *It's my fault, it's always my fault. I make so much trouble for her.* A tear ran down her cheek. She coughed and put her hand to her face, silently brushing the tear away so that no one would see her crying. "I hope I'm not catching a cold," she said.

It was a beautiful clear day. The lake was sparkling in the sun. Chicago was a beautiful city, but the weather could be problematic almost any time of the year. Summers could be hot, humid and rainy, the winters could be arctic, but today was wonderful.

Anne did not enjoy the drive out to the barn, even with a small amount of traffic it took about an hour, the roads could be jammed with cars on any given day and that time could double. Her mind was filled with the problems that this horse would bring. How could she make it work? The only solution she had come up with was working from home.

Ellie's unique abilities had been stressful to her marriage. Earl had never understood the challenges of their only child. He had not wanted the responsibility of Ellie. That burden had always fallen on Anne. Earl was proud of Ellie, but an exceptional child did not fit in with his reality. These children were difficult and fragile in lots of ways. Some could have mental health problems, and no one really understood how their minds worked. Most did not fit into the social structure of a regular classroom; it was wonderful to have a school like

Wilcrest right here in the city. Many parents with exceptional children came here to live just so their children could go there.

The staff at Wilcrest was doing remarkable work with Ellie. She knew that without the fine teachers there, Ellie would have a much more difficult time. Things had been going so smoothly until those dreams started. The dreams terrified Anne. Now the horse, Dream, was terrifying her.

Ellie was coming to the end of her time at Wilcrest, and would be taking some university courses in the fall. It was in the city and it was convenient for a girl of Ellie's age. She was certainly not ready to be away from home. She had this brilliant mind, but still the social skills of a budding teenager.

Anne was jerked out of her thoughts by Ellie saying, "Mom you just missed the turn. Are you alright?"

"Oh, sorry, I was lost in thought." She turned around and kept her mind on her driving. *This will all work out. It has to work out,* she thought.

CHAPTER 16

Anne was afraid that Dream would hurt Ellie. That horse had looked docile enough last night but Anne did not understand horses and she was afraid of them. She tried not to show it, but Ellie often laughed at her. Ellie had developed a love of horses when she was ten. Look where it had brought them. Two years ago, she had given Ellie riding lessons for Christmas, and now they owned a pregnant horse that her daughter was sure she could hold a conversation with. Nothing involving Ellie ever turned out to be easy, she smiled to herself. Why should this be any different? She watched as Ellie and Mary ran for the barn. Then she followed along.

When Anne got to the barn, Ellie was already inside the stall with her arms around Dream's neck. "Mary, could you get a grooming box, Dream's mane is a mess," Ellie said. Then she turned to the mare, and stroked her. "We'll clean you up, get all these tangles out," she said. Dream put her muzzle into Ellie's neck and blew softly. Mary came back with the grooming box and both girls set to work, chattering away.

Anne stood watching them. Ellie looked so happy; there were no signs of stress. She was almost convinced that Dream was just as happy as Ellie. The mare had not shown one sign that she might injure Ellie, no skittish behavior or anything.

Just then, Jackie walked up to the stall door, and joined Anne. "She had an easy night. I put a foal monitor on her, and a camera up, just in case something happened. She indicated the wall where a small camera was attached. But every time I checked on her, she was relaxed and calm."

The camera intrigued Anne, "You mean you can watch the horses in your house on a TV screen?"

"Yes, it's useful if a mare is near foaling or a horse is ill. It lets you keep a close watch on them, without having to come out to the barn. The monitor attaches to her tail and will tell you when she is about to foal. That's convenient, since they usually foal in the middle of the night," Jackie said with a smile.

"Just like women," Anne said.

"Yes, that's what I've heard, middle of the night. Oh, and I called the vet, she'll be here about one this afternoon. It'll be a good idea to have Dr. Warner examine her. She can't have had very good care. The papers do say she's been wormed and vaccinated. That's good. I hope Rachel, that's Dr. Warner, can tell us how the foal is doing, and if the mare's general health is good. She appears to be in good shape, but it's best to get a professional opinion."

"Yes, thanks, that's a good idea. We're so new to this and having the foal just complicates things," Anne said

"Well, it certainly isn't what I had planned for you."

"No, it wasn't what I'd planned either. But the mare looks remarkably like Ellie's painting, don't you think?" Anne said. Anne was cautious in what she chose to say to Jackie. Particularly the fact that Ellie was sure the horse was communicating with her. "Jackie, let's go to the office and get the boarding contracts taken care of. It was so confusing last night that I didn't even ask about any of that," she glanced in at Ellie and then at Jackie again. She needed to talk to Jackie about the mare and Ellie's amazing connection to her.

She and Jackie went into the office at the back of the barn. Anne took a deep breath, "Jackie, do you know that Ellie says the horse is talking to her? She told me yesterday that the horse was inside her head asking her to come find her. She says that the horse speaks to her. Sometimes in language, but sometimes in pictures or emotions or something," Anne said. She was uncomfortable even saying such things and finding it difficult to express herself. Her daughter was claiming to talk to this horse. What was Jackie going to think about that?

"Yes, Ellie has said things like that in the past. We actually had a conversation about it yesterday while we were driving home. Ellie told me about how she found the mare. I think she told me everything. She and the girls were discussing something like that on the way to the horse show, too. They all seemed to agree that the horses understand them; at least on an emotional level. They didn't seem to think it was all that strange." Jackie was trying to reassure Anne. She calmly got out the contracts for Anne to fill out, offered her a cup of coffee, and took one herself.

Anne added cream and two sugars to hers. She was going to need the carbohydrates today. Sipping coffee and filling out the forms, Anne felt more relaxed; Jackie did not seem to be shocked by what Ellie told her. Anne sighed with relief. Maybe Ellie was okay. Maybe many horse-crazy girls thought they could talk to horses.

She was so out of her element here. She had never had a pet as a child. Her mother abhorred animals of any kind. Anne remembered wanting a puppy, but her mother would not hear of it. "Pets and city don't mix," she said and that was it, so her experience with animals was minimal.

"So, you don't think it's strange?" Anne asked.

"Well, there are people that believe horses communicate, it's not just girls. Horses seem to have an affinity for people. They are used in therapy for PTSS, abused women, and people with mental or physical challenges, all sorts of things like that.

There are even programs for prisoners. I feel that this connection maybe one of the reasons horses are so popular, particularly with girls and women in the States. There are books on the subject. I think I've got one or two somewhere. I'll look and see. It's not too far-fetched. I wouldn't worry too much about it if I were you. Ellie's pretty special, you know."

"Yes she is. It's both a blessing and a worry," Anne said

Later that day Dream got a clean bill of health from the vet. The horse had been relaxed during the exam. There had been no trouble from her at all. The foal was in position and ready to be born at any time. Rachel Warner told Ellie and Anne that mares produced their babies easily and very seldom were there complications. If there were, she could be there within twenty minutes. Anne and Ellie liked her no nonsense, competent manner. It reassured them both and made them feel better.

Anne left soon after the vet did. She had a lot to do if she was going to try to work from home. She would see Jerry Lenton in the morning to talk about that. Triana was picking the girls up late in the evening, so she had a few hours at home.

Ellie and Mary took Dream for a walk around the property. They ate deli sandwiches for lunch outside Dream's stall door. Ellie had offered Dream a bite, but the mare, tossed her head in disgust. Dream showed her displeasure in a loud snort. They were going to have dinner with Jackie, so they would be able to help with the evening chores.

Once home, Anne spent her afternoon organizing her computer and work-space in anticipation that she could work out of her apartment. Late in the afternoon her cell phone rang. She got chills when she saw the number on her cell phone. It was Jackie from the stable. Surely, nothing had happened to Ellie. "Jackie, is anything wrong? Is Ellie —"

"No, Anne, everything is fine. I just called with an idea. We have a vacant house on the property. It's behind the old barn. I've not had anyone in there for a while. I don't know if you'd be interested, but I could rent it to you if that would help you and Ellie. I know how much she wants to be out here, and truthfully, she would be helpful this summer. I don't know anything about your work, but Ellie said that you were going to check into working at home. You could come out to look and see if the place might work for you."

Anne was stunned. She had never thought of moving out to the country. She had always lived in the city. How would she cope in the country? Yet, it would solve so many of the problems that owning a horse presented. Ellie would be overjoyed. She would be in the country, with the horses for the summer, but Ellie would need to commute in the winter. More problems, more decisions, but she would definitely have to think about it.

"Thanks for the offer. It would solve a lot of problems. I'll look at it tomorrow when I bring Ellie out. Thanks so much," she hung up the phone.

Anne looked around her apartment. Moving would be difficult. Just moving Ellie's piano was a major obstacle. There would be getting Ellie to school, and winter could be brutal without public transport. In the depths of her body, she felt the cold fear rising up. The same feeling she had had when Earl had left her.

Ellie was always at the center of Anne's thoughts. Anne thought as a mother first, not what was best for herself, but what was best for her child. She could almost see why Earl had left, but was there any other way? Did all mothers think as she did? There were no right answers. All she knew was that Ellie was the most important thing in her life.

~~~~~~

Mary had gone off to help Jackie get horses ready for a lesson, and Ellie was finally alone with her horse.

I'll take you out to a place where you can graze. How does that sound?

Grass? That sounds good. I would like to move around.

A picture of the valley in Ellie's dreams came unbidden into her mind. She was riding Dream at a gallop across the grass. *Will we ever get to do that?*

We can do that, but not now, but it would be good to move around.

Ellie led Dream out of the stall and to an empty run. The spring weather had brought up the grass and the paddock was a beautiful shade of green. Ellie unclipped the lead rope and Dream dropped her head to the tempting green grass. They ambled around together, and then Ellie went to sit under a small oak tree. It was warm and somehow comforting to just sit here and watch Dream.

The quiet must have put her to sleep. She had to be dreaming. The small white foal was talking to her.

I'm Esophia; I've been waiting to talk to you. You were so scared and all, but now you seem more relaxed.

Who are you? Am I dreaming?

No, not dreaming. I'm Esophia.

But, I'm seeing you.

I want to show you what I will look like when I get out of here. It will be soon now.

Ellie was shocked. Now she had not one but two voices in her head.

I was waiting until you adjusted to her voice, before I spoke. I'm much better at it than my mother is.

Yes, I suppose you are. How did you get your name?

It's my name; my father gave it to me.

He talks to you?

Yes. He's waiting for me.

I wish he'd talk to me.

He will, just wait.

The voice and the image were gone. Ellie was still under the tree. Dream was calmly grazing a few feet away. Nothing had changed and yet nothing was the same. The unborn foal was talking to her. Actually showing her what she was going to look like. She had declared her presence as if it was the most common of things, which it most certainly was not. Ellie got up and walked to Dream. *She's talking to me.*

Yes.

You know her name is Esophia?

Yes.

Does her father come and talk to her, like she says.

Yes.

"Is that all you can say! Yes, yes, yes," Ellie said out loud. Obviously, she was much more upset than Dream about the foal talking and the unicorn coming to see them.

Ellie threw her arms around the mare's neck. *I don't understand. I don't understand any of this. What is happening here?*

Dream stood quietly, but there was no answer.

They were in the middle of the field when Jackie and Mary came down the fence line and stopped at the gate. "Would you look at that?" Mary whispered.

"I'm seeing it, but I still don't believe it," Jackie said.

They stood and watched the two for a while, then turned around and headed up to the barns. "That's no wild horse," said Jackie.

"Well, you know Ellie claims they talk to each other. She told me this morning the horse could reach her even in the apartment," Mary said.

"Yes, I know," Jackie sighed. "I know."

A little later Ellie came up from the field leading the mare. She groomed the already gleaming red coat, and put Dream in her stall. She filled the feed trough with sweet smelling timothy hay and a measure of grain. Mary and Jackie found her leaning over the stall door watching the horse munch.

"I'm sorry. I've been so involved with Dream I've not had time to help much around here. She's just so wonderful and I've waited so long," Ellie looked at Mary and Jackie. "I've not been much help, have I?"

"You're doing just fine, Ellie. Getting acquainted with Dream is what you're supposed to be doing. Mary has been helping me with the beginner's group," Jackie said.

"Yeah, only last year I looked just like those guys. A lot can happen in a year," Mary said with a smile.

"Will you help us take the school horses out to the pasture? The school string is finished for the day and would like to get turned out," Jackie asked.

"Sure, I don't think Dream will mind, she seems content with her new home," Ellie said.

Ellie, Mary and Jackie took the six school horses out to the large pasture. There was a small creek running through it. The horses were dancing on the lines with the excitement of being turned out. Ellie had George on her left and a newer dark horse on her right. The new horse was a little mare but Ellie did not know her name. "What are you calling this mare, Jackie?" she asked.

"Her former owner called her Sunshine, but I've been calling her Sunny. She's such a nice little mare; we're lucky to get her. Good school horses are hard to find. The girl was sad to sell her, but she's going off to college in the fall. She didn't have time for her anymore. Also, she needed the money to help with her school expenses. It's really costly now to go to school."

Ellie said a quiet "Oh." She'd be going to college in the fall, too. Although she would be only thirteen, she would be taking college courses at the university this fall. How would all that affect her and Dream? Then there was the foal. How was she going to deal with Dream and Esophia?

She was deep in thought as she turned out George and Sunny. The horses made a beautiful sight as they ran across the pasture. Shiny coats of bay, brown, red, and the black and white

Harlequin. A lovely sight as they disappeared over the knoll to the creek.

Afterward, Ellie and Mary went into the tack room to straighten up and clean the bridles used that day. Jackie was out with a private student, so the girls were making themselves useful.

"Jackie called your mother and offered her the empty house on the property. Anne's going to look at it tomorrow. It would be so much fun if you moved out here."

Ellie looked up from the reins she was cleaning. "What? That house on the road leading in?"

"Yes, the one behind the old barn, up by the service road. I heard her talking to Anne on her cell phone. Wouldn't that be great?"

Ellie felt a jolt of excitement. Living on the farm would be awesome. It was too much. It would solve the problem of Dream and the foal, but what would she do about school? It would be so easy if life were simple. If she could just be with her horse and did not have to think about school and all that was expected of her. She had promised her mother she would not let her schoolwork slide. There was the art, the math, and the other, the unfinished piece of music she was working on. She needed to be at the school to finish that. The programs she needed were there in the music department. Then, too, there was her mother's work to think about. Life could be so complex.

"Wouldn't you be happy? Think how much fun it will be to live out here. You'd have it all, Ellie. A horse, living on the farm, I'm so envious. I'll be stuck in the city and here you'll be," Mary said.

"Maybe, I'll be here. Mother has never lived in the country in her life. She's afraid of horses and there is her job. I don't think she will go for it," Ellie said.

"I don't know what I would do. I'd miss you like crazy. It would not be the same if you weren't there."

"I'd be there. We go to the same school. You'll stay with me and I'll stay with you."

"I know, but still it won't be the same," Mary said.

"Mary, I've got to tell you something," Ellie was hanging up the last bridle on the hook that had Sunny's name over it.

"What have you got to tell me?"

"Today when I was out in the paddock with Dream, the foal spoke to me."

"What? The foal can talk to you too?"

"Yes, she's not even born yet, but she can talk with me, actually it's much clearer than Dream when she speaks. It's much easier to understand."

"She? The foal is a girl, er, filly?"

"Yes, the foal is a girl."

"That's amazing; although, it makes sense that if the mother can talk to you the baby can too."

"Yeah, I guess. But it's so hard getting used to just one, and now there are two," Ellie sighed.

"Well you said it was easier today, so maybe after a while it will seem normal. You know, like we're doing right now."

"Maybe," but Ellie sounded doubtful.

Jackie provided pizza for dinner. They all sat around the kitchen and talked about the day. By that time, it was dusk. The girls said goodbye to Jackie and walked down to the barn. They stopped by Dream's stall and stood watching the mare, as she settled in for the night.

Triana arrived, "You girls ready to go? I've got a lot of things to do tonight, so gather up. How's the horse doing, Ellie?"

"Oh she's fine the vet says the foal is due any time, but everything looks good," Ellie said.

"Oh, that's good news. I'll bet you can't wait. It's exciting," Triana was helping Mary gather up her backpack. "Ellie get your things together. We've got to get back home. Have you had dinner?"

"Jackie brought us pizza and drinks and we had sandwiches for lunch. All taken care of," Mary said.

"Good," Triana said, herding them toward the car.

CHAPTER 17

*T*he Spheres were glowing with vibrant color. *Ellie felt the color as music, or maybe, the music as color. She was amazed at the pulsing globes. Each of the seven was a note with major and minor vibrations and glowed with the shades of a color. The black space they hung suspended in gave them a magical appearance. The music was in her very being. She could feel the vibration flowing through her, becoming her or maybe she was becoming the sound. It was similar to the piece she was scoring at school, yet the colors pulsing with life made it all the more beautiful. Ellie knew she was in her dream world. She had thought that perhaps with the coming of the red mare the dreams would cease, but obviously not.*

She was more comfortable now with being in this state. She knew whatever came to her here was orchestrated by the unicorn Phell—Phell something.

"Phellsome," rang in her head. "My name is Phellsome and you are Ellie. You and I have a lot to

discuss. I wanted you to see the Spheres again. They represent the fabric of the universes. The vibrations flow into them and out of them. They are the vibrations or music of the whole, melding it all together. Do you understand?"

"No, not at all, although I'm getting some information on them from my math teacher. There was a mathematician a long time ago that believed music and numbers were the source of the universe."

"Well, he was somewhat right. All the expanding space and all the objects in the space make tonal vibrations. Those vibrations are centered here in the Seven Spheres. Each and every part of space vibrates to the spheres. That music is the balance of the whole. We unicorns are the keepers of harmony. The systems of the whole are in the music. We hold that lore in our very fiber." Phellsome shimmered and changed into a glowing color that pulsed like the spheres shimmering above.

Ellie forgot to breathe he was so beautiful. *"Okay, you are like the spheres,"* she said.

"Yes, but more than that. We are the spheres and so are you and all things. Musical vibrations make the patterns of the whole," he said. *"There is much you must learn and little time for you to learn it. Shortly the mare will foal. My daughter, first of her kind, first to be born off my world. She will be very special. I will help you with her, so don't be concerned. I must go now, Ellie, but remember what you have seen and think on it. Finish the music score. Attend to the mare. She is also very special."*

"I know she is special. I have loved her for quite a while. You will keep coming to me? You will help me with the foal?"

*"Finish the score. You have the music.
Remember that music is the answer."*

Music is the answer? To what? Ellie wondered, but only for a short time. She slowly slid into a normal sleep. She was so accustomed to the dreams now that she slept through the night. The alarm went off at six. She groaned as she came awake. "Ah, this new schedule is going to kill me."

Then the dream came back to her. Those spheres, she wanted to paint those spheres, the spheres in the dream. Those colors, that harmony, the music, she wanted to paint them just as she remembered them. The thought of somehow incorporating the feeling of the musical harmony into a painting stopped her for a moment. *Was there some way? No, of course not.* She shook her head to clear it, and instead, reached for her journal and wrote the dream down. She even wrote down the conversation with Phellsome. She stumbled over the spelling, it was hard to put the thoughts into language, but it was close enough, she supposed.

He was such a beautiful creature; he had melted into a rainbow of colors that pulsed with the music of the spheres. She would have to ask Mr. Gregory to hurry up with the information on the Pythagoras and his work on music and math.

Phellsome had said many things that puzzled Ellie. Why would he want her to finish the music, what was so important about the musical score that he was driving her to write? He had said that music was magic. No not magic, more like harmony, or a harmonic vibration. Magic was the word Ellie's mind chose for her because she had no better word. In the real world, there is no magic. There is scientific exploration, there is math, and there is music. Mathematicians consider themselves creative, but to them math is the foundation, the language underlying the whole. Ellie was not sure how to think about magic. It did not feel to her as just mumble, jumble, with no credibility. The question hung in her mind, "How does it fit in?"

After she had written down all she could remember of her dream, she thought how very strange it all was. Something was happening and she had no idea what. She had seen what the foal would look like in the dream she had of the river. She went back through her journal to that dream. She was under the water and Dream was standing on the bank of the stream that had become a river. By her side was a pale almost white baby, tiny, with huge eyes and a slight bump on her forehead. Dream's foal, Dream's and Phellsome's foal. Now she had seen her again, and spoken with her. She had a name and the name was Esophia. She was a beautiful baby.

Reflecting on the dream sequence, Ellie understood that Phellsome was orchestrating everything that was happening. She began to realize that it would take music and lots of magic to make whatever was happening happen smoothly. Ellie hoped Phellsome would be able to bring it about without anyone being hurt. She did not want her mother to be harmed in any way. Yet, she knew that Anne was already stressed by all of this, and that was a worry.

CHAPTER 18

Everything had been going so smoothly that Anne was thinking her luck would surely run out. This move seemed preordained. There had been no obstacles, none. That in itself was beyond strange. She asked and she was given. It seemed that everyone was determined to be helpful and agreeable. Jerry agreed to her working at home, and she had found that a transit bus left for downtown Chicago three times a day, stopping almost at the stable door. All the worries of work and Ellie's transport were taken care of. Anne liked the house, it was a lot bigger than the apartment, and the three bedrooms and two baths with an eat-in country kitchen was a delight. Also, the views and the grounds around the house were quite beautiful. Of course, she was not sure she would like living in the country. She had never lived outside the city.

The big worry at the moment was the piano. The baby grand was a problem and had only been moved once before. It took a special crew and its own moving van. She did not want to watch them bring it down and out to the farm. So far, luck had been with them and she hoped that it would continue. Once the piano was loaded, she could breathe easy. Ellie did not seem to be worried at all. She was so excited to be moving out to and be with her precious horse, that nothing could bother her. The piano could fall on her head and she probably would not notice.

The rest of the move was going like clockwork. The furniture and boxes were leaving as fast as four men could carry them down. They would be in their new home by this evening. It had only taken two days to organize everything. She still could not believe her good fortune.

She had made this important decision by herself. She had not even thought of Earl. The move from one apartment to another in the same complex was nothing like this one. Then Anne had been in agony and so indecisive. She remembered all the phone calls to Earl. Now she had made all the arrangements by herself. She smiled. Even where Ellie was involved, she had not thought to talk to her ex-husband. Maybe she was making progress after all.

There was a surprise waiting for them on their first trip to the new house when they pulled into the driveway behind the van with the piano. There stood Allen Edwards, the man from the BLM, the one who had made it easy for them to buy Dream. He and Jackie were standing in the driveway to the house. Anne jumped out of the car and hurried toward them.

She must have looked startled because Mr. Edwards said "No, no problem, but I was in the area and just wanted to check in to see how everything is going. Jackie has been filling me in on the horse and Ellie. And, I see that you're moving in, too. That should make it easier for you guys."

"Oh, I thought that something might be wrong with the paperwork on the horse or something. It's nice that you're taking an interest in Ellie and the horse. Would you like to see our new house? This is such a pretty area," Anne was babbling. *I'm behaving like a schoolgirl. Have I forgotten how to talk to a man?*

"Yes it is, pretty that is, and actually, I live fairly close to you, so it wasn't a problem for me to come and Jackie said it would be fine," Mr. Edwards smiled at Anne and Ellie.

"Yes, I knew you wouldn't mind, so when he called, I told him to come on by," Jackie said.

"Not at all," Anne said, "although getting this piano in will be the major priority of the move. I hope it stays in tune. Ellie gets frustrated if it has even one note off. Well, here we are." She led them inside the back door.

"So, Mr. Edwards, what do you think of Dream?" Ellie asked.

"First, I'm not Mr. Edwards, but Allen, okay? Second, I think that your Dream is fine, very fat, but fine. Jackie tells me that you are getting along extremely well. You have such rapport with that horse. Mustangs can be difficult, but maybe this one was a domestic horse gone wild."

"I could ask, er, well maybe that's what happened. She is so quiet and sweet, Mr. Allen," Ellie replied.

They watched as the men brought the piano into the living room. Everyone followed the men into the house, where Anne and Ellie finally decided on a space by the front window. It was a large room, much larger than the living room in the apartment, and the piano fit nicely in the bigger space.

"I grew up in this house; my grandparents built it for my mother and father when they married, and I lived here by myself when my parents took over the big house after my grandparents passed away. When my parents retired to Florida, I moved into the big house. I've rented this one occasionally, but mostly it's been empty. Finding good tenants is not easy," Jackie said, "which is why I'm so glad that Anne and Ellie wanted it. It's a win for all concerned."

"It looks like the move is moving right along," Allan laughed at his pun. He was admiring the piano. "That looks like a serious piano. Who plays?" he looked at Anne. "You?"

"No, no not me. I can't carry a tune. Ellie is the pianist in the family. She's very good. You'll have to come hear her sometime," Anne actually blushed.

"I'd love to. We'll make a date, but now I must be going. This was a business stop. I'm working, you know. Let me know when the foal is born. Sometimes the color gives us a clue to the father. I've some knowledge of that particular herd. Although I don't remember that red mare. I've done some research on herd management there in the past."

"Yes, we will. It would be nice to know more about them. I'll definitely call you. Please come out any time. I'll have a new phone number but my cell is the same, so just call. I'm so looking forward to living here. It will be strange for a city girl like to me to be living in the country, but we do what we have to do when we have children. I'm sure I'll adjust."

"I'm sure you will," he said smiling.

Jackie and Ellie exchanged glances and smiled at each other. They were both thinking that Alan Edwards and Anne Miller were getting along very well. However, Anne was wondering if Mr. Edwards, Allen as he had insisted she call him, was interested more in Jackie than in Dream. Jackie was a lovely woman and completely unattached. All around a good catch, not an over-stressed working Mom whose first interest always had to be her daughter. She sighed. She thought that Allen Edwards was a nice man. It startled her to find she was wondering if she might be ready to think about a new relationship, another man. Now that was a thought!

~~~~~~

Ellie was so happy that the last of the furniture and boxes were unloaded. They had spent the whole day moving their things to the new house. She loved the house. It was big, the front looked out toward the road and from her bedroom window, she could see into the paddock where both the foal and Dream would be during the day. She felt like she had been released from prison. Fun, she was going to have so much fun this summer.

The house sat close to the main road that led to the interstate and a bus stopped there so that she would be able to get to school. The commute was just over an hour, but it would give her time to read. She was concerned about her mother, however. Anne had always lived in the city and felt uncomfortable in the country. She had never had any relationship with animals, never owned a pet, not even a fish, and yet here she was moving to the country so that Ellie could be with her horse. Her mother was giving up a lot so that Ellie could be happy.

It took them several days to get the house organized. They worked steadily and things were finding their place in the larger space. Ellie loved her bedroom. It was large and there was plenty of room for her computer, books and even space for her paints. Even Anne was finding the large house a luxury. The big kitchen had room for a table, and windows that looked out on the pastures. She was getting used to the quietness and the dark of the country nights.

CHAPTER 19

The foal alarm was going off. Somewhere in Ellie's mind, the warning is heard and translated into a wake up response. "Wake up! Wake up!" Ellie was already putting on her jeans before the significance of the alarm registered in her head. Her body had just done its thing. She was dressed and putting on her boots before her mind caught up. It was time. The foal was coming.

Just as Anne was entering her room, Ellie was throwing a jacket over her shoulders and heading out the door. "Mom, she's coming, the foal. Dream needs me. I've got to go."

Anne looked bewildered, but she moved aside and let Ellie leave. Then she glanced at the clock and the bleeping alarm. 3:00am. almost exactly, yes, that was the time of babies, when the world was dark, quiet, relaxed. That is when babies came. She remembered that. Oh well, nothing about labor was civilized. It was heavy, primal, painful and ancient. She turned off the alarm and went to the kitchen. She would make coffee and chocolate. The night was over. The new order was here.

When Ellie raced into the barn, she found Dream drenched in sweat and pacing round and round her stall. Ellie stood at the stall door and realized that she did not know what she was supposed to do. She looked into the place in her mind where she could always find the contact with Dream and her foal, found it was closed and dark. There was nothing, just an empty space. She realized then that she had come to rely on the touch of them, the comfort that she could always count on. She was so used to them in her mind, a private place that kept her from ever being alone.

"Dream, I'm here. I'm coming into the stall with you. I need to remove the foal monitor. Okay?" Ellie moved inside the stall to her horse. She laid a hand on the sweaty neck and snapped a lead on the halter ring. "I need you to stand still for a moment, please." She ran her hand down the side of the mare and raised her tail to remove the clip on the monitor. She then removed the device and turned it off.

Dream shook her head and moved off as if Ellie was not there. Ellie could see the muscles in her flank ripple in waves and when they did, the mare made a sighing noise and shuddered. Suddenly the foal was making sounds in her mind, not the voice she had come to know but other strangling, frightening sounds. Ellie did not know what to do.

The presence of Phellsome seemed to come all at once. Ellie could see the shimmer of rainbow light, feel the lightness, and then her fear was gone. The sound of the foal in her head was gone. He did not appear as the unicorn but only as a rainbow shimmer. Dream seemed to relax and the most beautiful music seemed to envelope them.

The music was inside Ellie's mind mesmerizing her. Suddenly, her head seemed to be expanding, exploding, and then pain came. Starting at the top of her head, but it was sound, color, bright pain. It seemed that all her senses were connected together and fusing into something more. Her head became nothing but circuits forming and re-forming. Lightening like flashes bolted through her, she put her hands on both sides of her head to keep it from shattering. It was like feeling the inside of your brain glow, form itself into a new configuration. It seemed to last for a long time, she lost consciousness and collapsed in the hay.

She awoke walking in a field of flowers with her arm on Dream's shoulder. All was shimmering in a light that her artist eye longed to capture. It was the valley where she had first met the red mare. She could not feel the foal's mind anymore, but that did not bother her.

The music was beautiful, a song of love and light. The music was vibrating and pulsing with life. She only hoped that she would remember some of it. There was part of her, that intellectual part of her that was trying to commit it to memory. Then for the first time in her remembered life she was not thinking, she was fully in the moment, the moment of the foal's birth, a new being coming into the world.

Time was irrelevant; Ellie and her horse were together in a place of sound, light and for the moment, total trust. Together they were seeing lines of golden color connecting a web that seemed to hold points of pulsing music, and it stretched out from them through a void of nothingness. Somewhere, the Seven Spheres were gathering it all together and sending it back out. How Ellie understood this she did not know, but know it she did, and it seemed that Dream did too.

When the golden web of light drew them down, they were back in the stall. Dream was laying in the bed of straw that had been prepared for the birth, and lying in a wet heap was a small being, wet and struggling. Phellsome was there, a shimmering presence, but no one else was. Jackie had a monitor and her mother had known that Ellie was coming to the barn because the birth was imminent. *Where were they?* Ellie was confused and did not know what to do. She looked wildly around, and tried to stand up.

Ellie, don't panic. Everything is under control. I had to sing the foal into her new place. She did not understand the birth process, and would have struggled in her fear. The parents of a new life on our planet sing the young into their new place. There is a gathering of others to keep the young one protected from the sensations of sound and light. Here I am alone, and as Esophia's male parent, it fell to me to nurture her birth. We have about an earth hour to acclimate her. Don't worry I will guide you, he was speaking inside her mind.

Dream turned her head and began to nuzzle her new baby. She was making soft whickering noises, and licking the foal all over. This seemed to comfort the foal and after a few moments, Dream stood up. *She's very beautiful, don't you think?*

She's the most beautiful baby in the world. Ellie answered, looking at the small creature lying in the straw and for the first time it became real. She was a filly foal, wet still, creamy white with a golden glow to her coat. Her eyes were huge and dark, with an unfocused haze, and her tiny head was lifted and gazing around at her new environment. Ellie could tell she was going to be lovely, but definitely unusual. White was common in adult horses but very unusual in a newborn. Her tiny hooves were soft looking, and she was so delicate that she awed Ellie.

As you know, she can communicate with you already. I understand that she has been doing that, Phellsome said.

Yes, sometimes, Ellie said. *She talks to me, and I assume she talks to Dream.*

Of course she talks to me. I'm her mother. Dream moved between Ellie and the foal. Ellie left the stall and came back with several clean towels. Kneeling down by the baby, she started to rub her dry. Suddenly Esophia lunged forward out of her hands onto her forelegs, attempting to rise. Ellie moved backwards out of the way. Phellsome was still there but he was insubstantial just like a glowing ghost.

Where is everyone? I could use some help here, Ellie thought.

They won't come for a while, came into her mind. *We must have quiet here for the bonding time. Like all our species, she has the ability to communicate mind to mind, but she has not learned how to shield herself. We've got to protect her until she has control over her own mind. I have given you the ability to shield her. I'm sorry that it caused you pain. She will be different; she will combine traits from her earth mother but will carry the magic of my kind, bringing something altogether new. She will be of the earth, but also of the unicorns. We must bond with her,* suddenly Ellie felt the big unicorn in her mind, and she was drifting away again.

The music was at first soft and came with the colors of a rainbow. All was quiet in the stall. The new being became still as her father sang the birth song to her. Ellie pulsed with warm radiant light, and the colors of the rainbow, swirling around in her. The music was so beautiful a tear leaked out from her closed lids. The expansion she had experienced earlier had given her a new understanding of the music that had been haunting her for so long. She drifted in the sound and color. She had never seen or heard such beauty. The music became part of her and colored her mind.

How long it continued she did not know but when she became aware of her surroundings, she was kneeling on the stall floor with Dream standing to one side and Esophia nudging at her mother's flank. Dream sighed as her new daughter took the first milk into her greedy little mouth.

The barn door opened. Anne and Jackie came in together. Anne was carrying two thermos bottles and boots. "Ellie, you forgot your boots. It's freezing out here," she halted and just stared.

Jackie stood rooted at the stall door, her eyes wide with shock. Both women were quiet as they looked over the stall door. The cream-colored filly was standing by her mother nursing and twitching a fuzzy golden tail. She did not stop her first meal to greet the newcomers.

"She's beautiful," Anne breathed.

CHAPTER 20

Rowen's long, dark hair was tangled from her restless sleep. She came awake suddenly and blinked her eyes in the dark bunk of the horse van. It took a moment for her to remember where she was. The rumble of the truck motor and the swaying movement of the van brought reality. She was in the sleeping unit of the van, speeding along with six of her horses toward Chicago. Hopefully, the other two vans were right behind this one, and all her beautiful Gypsy Vanners were doing as well as these.

She was awake, remembering the dream. It was beginning to recede but the music and color seemed to stay just behind her eyelids, a wonderful dream but somehow disturbing. It was not quite clear why. She moistened her mouth with her water bottle, trying to bring the dream into focus, but it was vague.

The van swayed to the movement of the road. She sighed and listened to a different music, the music of the horses in the large van. Smiling, she allowed herself to think, *I've come a long way for a Gypsy Girl.* As in affirmation, a large hoof stamped and sent a dissonant noise jarring through her ears, displacing the dream notes with reality music, the music of being close to her horses. Her horses were stomping and whuffling, giving an undercurrent of sound that made her feel complete. Rowen placed the offbeat noise. She knew it was Calipher being impatient in her tie stall. *Calipher, be quiet you'll wake everyone up,* she thought.

She looked at the small light on her cell phone, 4:00am. They were due at the new barn at about 5:00 this morning. She did not know what was going on up front, or how far they had come. The six big horses in the back, one stallion, three mares and two foals were traveling fine. *"Gypsy Vanners, I love you,"* she thought. Gypsy Vanners were an old breed of horses bred by the Romany, or Gypsies as they were commonly known. The big horses were used to pull their colorful caravan wagons, as they moved across the countries of Europe.

Rowen thought it was appropriate that she, a Gypsy girl, was raising these beautiful horses. Their temperament made them wonderful to deal with, and as the horse world was taking note of them, they were becoming popular and profitable. She was bringing this group to a place called Whispering Trees just outside Chicago.

I should go back to sleep if I can, this will be a very busy day. Twelve horses in two vans moving into a new environment, with all their gear in another van with all the carriages, and her pride and joy, a Romany wagon. A labor of love that. She lay content in the bunk. With the rise of popularity of her horses, she had made a lot of money in the last two years. The small New York farm where she had first started her herd was just too isolated and distant from the market. When she had heard about the Chicago contract for carriage horses, she had bid on it and she had won. A real gamble, even now it made her stomach tighten, all that money and all that debt. *Think positive, be positive and work hard*, she thought.

She smiled to herself; these were not traits her people were known for. The Romany people had many names most of them derogatory: Gypsies, travelers, thieves, fortunetellers, baby snatchers. Mostly this was from their wandering ways. They were travelers and they moved around Europe and the Middle East. They were an ancient people who had managed to keep their identity and culture for better or for worse, mostly worse.

Rowen's family was not the norm. They had not been nomadic for centuries. They were part of the Three Families of Rome, rich and famous. Not many outside the families knew of their Romany heritage. They had many interests, banking, manufacturing, and sometimes politics, but they were known worldwide as the founders of the Institute of Music.

Rowen had broken from her family and struck out on her own. Her skill with horses had helped her. Her grandmother said she carried the Romany horse spirit in her blood, but she carried other things in her blood as well. Her mother had brought her to New York City as a baby. A noted psychic, she had started to train her daughter even before she was born. She contended that Rowen was a strong psychic, "You could be better than I am, Rowen, you could be a powerful shaman of the people. Our line from ancient times has been privy to the secrets. In your blood, you have the horse spirit and the gift of sight. Don't throw it away, stay and learn. Please stay and learn."

Her voice was still in Rowen's mind and soul, but she did not want to enter her mother's world, which was mysterious and unstructured. She wanted the today world of horses and reality. She had left her mother as soon as she finished high school. She had apprenticed to a well-known horse trainer and learned. It was true; she had the horse spirit in her blood. Horses trusted her, and she had become a very talented trainer and rider. Now she was emerging as an entrepreneur. She was on her way to a business in Chicago. The Gypsy Vanners would pull the ornate carriages around the downtown area, and her breeding program, training, and all the things associated with the Vanner breed would be her life's work. She was bringing the twelve horses and all the equipment to a place called Whispering Tree Stable, owned and managed by Jackie Long.

The van was slowing. Oh well, so much for any more sleep. She heard the horses stirring. They too had felt the van slowing and knew the ride was about to be over. Calipher neighed to make sure all were awake. Always the leader that mare, Rowen smiled.

The van came to a slow stop and Rowen heard the van door open. She sighed and jumped down from the small bunk. *It's going to be an exciting day*, she thought the horses were getting agitated and moving around in their bedded tie stalls. Calipher was whickering softy to keep the others from getting too wound up. Rowen heard the blowing whicker as, *Okay, now, we're here, I'm looking out for all of us, it's fine.* A picture of green grass and shady trees came into Rowen's mind. *Atta girl, let them think of exercise and food. That'll get 'em co-operative.*

She opened the small door and jumped down. The cool early breeze blew her hair and taking a deep breath of fresh air, she headed for the barn. She had talked to Jackie Long only yesterday to give her an approximate arrive time. The office door was open but no one was around. Where was everyone? It was early but then stables woke early. Horses loved a routine. Mornings were pretty much the same in all the barns in the world. Feed, clean, water, turn out, whatever, so she was surprised to see the place deserted.

She looked around. It was a pretty farm, well cared for, very neat and tidy. She moved around to the large sliding doors that led to a covered arena. There were a double row of stalls on each long side, another barn down a short road, a large storage shed, and several large pastures. The horses in the barn were beginning to answer the calls from the new ones in the van. *That should get someone's attention*, she thought. She opened the doors to the double row of stalls. At the far end, stood several people in front of a stall. They all seemed intent on whatever was happening in it. They did not even look up to see her.

She started walking toward them quickly. *This is some greeting. I've a trailer full of big horses that have been traveling a long time and they need attention. Moreover, they want to get out.*

Just as she reached the middle of the stall row, a striking brunette, turned and saw her. "Rowen Martinelli, here already? Come on down here and tell me what you think of this."

Mystified, Rowen hurried down to the stall where a petite woman and young girl who had to be her daughter because they looked so alike, smiled at her with puzzled expressions. Obviously, they had no idea who she was, or why she was here.

Rowen looked inside the stall. There was a newly born foal standing, nursing what must be her first meal. *Strange coloring*, she thought. Her horseman's eyes were making evaluations about this new entity, when the world shifted around her. She grabbed the stall door with both hands to keep from falling. These were not horseman's eyes, these were psychic's eyes. The mist was grey white and the glowing being was a rainbow of colors. *Welcome, Rowen. See my child? Is she not beautiful?* The shifting world did not settle and Rowen was trying hard to breathe and accept. She heard her mother's voice, and it steadied her. *Focus, Rowen, dear, focus. Breathe, accept.* The rainbow took the shape of a unicorn, the mythical beast from the lore. *He's not real; he's a metaphor*, her mind reasoned with her.

Oh, I'm real enough, his voice smiled in her brain. *Definitely real. Thank you for coming. You are needed here. Ellie, Dream and Esophia, will all need you. Welcome, earth horse spirit,"* the voice was gone.

The world shifted again and still holding on the stall door, she was back in the present. She took a deep breath, opened the stall door and entered to get a better look at the small filly, she said, "Welcome, little one. On behalf of my people, I welcome you," she bowed gravely to the mare and to the foal, dropped to her knees, slowly extended her hands toward the small filly with the strange coloring. The foal stopped nursing, turned her head and seemed to acknowledge the kneeling woman.

The filly had huge dark eyes and they seemed to swirl with the rainbow colors of her sire, and neatly placed in the center of her forehead, just below the fuzzy golden forelock, was a small dark golden bump. Rowen rose and backed to the stall door.

It was then that she turned to face the two women and girl looking at her with startled eyes. *Well, you've done it now, Rowen; everyone here will think you're strange for sure,* raced through her mind.

"It looks like I've arrived just after," she pointed toward the mare and baby, "she arrived." Jackie and Anne were looking at her startled. She tried again, "Jackie, and you are?" looking at Anne then turning to Ellie, "and you?"

Ellie recovered first. "Oh, hi, I'm Ellie and this is my speechless mother, Anne, and Jackie you know already, and you are?"

"Oh, well, I'm Rowen, I'm expected. I think I'm expected, because I've got twelve anxious horses out there in vans that have been on the road for several days. They would very much like to get out and stretch their legs, have a drink and get acquainted," Rowen smiled glancing at first one and then another.

A tall, broad shouldered man with dark hair and eyes, stepped into the barn, looked down the long row and quickly started toward them. "Gotta get them out of there. That Calipher mare is havin' a hissy in the trailer," he said in with a southern drawl.

Rowen turned to Jackie, who seemed to be coming awake at last, but still looking confused, "Could you show us where you want us to take the horses? They really do need to get out. It's been a long ride for them."

146

Jackie came to life at last. "I don't know what happened just now, but we'll talk about it later.

"Ellie are you and Anne all right?"

"Yes, of course we are, you don't need us, do you?"

"No, you stay here and take care of your horse, or should I say horses?" Jackie smiled. "You'll be okay?"

Ellie nodded and smiled. "I think we'll be fine."

Jackie turned and started out of the barn with the man following. Rowen looked at the girl and her mother, bowed to them and then again to the mare. Then she went to her knees in front of what appeared to Anne an empty corner, touched her head to the straw stayed there a moment, rose and backed away.

Ellie frowned, did she see; really see the swirling colors of the unicorn in the corner? Rowen smiled at her, nodded thoughtfully, and hurried out of the barn.

"What just happened here?" Anne asked.

"I don't know, maybe that's the way she welcomes a new foal," Ellie said.

"Strange, but maybe so," Anne said with a frown. "Strange woman," then she asked Ellie what she could do.

Ellie wasn't so sure but they cleaned up the stall, then drank the hot chocolate Anne had brought from the house and watched the foal and Dream bond.

CHAPTER 21

Ellie stayed close to Dream and the filly most of the day. She would catch herself staring at the new tiny foal, as it went about its first day in the real world. The foal would nurse, stamp her feet, lie down, twitch as she dreamed of — "What do you dream, little one?" she smiled her question.

It was a wonderful day; Dream was preoccupied with her new responsibilities. She paid no attention to Ellie at all. She would nuzzle her baby, circle her, make soft noises to her, and stand patiently as the foal looked for the right place to nurse. *Such patience,* Ellie thought, *is that what all mothers do?*

Phellsome had left as quickly as he had come, and the foal did not seem to miss him. She seemed content to explore her much larger space. She would jump and then fall flat, thin little legs at strange angles, then she would reorganize, get her tiny front legs out in front of her and try to stand up, only to fall over and make the effort again. Dream walked circles around her, and talked to her in short huffy whickers. She did not speak to Ellie, but she seemed happy that Ellie was there, taking up the left front corner of the stall.

The foal was now dry and the color was somewhere between pure white and white with a hint of pink gold. She would come over to Ellie and put her little head down and sniff, turn, jump and then run back to her mother. Dream seemed immersed in her new offspring, as was Ellie.

Anne brought out a picnic lunch and stayed to share it. "She is such a little darling, isn't she?" she whispered, as the foal came over to nibble at the paper that was crackling around the sandwiches. "No sweetie, this is people food. Yours is over there." She pointed at Dream who was having a warm mash of bran and oats. "That's your lunch wagon, dear."

"What are you going to call her, Ellie?"

"Her name is Esophia," Ellie said, but we'll have to come up with something as a stable name, maybe 'Sophie', what do you think, Mom?"

"Esophia? What a strange name, but Sophie is nice. She is such a delicate little thing. Those long legs, I don't think I've ever seen such a young horse before. Who do you suppose her father was?"

Ellie looked at her mother, realizing that Anne had no idea of what had taken place around the birth. Phellsome had worked his magic and no one knew what had happened. He had been able to keep them from knowing anything about his presence.

It had been so hard and so real for Ellie. Phellsome was able to work with her while Anne and Jackie were standing there without seeing anything that was going on. Somehow, he had given her a new type of power. It had exploded in her head. She realized now that it was still there, and that she was the one shielding the foal with part of her mind. Dream wasn't doing it, she was.

What had Phellsome said? Yes, she remembered. *We will have to shield her from the stimuli of the world around her. She has the abilities of my race as well as her mother's. She is able to read thoughts and see with a different reality, my reality and power have been born into her. Until she is able to handle all that we must shield her. I have helped you expand your mind so that you will be here to do those things for her.* She was remembering more and more of what had transpired in the stall, while everyone else was in some kind of trance or something. It was frightening and, she felt herself go cold with anxiety.

Ellie would need to have a talk with the unicorn about all this, she just did not understand these new abilities he had given her or how she was able to use them. She needed to be alone to explore them.

How was that happening? She felt tired, but the lunch was welcome. She ate two sandwiches and drank a thermos of tea; the homemade cookies went down too. "That was good, Mom. Thanks, I was really hungry."

"I can see that," Anne said. I only got one cookie!"

"Oh, I'm sorry. I didn't think."

"Well, I'm glad; you were white as—as that baby."

"She's really beautiful, isn't she?" Ellie said.

"She certainly is, dear. Although I don't know anything about horses. I think she's exquisite," Anne replied. "Will you stay here all afternoon or are you coming back to the house? I've got a project to get ready, so I need to get busy," Anne said.

"I'll probably stay here the rest of the day, but I'll be home for dinner. At least, I think I'll be home for dinner. I should wait for Jackie to come back and see if there's anything that needs doing. I think she called the vet, and would you call Mr. Edwards and tell him about the filly?"

"Who? Mr. Edwards, the BLM man? Why?"

"I think it would be nice for him to know, and he asked us to call, remember? Maybe there's paperwork for the baby? I'm not sure why he wanted to be called, but he asked. His card is in the folder with the paperwork on Dream."

"Well, yes. I suppose I can do that." Anne said slowly.

When Ellie was alone she began to think about the birth again. She wished she had her journal so that she could record it, as she did with her dreams. *I should write down all our meetings and try to remember their order, and what he says. Sometimes he talks in riddles, at least they seem that way to me.* She still felt drained because of the energy she was expending to keep the force field up around the stall. If she looked hard at a spot in the stall, she could see the slight glow of it, like a golden thread covering the whole area. She was not sure how she was doing it but she knew she was.

She would have to ask Phellsome, but she had no idea how long she would have to stay here. He had just gone and that was several hours ago. Also the woman with the long dark hair, Rowen? Had she really seen him? She had certainly acted as if she had. She had bowed to him before she left, but then she had bowed to Dream and to Esophia, too. How could she have done that if she had not seen him?

Then Jackie and her mother had acted as if they had not seen anything. It was as if Phellsome had just suspended time for them. It was a long while and they were just standing there so still. They had not even known that the Rowen had come in.

Strange happenings, but then how could it have been otherwise? The birth of this foal was unique. What did the birth of the foal, the unicorn, the dreams, mean? What was it all about? The music, the colors, if only it were clear, but if the Rowen had seen the unicorn—maybe she would be someone to talk to. Maybe there was someone else and she would not be all alone.

CHAPTER 22

Rowen flexed tired muscles and sank into the steamy water; let her body slide slowly into the wonderfully hot tub. She sighed and closed her eyes. It was nice of Jackie to let them stay at the farm. Anton was in the sleeping quarters of the huge trailer, while she was in the guest room of Jackie's house. She drifted in the tub and let all the tension from the day rise into the iridescent bubbles floating around her exhausted body.

What a day. She had existed on little sleep for the last week, and the work had been taxing to both mind and body. Nevertheless, she was here and the horses were settling in nicely. Funny what a lot of green grass and room to kick up your heels could do for a horse.

She had the carriages in the appropriately named carriage house. It was a long building that in a former time had actually held carriages for the landowners. It seemed apt for the ornate carriages to be there once again. There were some old harnesses there she wanted to look at, she reminded herself, if and when, she had time.

Let it go, let all go. Just relax. Just be. She was here at last. Her new life was in front of her. She was keeper of her own destiny. *I'll make it or I'll break it, no excuses. My horses are settled into the large, lovely old barn.* She had chosen well and it was going to be fine.

The water was working wonders on her tired self. She soaked until she felt the water getting cold, then climbed out of the claw-footed tub, and dried herself off. Put on a fluffy robe and dropped into the bed that did not move like the bunk in the trailer. She curled up in the fetal position and fell into a dreamless sleep.

Twelve hours later, she came awake. Whatever time was it? She felt drugged from such a long time in an unconscious state. Quickly dressing, she headed down the stairs of the two-story house. "Jackie?" then louder, "Jackie?" Her voice echoed and she arrived in a large kitchen that smelled deliciously of coffee, bacon, and yeasty bread. A note left by the pot of coffee simply said, HELP YOURSELF! Jackie. A smiley face graced the bottom of the note.

The smells were too tempting. Pouring coffee and filling the plate from the stove with scrambled eggs, bacon, some excellent soft toast, with what looked like homemade jelly, she ate and then ate again, finishing all that was on the stove. She rinsed the dishes and carefully put the dirty dishes in the dishwasher. Turning off the coffee pot, she poured the last steaming cup and went out the door. The rather large house sat on a hill with a veranda all the way around it. Built in the late eighteen hundreds, she guessed.

What a beautiful place. She sipped coffee and walked around the whole house slowly taking in the panoramic view. To the left from the front entrance were the large new barns of the boarding stable and covered arena. The paddocks stood out in white board fencing, clearly defined from the higher ground advantage. She saw that her horses were stabled in an older barn with the large stalls that had housed horses from a time when horses were a necessity not a luxury. A barn for horses that worked, plowed the land, pulled the heavy equipment, took their owners to church, and that now housed the Vanners' ample size. It looked like the original barn that went with the big house on the hill. Next to the old barn was the carriage house.

The barn itself was newly cleaned and refurbished in anticipation of the Gypsy Vanners, and the woodwork, true to the last century's craftsmanship, was lovely, old and ornate. It was a beautiful place.

Jackie had mentioned last night that there was an apartment over the barn, but it had not been used for ages and ages. She had said that Rowen could look at it and see what kind of shape it was in. If it could be made habitable, she was welcome to rent it for herself. Rowan made a note to herself to look at the apartment. It would be perfect if she could make it work.

Then there was the strange new filly, and the girl and her mother whom she had met yesterday morning. That was something. Had she actually seen what her eyes told her she had seen, a unicorn, a large male unicorn and his child by the mare? He had seemed very proud of his new daughter.

An old story came to mind and with it a picture of her great-uncle Rory, old when she was very young, talking to her about unicorns. He was a horse master, what is now called a horse whisperer. He had the spirit of the horse in his being. He could talk to them, and they trusted him. He was also a psychic as many in her family were. He took a special interest in her from the day he found her at the age of two sitting between the legs of a black and white Gypsy Vanner stallion. He had recovered her, laughing and taken her back to her mother's house, "She's got the gift. She's got the gift." Her mother had often told the story to her, always with the warning to take care, for the horse gift was a dangerous gift, wild and undisciplined.

The story of the unicorn was very famous in the three families. It was an account of how they had become the keeper of a magic older than time. Long ago, a unicorn had come and taught them a magic of the harmonies. The vibrations could be made to change basic elements, a secret they had kept from the world. Only a few were selected and then trained in the way of the unicorn's teachings. From that time forward, they had kept the secret, and developed the teachings. There was danger in power, and the three families had a lot of power.

She had been thrilled that her uncle was teaching her about the beautiful horses. They were her friends and she loved them. When she was eleven or twelve her uncle had become ill. He knew he was dying, but he continued to teach her all that she could absorb. On the last day of his life, she was sitting by his bed, when he began to whisper to her. She leaned in close to him to hear his words.

"Someday, one of the horse masters will play a very important role in helping our people regain their place. The horses have told me this." Then he sent a picture into her mind as they did when talking with the horses. A pure white, very beautiful unicorn, with a gold tinged horn in the middle of his forehead. He is not of our world but the horses are his cousins, just as we are related to the chimps and gorillas. When he comes, it will be a time of extreme danger. He will guide us and help us, and we will desperately need his help."

She remembered asking him to give her more information, but that was all he would tell her. It was his final teaching. Remembering him even now brought a deep sadness.

She had seen a unicorn in the stall with the young girl and foal. Could it be that she was the horse master of whom her uncle spoke? There was no doubt that this was a time of danger, over population, wars, greed, the danger to the environment, all these things were a real threat to the planet and all living on it.

There had been some dreams from time to time. Mostly, she was so busy with her life that she would just put them aside, to think about later, when there is more time. She had heard music in her dreams, always the music seemed to be floating on moving waves of color, floating, floating. She shook her head. She did not need this now. Now she needed to focus on the new business, the horses, and hopefully, a new life.

CHAPTER 23

Ellie was up early, just as the sun was coming up, beautiful and cool. Not for long though, because the day was going to be warm with maybe some showers. She looked up at the sky and saw that the weatherman was going to be right. Maybe she would not let Dream and Esophia out today.

It was as if the foal were growing with every minute of the day. She had been born in the early morning, but was already steady on her tiny legs. One day made a big difference in Sophie. She no longer fell over when trying to either stand or lay down. Her small cream-colored body looked like it was gaining weight with every hour. Dream was looking with longing out the stall window at the green, grassy pastures. She would watch the weather but she could no longer deny Dream the grass and Sophie's first trip outside. It should be hysterical.

Ellie had not seen Phellsome since the birth and she had been reluctant to leave the stall. Not knowing if she could maintain the protective field if she left them alone. She was not sure how far away it would work. In the late evening, she very carefully left them and slowly made her way home without losing the shield. She did not know how she was doing it but she was. Now she took for granted that the shield would be wherever the foal went.

Phellsome had changed things inside her head during the birth. Now it seemed that she had compartments inside her brain, they seemed to work without her consciously thinking about them.

Hopefully, Phellsome would come again soon. She wondered how he would act with Sophie. She had so many questions and he had not given her much information. Would Sophie be like a normal horse, or would she be more like her father? He could just appear, get inside her head and there was the episode where her mother and Jackie seemed frozen, when time moved for Ellie, but not for them. They did not remember anything until that Rowen had shown up. She wondered how Phellsome could do that. Her mother and Jackie had lost about an hour. Even more strange, they had not seemed to realize it.

If Esophia had his abilities, how would she be able to keep her safe? It certainly would be a challenge. Maybe that was why he had done whatever he had done inside her head. Just remembering that time caused her to remember the pain, the agonizing flashes of light, and the music.

She had questions but no answers. She would just have to wait and see what would transpire. She hoped the unicorn would not leave her alone with the foal. Dream did not seem disturbed. Everyone was taking the birth as something normal, so maybe it was.

Dream was munching on hay when she got to the barn. Esophia was having a little breakfast, too. With her nose, she bumped her mother's flank to bring down the milk, and sucked greedily. Ellie stopped at the stall door and just watched. What a beautiful picture they made.

A man came walking quietly toward her. He was the guy from yesterday, the one who worked with Rowen. He came up and stood by the stall. "She's a beauty, truth be told," he said,

"I've never seen one born that color before. Almost gold, but not palomino, not cremello, either. Wonder what color her father was," he looked quizzically at Ellie.

"Her father was white, I think," Ellie said with a small smile.

"White, as an Albino, you think?"

"I don't know for sure, maybe. Dream was a wild horse from Montana. We bought her from the BLM."

"That so? Well, you got a lot for your money. She's beautiful."

"Yes, she is. I'll ask Jackie if we can let them out in the pasture today. I know that Dream would love some grass and sunshine. The vet said they were fine when she visited them yesterday. She commented on her color, too."

"I'll just bet she did. My name is Anton, Anton Wheeler. I'm here with Rowen. We have the Gypsy Vanners in the old barn."

"Oh, Gypsy Vanners. They're so beautiful. Are they all pintos? I've never seen a solid colored one, but then I haven't seen many. They are rather rare here."

"Yep, mostly all pintos, but not all. We're going to do carriage rides in the city. They are wonderful driving horses," he said.

"I've heard that they are, but I don't know anything about driving. It will be wonderful to have them here. How many do you have?"

"Well, we brought twelve in, and one of the mares is in foal, so the herd is growing. The geldings and open mares will try to earn our keep while the others raise babies and make more. We have a wonderful stallion, and he'll be standing at stud here."

"I can't wait to see them," Ellie said

"Anytime; we start working early next week. Well, gotta get moving, they're restless and want to be out on that beautiful grass."

"Yes, grass and sunshine," Ellie smiled and moved inside the stall, the new people were very nice. She needed to talk to the woman again soon. She knew that Rowen had seen the unicorn. She just knew it.

Ellie groomed Dream and put on her halter, snapped on the lead rope and opened the stall door. "Okay, you two lets go eat grass." Dream moved out the stall door by Ellie's side, they moved on out to the center and waited for Sophie to follow. She stood inside the stall and shook her head looking frantically out, trembling with fear. Dream nickered *Come on,* but the stubborn little body went rigid.

Ellie was stumped. "Any ideas, Mom?"

Dream bumped her on the shoulder and started walking down the barn aisle. Sophie was beside herself, calling and running circles. Dream paid no attention to her, slowly moving away. Just when they disappeared from Sophie's vision, the filly screamed a whinny and jumped out, her eyes huge and her trembling little body scrambling to get to her mother.

"Well, that got her out, didn't it?" Ellie was smiling. "Sophie there's a whole big world out here; it's beautiful and full of wonderful things. You're going to love it. I guarantee. Dream and I will keep you safe while you learn your way around in it. Also you have a father to help, if he ever shows up."

~~~~~~~

Phelistia

The beautiful swirling eyes were damp from tears. "Oh Phellsome, why didn't you take me into your plan? We're as close to being one as two can be. If you are in this so am I. I can feel the wrongness on that planet. I can hear the fouled music. Why can't we just work it out together? I could come there with you. Together we could sing it right, change it. Make it beautiful again."

Phelistia gave a shake of her head. The disharmony of the vibrations rising from this planet, was that the reason they were twins?

What had happened there? She had followed the thread up to the spheres and saw the spheres tremble with the task of correcting the tones. All seven had dimmed and struggled. What would happen when they could no longer change the flow?

Music-like vibrations held the whole together. She let herself meld into the last sphere as it changed each discordant note. How long had this been going on?

It was a beautiful planet, with something very ugly going on, something had changed it, the harmony that was integral to the whole of the universe, was missing there. She wondered what had happened, what had made this madness.

The dominant species, while sentient, were seemingly unaware. How had we, the unicorns, charged with keeping the balance, let this small planet lose its harmony? Why had there been no intervention?

She wanted to help but was not being asked. The youngling, her niece, (she shuddered) was already born and Phellsome had not notified anyone, not even her. Why had he excluded her from this? They were bound by spirit and by *blood. What he did would reflect on her as much as on him. The whole matter should have been handled by the Elders.*

There were those here who thought that she and her brother were abominations. Twins had never been born before. There was a prophecy about two born to make a harmony that would save the spheres. Nevertheless, many were left uneasy with the twins.

What would they think about a half-breed creature from this damaged world, half unicorn, half — well, Phelistia was not sure what the creature was called there. Anyway, the small female was without precedent. She did not have any notion about how this would play out on either world. She had to trust that Phell knew what he was doing. If he did not, they were in serious trouble.

CHAPTER 24

The dreams had been coming every night for the two weeks since Sophie had been born. Ellie was tired, so very tired. Her mother and Mary were concerned. She would fall asleep and immediately the sequence would start. Music would pulse through her and the brightly hued colors would coalesce into—she was not sure what. Perhaps Phellsome was conducting the orchestra that played in her dreams. Colors and musical notes, numbers and colors and musical notes all became one. She was taking in so much that she had no chance to rest.

What she needed to do was talk to Phellsome. She could feel the energy draining from her. Ellie was spending her days with her horses, helping Jackie with the summer schedule and at night when she was supposed to be resting these dreams kept coming. It was a lot of stress. She was trying to write some of the music down but it slid away with the morning.

Mary had come at Anne's request to spend a week or two. Anne was hoping that Mary would be able to help, that Ellie would at least talk to her about what was going on. She knew that Ellie was not sleeping very well. Anne would come into the room to check on her daughter to find the bed a tangled mess and Ellie mumbling in her sleep. Ellie would be up early at the piano or her computer. She was not painting, and she was not laughing anymore. She had an appointment with the therapist next week, but maybe Anne would call and see if they could get in earlier.

In the morning after a huge breakfast of cereal, scrambled eggs and toast, Mary and Ellie walked out to the barn. The routine was that they would feed Dream and Sophie their grain, and while they ate, would groom them. It was a quiet time for Ellie, time with her horses.

Sophie acted like any new baby. She was full of energy and ready to be out in the sunshine. She would let Ellie groom her but not pick up her feet. She was never mean but she would stamp her feet and pull away. She would grab Ellie's shirt in her mouth and pull, toss her head, jump straight up in the air.

Ellie loved the joy that was the young foal. There was a place inside her brain where Dream and Sophie resided. Ever since the night of the foal's birth, it felt like her head was expanding in some way. She was using her mind in ways that she had not known she had, and it was scary and tiring. Whatever she was doing, it was draining her of energy. She could not get enough to eat, and she was not sleeping. She was disturbed by the dreams, making her tired all the time.

It was a widely held theory that humans only used a small percentage of the capacity of their brain, and Ellie knew that she was beginning to use more and more of hers. She was aware of new abilities now. She could see shimmering lines of gold if she let herself. She could touch them almost. Even more strange, she could use them, but for what? Had these abilities had been latent, and Phellsome awakened them? It felt like exercising muscles that had not been used in a long time. Expansion was going on inside her and it was difficult to understand.

Ellie had been deep inside herself when she noticed the silence, and saw that Mary was holding a grooming brush looking at her as if waiting for a reply. "Um — I'm sorry, I — I was thinking, I guess. What did you say?"

"You're always thinking. What's going on with you, anyway? Where's my friend? The one I used to know. I've been here for a week and you've hardly talked to me. Is it Dream and Sophie? Talk to me, please, please talk to me. Ellie I don't understand!"

"Well I don't understand, either," Ellie snapped. "Something happened the night the foal was born. Something changed inside me." Ellie's eyes were wide and moist with tears. Once the tears started, she could not stop them. She leaned into the wall and sobbed.

Mary dropped her brush and went to her friend. "What's the matter, Ellie? Talk to me." She threw her arms around Ellie and pulled her close.

Dream had stopped eating. She turned around and she too put her head into Ellie's back and blew her warm breath into her neck. Even Esophia stopped and looked at the scene going on in the stall.

Ellie was shaking and crying, "I don't really know what's going on. During the day, it seems okay, even if it is weird, sometimes. But at night, I've been having dreams again. Dreams that aren't dreams, but something else. I'm not sure what. Music, color, numbers, like a universe of expanding light. Oh, it's just so hard to explain. Something happened the night Sophie was born. Her father was here and he did something, and now I'm all different!"

"Her father? Sophie's father? Here in this stall? How could that be, Ellie? Have you lost it?" Mary was looking at Ellie with amazement.

"Well, you asked, and now I've told you. Now you think I'm crazy. Maybe I am. I don't know any more," Ellie said. "I'm just so tired. I just want to be a normal girl. I want to ride

Dream and groom her. Take care of Sophie. I want everything to be normal," she stood there face bright red, with tears streaming down it, glaring at Mary.

Mary pushed her against the wall put both hands on her shoulders and shook her. "Get a grip, take a deep breath—breathe," she said. "It will be alright. We need to talk and we will, but now we need to get these girls out to the pasture. Your mother is going into the city today for a meeting. We'll pack a lunch and go out to the pasture with the horses and you're going to tell me everything. Do you understand? Everything."

Ellie wiped her face with a grooming cloth, breathed a sigh. "Okay," she said.

CHAPTER 25

They sat in the shade of a large old oak tree, with a thermos of lemonade and a large sack lunch. There were ham and cheese sandwiches, apples for themselves and Dream, a small jar of peanut butter, which Dream liked almost as much as the girls, and chips and cookies. It was a feast. The day was not overly hot; there was the drone of insects and from the pond the croak of frogs.

Dream and little Sophie were shining bright in the sun with Dream ambling along, head down grazing. Sophie was doing her best to get to the grass, but her legs were too long, and her neck was too short. She splayed her front legs wide and put her tiny white muzzle down as far is it would go. It was about three inches from the lush grass her mother was chopping away on. The girls under the tree watched as Sophie tried again for the grass, over reached and toppled over. She was all legs, but her balance was getting better and she sprang up like a jack-in-the box, tossed her head and kicked out at her mother. Dream raised her head from the grass and calmly stared at her child.

"Are they having a conversation?" Mary asked, looking at Ellie.

"Not in words, it's more like pictures, but not quite." Ellie responded.

"How do you manage, I mean how do you keep those silent conversations with them," she pointed to the two horses, "and us separate in your head?" Mary asked.

Ellie frowned, sighed and so the conversation began.

"It is so difficult, Mary. On the night of the foaling, something happened. There was a unicorn there. I've seen him before. Well, actually I've dreamed him, and talked to him a lot, but that night I was awake and he came. He did something to me. Since then it is like—so hard to explain. It's like an explosion happened inside me, an expansion of some sort. You know that we're different from most people. They say we're smarter, but I think it's more than that. I think that somehow, some of us see, hear, and think in a way that is not common to others. A lot of kids like us grow up outside the norm. At school, you see it all the time. Sometimes we lose touch with what most people would call the real world. Certainly, we think differently and behave differently than other kids our age.

"Well, with that and what is happening, I don't know what is real and what is something constructed in my head. Is the unicorn real? His name is Phellsome, by the way. Did he sire a foal with the mare Dream? Does he send me dreams, and give me the ability to hear and speak to her? The night Esophia was born, was he there? Did he stop time for a while? Did he give me new—I want to say, powers, for lack of a better word, like some kind of magic? Or, am I losing touch with reality? I don't know." Mary was looking at her with wide eyes.

"Mary, come over here with me. I want you to look at Sophie. Really look at her. Stare at her. What do you see?" As she said this, Ellie stood up and started walking toward the mare and foal.

Mary followed Ellie out into the sun and stood in front of Sophie. She stood there for almost a minute. Suddenly, her eyes widened, "Oh, oh my," she whispered. Mary was staring at

Sophie wide eyed, "Yes, I see it, when I look at her very closely I see something different, but only for a second. I have to concentrate hard to see the eyes swirling, the iridescent color, and the gold tinged horn. I only do that because of what you just said.

"Other people see what they expect to see. What's normal, what their mind makes real. Your mind sees what is there. I see her as I want her to be, but that's my mind constructing what it wants to see, this is only a baby horse. I have to make an effort to really see her, as I know you see her, but it's getting easier for me. Sometimes she glows, blurs, becomes like a rainbow of colors. I blink and she becomes a baby horse once more. I know that's what you see. I know you can understand them. Look at the small bump on her forehead. That is not a horse thing that is a horn. Is her father a unicorn? Yes, I think he is." She leaned over and gave Ellie a hug, squeezed her tight for a moment, then leaned away from her. "Let's eat; it's going to be okay. I'm here and you can tell me anything, all right? Anything. We are best friends, and we always will be."

Ellie looked at her friend, maybe it would be all right, now. Mary had seen Sophie as she really was. She had accepted the fact that there was a unicorn and that he was Sophie's sire. She breathed a sigh of relief. Maybe all this was true. Maybe she was not hallucinating after all.

Ellie and Mary ate the huge lunch, munching and laughing at the antics of Esophia, who was still all legs and not always sure of where those legs were. She would fall down, shake herself in anger, jump up, run, kick up, try to talk her mother into a game of tag, try to eat the lush grass, run away, then gallop back, nuzzle Dream's flank, bump her udders and suck noisily, as much for comfort as from hunger.

Ellie and Mary learned a lot about motherhood watching Dream with her child. The mare was long-suffering with the young filly. She never lost her patience with Sophie. Sometimes she would stamp a hoof on the ground, or lay back an ear. Ellie, who could understand the communication, knew the mare was saying, *That's enough of that. That hurts, stop it,*' when Esophia would bump her full udders too hard. They were learning the fortitude required to be a mother, how much fun baby horses could be to watch, and how much their friendship meant to them both.

CHAPTER 26

Anne was happy to be in the city. She was surprised at how well she had adjusted to living in the country, but moving about downtown with all the people on the streets made her feel excited and busy. She had been in the office for the morning. It had been good to meet with others from her team and discuss their latest project. Their input had been invaluable.

She glanced at her watch to make sure she could make her appointment with Ellie's adviser at the school. Ellie would start transitioning into university in the fall. This summer she had elected not to go to school at all. It was the first time since she was three that Ellie was just spending the summer being a kid. Although, Ellie was in deep with all the responsibilities and work the horses made, Anne was more than a little worried about Ellie's health. Anne thought it was a good thing, but she always had doubts about what would be best for Ellie. What if she made a mistake, what if her decisions were wrong, she could 'what if' herself into worry. *I don't want to think about that now. I'll just put it out of my mind.*

She was startled to hear someone calling, "Anne, Anne," someone was calling her name. Could they be calling her or someone else named Anne? She stopped in confusion, started to turn around and someone collided with her almost knocking her down. Reaching out with both hands, a man grabbed her shoulders and pulled her toward him.

Anne felt herself pulled into a very close embrace, "What, who, hey," she was trying to pull herself away.

"Ouch, I'm so sorry," as he steadied her.

Anne went rigid in his arms. She looked up and into the face of Allen Edwards. It took a moment to register, but there he was, the BLM officer who had helped them with Dream. What was he doing here on Michigan Avenue? He was still gripping her shoulders as if she might disappear, fall or something.

She took control of herself, "Mr. Edwards? Allen? What are you doing in downtown Chicago? You are so out of context, what are you doing here?"

He was still holding on to her. He looked uncomfortable. "Well, I didn't mean to run you down. Are you alright?" He slowly dropped his arms from her shoulders and let them hang at his sides.

She took stock of herself and figured she was back on solid ground, "Yes, yes I'm fine. What are you doing here?"

"Well, even country folk have to come to town, once in a while," he smiled. "It's funny that we should meet. I've been thinking about you."

"You have? Oh, right, I remember now. I was supposed to call when the foal was born. Yes, I remember. Even Ellie asked me to call you to tell you that she was born, but I've been so busy that I forgot."

"Well, that's okay. I just thought it would be nice to see the foal. I take it the foal is here? Did everything go well, with the delivery and, and, well you know."

Anne frowned. *Was all well with them?* She did not know. Ellie walked around like a ghost, she was tired and silent at home. She just did not know if all was well with them.

Allen was looking at her with concern. "Is something wrong? Did something happen?" he asked.

"No, no, not anything like that. The foal is beautiful and the two of them are doing very well," she glanced at her watch. "I've got an appointment in a few minutes, so I must be going," she said.

Allen Edwards looked closely at Anne. She had such an expressive face. He had seen the concern over his question. There was something wrong, he decided.

"Hey, how about an early dinner or a drink, or something, I've got an appointment, too, but it will be over about 4:30. How about you? We could have an early dinner and you can show me your baby pictures," he smiled down at her.

Anne swallowed, and thought, *What can it hurt?* "Yes, that would be nice."

"The weather is so nice, let's eat on the river outside at Michael's about five? How does that sound?"

"Okay, sounds great. See you there," Anne was hurrying away.

"Good, I'll see you there at five," Allen Edwards was saying that to her back as she sped down the street. However, he was very pleased that she had said yes.

He stood watching the petite, blonde, well-dressed woman walk away from him. He had been thinking about those two, mother and daughter. Something was strange about that incident with the horse, but that was not why he wanted to see Anne Miller again.

At 5:00 o'clock, Anne hurried down the stairs to the outdoor restaurant. She liked to eat here in the summer, the water sparkled with sun diamonds from the warm breeze, and it gave her a feeling of joy in just being alive. There were groups of people laughing and like her enjoying the day. It was beautiful, the food was good and everything had a fresh feeling.

It had been a long while since she had been here last. On one of his trips back to see Ellie, Earl had told Anne about Sandra here. Anne had managed to get through that. Actually, she had not given Earl a lot of thought lately and now she was here meeting a very attractive man. She was excited and a bit nervous.

Allen was waiting at the outdoor bar with a cool drink in his hand. He turned to see her scanning the crowd and waved her over. "Welcome, it's a bit crowded. We have about a twenty-minute wait. Would you like something to drink? Wine, soft drink?" he was smiling down at her.

"I think an iced tea would be wonderful," she said taking a stool. "I could use something about now." She gave a sigh as she settled herself.

"How did your meeting go? Everything okay?" Allen asked, settling on to a stool at the bar next to her.

"Well, as you know we've moved out to the farm. I'm settling in and Ellie is so happy there. I can work mostly from home anyway. Today, I was in meetings all morning with my design team and then a conference with Ellie's adviser this afternoon. I've hardly had time to catch my breath. What are you doing in the city?"

"I'm in the city every day this week. We're having a conference, but I live north, out close to the stable actually," he said.

"I'm so sorry that I didn't call you, Ellie had asked me too. She wanted you to know that the foal was born and all was well. She's a beautiful little thing."

"Filly, then?"

"Yes, she's all white and feisty. She is healthy and leads her mother a merry chase. You must come out to see her, Ellie would be so pleased."

"I'd love to come out. White, you say. That's a very unusual color. Foals born white normally are defective and do not make it. Her mother is chestnut, isn't she? That's a dominant color, very strange. What did the vet say?"

"Just about the same thing you just said. Very uncommon color; I think she called her a cremello or something. Not white, but certainly not palomino either."

"Well, I'm glad she's healthy and thriving. You never know with these wild ones. Not sure about the stallion, and they are sometimes run a long way to the holding pens. How the mare managed to get to Chicago is a mystery to me."

"Yes, and to me, too," Anne said.

"There was a real bond between that mare and Ellie, wasn't there?" Allen said, remembering the day he had let them buy the horse. He had watched that young girl halter the horse and lead it out of the truck right into the horse trailer, the mare walking along like a veteran traveler.

"Oh, my, Allen you don't know the half of it." Anne said. "Do come out and see for yourself. We'd love to have you."

They talked of their work and about themselves through dinner and dessert. Allen had his car and offered to take Anne to the farm. She thought about the bus, and then decided that she would accept a ride home. It would be quicker, and she was having a wonderful time. It was nice to have someone else to talk to who was not so closely involved, and get an objective view of what was happening in her life and to her daughter. It gave her pleasure that he was showing an interest.

They continued the conversation all the way home and when he parked the car and came around to open her door; she realized that she was sorry the evening had ended. It was so nice to talk to someone about something besides Ellie and the horses, another adult and quite a handsome one at that.

He gazed down at her, "I had a good time, thank you. I'm busy for the rest of the week, but I'd like to come out on Saturday to see Ellie and her foal. Would that be alright?"

"Ellie would love to have you come out," she said, thinking that she would be glad, too. "Call me; we'll set a time, maybe lunch or a picnic?"

"Thanks again. I'll call," he got in his car and drove away.

Anne stood on her porch and watched until his car drove out of sight. She sighed; Allen was a very nice man, divorced for several years, although he had not talked much about his own life. He had drawn her out about her life, and being a single parent. It was nice to have someone to talk with.

Ellie woke up the next morning hearing her mother speaking to someone in the other room. She looked at the clock; it was late she must have overslept. She jumped up ran out of her room to see the sun streaming in the kitchen window and her mother laughing into the phone. Something in her mother's voice made Ellie stop and listen. There was a lightness to it, musical. Ellie had not heard that happy sound in a long time. Then she remembered, Mr. Edwards had driven her mother home. Well, that was an interesting development. She would need to think about that.

She wondered if her new abilities would allow her to listen in to her mother's thoughts, similar to how she heard the horses in her mind. Maybe, she should try that out with Mary, now that Mary was an ally. Too bad Mary had left with Anne yesterday morning to return to the city, but she and Triana were leaving on vacation in a few days and they had to get ready.

"Hey Mom, sorry I overslept. I'll run down to the barn and put the girls out and then we could maybe have breakfast together?" Anne gave her daughter a guilty look, pointed to the phone in her hand, and nodded in affirmation.

Ellie threw some clothes on and ran out the door. As always, she could feel the horses in her mind. She wished that she understood more about what she was doing. It was very worrying and strange. She put it out of her mind and hurried into the barn. *Why didn't you wake me up? Are you starving? I'll hurry with your breakfast.*

I wanted to wake you up but we decided that you were very tired so we let you sleep. Sophie was getting very good at speaking directly to Ellie now.

I wanted to let you sleep, Dream nuzzled Ellie's shoulder.

Thank you both for your consideration of my beauty sleep, then. Ellie checked the automatic water dispenser and hurried out of the stall to bring in the grain mash for Dream and another small bucket for Sophie. Sophie wanted to eat her mother's ration and every time Dream raised her head from her bucket, the foal would push in and stick her head into the grain. "Greedy little girl," Ellie said. *Let you mother have that, she's making milk for you. Eat your own grain.*

She quickly brushed the mare and picked out her feet. She tried to brush the foal, but Sophie was having none of it. *You have to let me do your feet, Sophie.* Ellie slowly ran her hand down a tiny leg. *Lift it up for me and don't you kick me*, as the foal let fly with a hind leg. Ellie tried again for the leg and again Sophie kicked out. *Dream, help me out here, tell her to let me pick her feet up.*

She will learn in her own time, Dream continued munching her grain.

Yes, I guess you're right. Okay little one, you win today. We'll try again tomorrow. She put a halter on Dream and led her out of the barn with Sophie gamboling along behind, running ahead, then back, racing off and then pushing her nose into Dream's rump.

"What a little terror you are becoming," Ellie said, out loud.

"You're going to have some trouble with that one," a voice came from the side of the path leading to the arena.

Ellie looked over and saw the new tenant, Rowen. "Good morning, Miss—I'm sorry I've forgotten your last name," Ellie said.

"Martinelli, Rowen Martinelli. We met the night this little terror was born, as I recall." Rowen said. "How are they doing?

She's really quite a beauty." She gave a critical look at the foal and at her mother. This is a BLM mustang? Wow, you really lucked out with her. She's lovely, and this little one is a beauty, too."

"Well, yes I was very lucky to get her. Her name is Dream and this is Esophia. I'm having some trouble getting her to let me groom her and pick out her feet. But we'll get there eventually." Ellie smiled at Rowen. "Are you settling in? You're horses are beautiful. I hear you are using them for the downtown carriage rides. That must be fun." Ellie said

"Well yes, it is fun and a lot of work. I have a mare that's about to foal, too, and a yearling colt, but he will make two of Esophia, but I imagine the mares would like each other's company. We'll have to introduce them when she foals, which will be in about a week or so."

"I think Dream would love company. Esophia is a little terror and having another foal around might teach her some manners." Ellie smiled at Rowen.

"It's good to let the mares and foals be together. They learn a lot about being a horse in a herd," Rowen said.

"I heard that you are renting the apartment over the old barn. My mother and I rent the house on the easement road; it's very convenient to be here all the time. It's a lot of work having the two of them and commuting would have been awful. We are so lucky to be here. We'll have to get together. I know my mother would like to meet you. Maybe dinner some night," Ellie said.

"Well, that would be nice. Although I'm busy most of the time. We work seven days a week, but I'm lucky to have Anton to help out, otherwise I would be up 24/7. With the two of us, and the drivers we've hired, there is some room for eating at least. Maybe we can arrange something. Surely, the work will settle into a routine. After all, eating is important. It would be lovely to eat something not from the microwave or drive thru. Thank you." Rowen smiled at her. "We'll have a conversation as soon as I get some kind of routine down. Also, I think we have something in common, don't you," she gave Ellie a smile and moved away.

Ellie remembered how Rowen had bowed to Phellsome in the stall that night. She had thought at the time Rowen had been able to see the unicorn. Could that be true? Was there someone else that saw what she saw? If so, that would be something.

She put the horses out and Dream cantered off with Esophia running along beside her, bucking and rearing. How beautiful they were. She left the lead rope on the fence and hurried back to the house to have breakfast with her mother.

CHAPTER 27

When Ellie hurried into the house, she carefully removed her muck boots leaving them in the mudroom at the back door. She went into the large, old-fashioned bathroom that set between her bedroom and her mother's. The claw-footed tub was deep, good for soaks, but she wanted a shower, one that you could run through like a car wash. Horses were dirty work and a quick shower would be so nice. She washed up, quickly ran a comb through her hair, brushed her teeth, and came out to bacon, eggs, and blueberry pancakes.

"Wow, and wow again. This smells delicious," as she sat down to the feast.

"Well, you're skinny as a rail; I don't think I'm taking very good care of you," Anne said.

"Oh, I'm just fine, Mom, but I really miss Mary. She was a lot of help." Mary was taking a week vacation with her mother, and they were going to the coast. In a normal year, Ellie would have gone with them, but now Ellie was up to her neck in horses. She thought of her friend at the ocean with nothing to do but swim and laze in the sun and sighed.

"Well, having Dream and a foal, is not all fun and games, is it?" her mother said.

"A lot of work, but I wouldn't trade it," Ellie replied, "I would not give them up for anything. Dream is the most important thing in my life, except you. She's like a soul mate."

"What about Esophia?" Anne said.

Ellie frowned, "Of course I love her, but she is—"she paused, "she is something very special. I'm more hers than she is mine. I am her caretaker, something like that."

Anne looked over at her daughter who was consuming the food like there would be no more, "What do you mean? Isn't she just a horse, albeit, a special horse?"

"I'm not sure what she is," Ellie frowned into her plate. "She is — is herself. There is music all around her, beautiful music." She paused for a time but then shook her head. "We have no idea what's out there, none at all."

Anne sat and looked at her stressed child, what could she do for her except nurture her, be there for her. She frowned, and after a long pause, spoke. "Well, I had a conference with your school advisers yesterday. I would have taken you with me but we've both been so busy. Dr. Hansen and Dr. Gregory have arranged for you to take two classes at the University, in their math department, also their music department may be useful to you. You need to look over the curriculum and see what will work for you. You will still go to Wilcrest in the mornings, and go from there to your classes at the University. This should be your last year at Wilcrest."

Ellie looked down at her empty plate. "Look I've eaten everything. It was so good." She paused, then said, "I'll be thirteen and going to college. It looks like I'll be a college grad, before I'm sixteen," Ellie looked up at her mother. "When you want things to go slow, they go fast. When you want them to go fast, they go slow. Go figure," she said softly. "Now, you have to tell me how you managed to get a ride home with Mr. Edwards?" she smiled across the table at her blushing mother.

"Well, I was on Michigan Avenue coming from work and lunch with the team, and he literally ran into me. I was so confused, seeing him there in a business suit and looking so very professional. Anyway, he's attending a week-long conference downtown, and he invited me to have an early dinner. It turns out that he lives out this way so he gave me a ride home. I have invited him to come out on Saturday about noon to see the horses. I thought maybe, we could do a picnic lunch for him. What do you think?"

"Sounds fine, Mom, he's quite good looking," she glanced over slyly at her mother.

"I really miss Mary," she said again. "She's just so helpful with everything. I don't know what I'll do without her." Ellie was remembering the day she had shared all her concerns with her friend. It had been cathartic. She hadn't known just how scared and troubled she was until then. May had reassured her that she wasn't losing her mind, and that she would be okay. That she would be able to handle the stress, and that they were best friends. She was the best.

Mary would be back on Saturday. Ellie hoped that she would be able to come out on Sunday. Maybe they could have a party in the evening. Invite everyone, Mr. Edwards, Mary, her mother, Jackie, Rowen, and her partner, others from the barn. It would be fun. She would ask her mother and see if they could do something normal for a change. They hadn't had any company for a long time, since before her father left, just some evenings with Trina and Mary. It was time they had a more normal life. Maybe this Mr. Edwards would be the one to bring her mother out of her miasma over the divorce.

She wondered how that would be. What did she really think of her mother and another man? What would that do to her life? Not much, she realized. Her mother had been fixated on her for so long, it might be nice to have her focused on someone else for a change, or would that be like missing Mary?

Would she not know how much she missed it until it was not there anymore? Well, it would be good to find out.

She had always thought that she was the cause of her parents' divorce. If she had been normal, her father would not have left them. Her mother had been too involved with Ellie, and that was why her father had left them. Now she hoped that she would not stand in the way of her mother's chance with another man. After all, she was almost an adult.

College was here. Ellie would be starting on a path to independence. That was scary, she was still only twelve and as her mother was making clear, she needed to start focusing on what she intended to study there. It was not fair, but then settling on a course of study was a good idea. In some ways, she felt she was still a child, but in others, she felt grown up.

Ellie decided to put adult thinking away and talk her mother into the idea of a late picnic party. Surprisingly, Anne seemed open to having everyone over. She even thought it was an excellent idea. It would be a good time to invite her team from work to her new home, and repay Jackie for all she had done for them. In addition, the new people at the barn seemed nice, and this would be a good start to get to know them. So, the party was on.

CHAPTER 28

Anne and Ellie were calling and emailing their friends about the party. Since it was already Wednesday, they had a lot to do. They were going to need a grill, and a list was made of the food they wanted to serve. They decided on an outdoor party, very informal, just grilled steak and chicken, salads, rolls and dessert; it was ambitious, because Anne had never grilled anything in her life. She assumed that someone coming would be able to do it. Living in the city, she had little opportunity for this type of cooking. She would buy a grill and let someone else do the grilling.

Anne was as excited as Ellie. They spent the next day laughing, planning, shopping and generally having a fun organizing the affair. It would be a house warming, Esophia christening, pay back for past invitations, and an unacknowledged way to have Allen Edwards over without any strings or innuendos.

On Friday morning, Anne picked up the phone and called him. "I know you're coming out tomorrow about one, but I was wondering if you were free on Sunday late afternoon as well.

We're having an informal party at the house. Sort of a housewarming, meet the foal, fun thing.

"I'd love to come. I'm a good cook with a grill. So, if you would like me to be the grill master, it would be a pleasure. I don't get to do much of that anymore."

"Thanks so much you've just saved my life! I was hoping someone would offer to cook, since I don't know anything about using a grill. I'm going in the morning to buy one."

"I'll be out tomorrow, let me bring my grill over it's just gathering dust here. I haven't used it since my divorce. It'll be good to use it again," he said.

"Oh, well, if you don't mind. It will take one thing off the list. This last minute party is driving me to distraction." She felt a little jolt of pleasure that he had been so quick to respond in a positive way. Not only was he coming but also he was making himself a part of the plans. She was excited about it, but didn't want to explore the feeling in depth, just let it go where it would. That was best.

The next morning was ominous with a feel of storm, not dark but just sort of gloomy, with clouds, with that feeling of static electricity in the air. Ellie felt sluggish as she dressed to go to the barn and let the horses out. Mr. Edwards would be here about noon, and she took extra care to see that Dream and Esophia were looking their best.

Dream noticed the extra care. *What's happening?*

You have a visitor coming to admire you, and you, she pointed at Esophia. *The man from the auction yard wants to see you and Esophia. Do you remember him?*

No, I don't remember him. Is it trouble?

Not trouble at all. He just wants to see Esophia. I think he likes my mother, Ellie said with smiles in her voice.

There was a confused image in Ellie's head. Dream had not understood 'like' in conjunction with her mother. As easy as it was to communicate with the mare, there were many things that did not translate well.

185

Speaking mind to mind was easy, but sometimes things like expressing feelings or emotions were difficult. It was easy to talk about things, but emotions, relationships, things that people took for granted were hard when communicating them to animals. It made her realize how much people relied on body language, or facial expressions, when they were speaking with one another. She just did not know enough yet to make things clear to her horse.

When she was finished at the barn, she hurried back to the house for breakfast. Anne was at the stove frying chicken. The smell sent Ellie drooling in anticipation.

"Wow Mom. That smells so good. You're really making a feast. Mr. Edwards should come out every day." She snagged a hot chicken wing and went to wash her hands.

When she came back, Anne was looking out the kitchen window. "I think it's going to storm. You can feel it in the air."

Anne was making a nice picnic lunch, which they had intended to eat out in the pasture while watching the horses. Yet, the weather might not cooperate, which meant that she would have to bring the horses back into the barn. Then they would probably go back to the house and have the lunch indoors.

"Yes, I think so too. We'll probably have lunch in the house. I think I'll bring the horses in to the barn. I hate lightning and this feels like there might be some," Ellie said.

"Well, Allen is on his way here; he just called. I'm making potato salad and some of that fresh corn from the stand on the corner. Living in the country has some advantages. I wasn't sure I'd like living out here away from everything, but I'm getting more and more settled. The house is so large, and the countryside so pretty and quiet."

"I'm glad you are happy here, too. I felt like I was the cause, again. You know, causing you to do something that you didn't want to do."

"Oh Ellie, you should quit thinking those things. You didn't cause your father to leave, and though you are reason for this move, if I hadn't wanted to do it, we would have worked something else out. This move has been good for me. I needed to make some changes and this was a good one to make, for you and for me," Anne reached out and pulled Ellie into her arms. "We will be fine," she said, "just fine."

There were tears in Ellie's eyes as she gazed out the kitchen window with her mother. Pensively she whispered, "I hope so. Oh, I hope so."

They had buttered toast with a couple of the boiled eggs that were going into the potato salad. There was some blackberry jam from the same fruit stand as the corn. "Well, we are certainly eating well," Anne said with a smile. "I don't think I've ever tasted better jam in my life."

"Is there anything you need me to do before Mr. Edwards gets here?" Ellie asked.

"No, it's all done. I've got it under control. Simple is better. I just wish the weather were cooperating. This can't happen tomorrow. The house is big, but that's a lot of people to have inside. Although, I suppose we could put the grill on the screened-in porch, but that means that I've major cleaning to do out there."

"Well, I'll check the weather for tomorrow. Maybe it'll all be over by then. If it rains today the dust will be settled and that's a good thing," said Ellie, as she wandered off into the living room to the corner where the piano sat.

She looked at the piano and thought about the music that always seemed to be playing in some part of her mind, or in her dreams. She was aware of it all the time, just as she was aware of Dream and Sophie. There was the energy that kept Sophie shielded from what? She did not know. There was so much she needed to understand. She needed to ask Phellsome, when and if he showed himself again. She moved on into her room to check the weather on her computer. They were having a party.

Her mother seemed very happy. That was good, very good. She smiled to herself.

The weather continued to threaten a storm and the air was thick and clinging. Ellie was at the piano playing a bit of the music from her dreams about the Spheres. She had her hand-written score up, but was letting her mind drift aimlessly without focusing directly on her music. Her mind was on the spheres that she saw so clearly in her dream, but were so elusive when she was awake. She was so lost in thought that she did not hear the sound of a truck pulling up.

Anne was just out of the shower and was dressed in a new pair of red shorts with a matching top, but she heard the truck and walked quickly out the back door and into the muggy air. The red brought a lot of color to her bright blonde hair and made her cheeks rosy, too. Allen Edwards was just getting out of his truck.

"Hi, Anne, don't you look pretty this not so beautiful day."

"Oh," she looked down at herself, "Oh, thank you so much. It's getting ugly out, isn't it? Think we're going to have a thunder storm before too long," she was looking up at the sky.

"I think you're right there. I hope we do get some rain this muggy heat is awful. Feels like we're in a sauna. Well, I have a surprise, here. That grill of mine was in bad shape, so I stopped and got a new one. We'll have to put it together, but it should be easy. I filled the tank, too. So, you'll be all set for the big party tomorrow."

Ellie heard her mother calling her, "Come see what Allen has brought." Ellie hurried out the back door to see them at the bed of the truck. Inside was a huge box. "What is it?" Ellie asked.

"He's brought us a new grill, a beautiful new grill. Isn't it wonderful?" Her mother was excited and laughing.

"Wow, how nice," she was thinking her mother's laughter was the wonderful thing. She saw that Anne was wearing a new outfit, red, a color that Anne normally did not wear. She was very conservative when it came to clothes, Ellie did not think she had ever seen her in red before. It looked very good on her.

Mr. Edwards was dressed in jeans and a short-sleeved shirt in a light blue. He had an outdoorsy, masculine look. Ellie watched her mother and Mr. Edwards from the porch for a moment, then came down to help them with the grill. He had brought a toolbox with him. It was good, because they certainly did not have anything like tools.

It took about an hour to get the large grill assembled and set up by the porch. Anne had helped a bit getting the thing together, but mostly it was a mystery to her. When they were finished Mr. Edwards looked over at Ellie, "Shall we go to see the new addition now? I've been looking forward to it all week."

"Okay, I left them in the pasture. Would you like me to bring them in? It's a bit of a hike out there Mr. Edwards," Ellie asked.

"Please call me Allen, Mr. Edwards makes feel old and that's too close for comfort," he said. "I'd like the walk, this is such a pretty farm," he was looking out over the paddocks and dark fences.

"Right, Allen," she tried the first name out and it sounded just fine. "Mom, want to come along?"

"Yes, it's like every day that foal changes. It's hard to keep up." Anne said.

Ellie led the way out to the paddock where Dream and Esophia were eating the grass and ambling about. Dream always knew where Ellie was and what she was doing, so Ellie expected them to be close to the gate. She intended to bring them in as the clouds were getting darker and there was now a breeze blowing. It was definitely going to storm. Horses can get struck by lightning, and she wanted them in the barn when the storm hit.

They were close to the gate. Sophie raised her head up and pricked her ears. "Hi, Sophie, look who I've brought to see you.

This is Allen Edwards. He was instrumental in your coming here," she opened the gate and let her mother and Allen walk inside ahead of her.

Allen walked slowly up to the mare and her foal. He was speaking softly and holding out a hand. Dream reached out and took the sugar cube he held there. She nodded her head as she chewed. Sniffed him again with more sugar in mind, but he just reached up and scratched her between her ears. "Hi Dream, you've got a beautiful daughter here," Sophie had come up and was very close to the man. She reached out her nose gave him a quick sniff, snorted, turned and galloped off a short distance, stopped suddenly and reared up on her hind legs, pawing the air, whinnied, whirled and raced around.

"You little imp," Ellie said, "come and be nice. This is Allen and my mother. They want to see how you've grown. Be good now."

Sophie trotted up and posed prettily. Allen walked around her and she stood perfectly still as if a statue. She spoke into Ellie's mind, *Does he hear me? He's very nice.*

No, I don't think he can hear you.

Well, that other person can hear me. I talk to her sometimes.

What do you mean? Who hears you? You've never said that someone else can talk to you. In the same manner as we talk to each other?

Yes, in the same manner as we talk to each other, Sophie answered in a matter of fact way.

Ellie was trying to absorb this information and missed that both Allen and her mother were looking at her. She had been so involved that she had missed a question or a statement. She must learn to be more careful. It was hard carrying on an out-loud conversation and a mental one at the same time, but she needed to learn how to do that, and quickly. People would not understand if she did not.

"I'm sorry, I didn't hear you," she said.

"I was wondering about her color. It's very unusual," Allen said.

"Well, I suppose so. The vet thought that she might be what they call a cremello. Had she been born white she would probably have died at birth, is what she said. I think it's a beautiful color, kind of white but not quite, almost luminous. I wish I could capture it and paint her, but I don't think we will ever get that color down on canvas," Ellie said seriously.

"I've been around horses all my life, and I've never seen anything like it," Allen replied.

"She is so lovely," Anne said. "Simply, beautiful, she's grown a bit since I saw her last."

Ellie slipped a halter on Dream, grabbed some mane and swung up on her back. Anne opened the gate for Ellie and Dream. They walked out leaving the headstrong Sophie, who did not want to leave the paddock, standing inside the paddock nickering wildly. Dream stopped and turned around. It was quiet for a moment. Clearly the two were having a conversation, and then Dream turned back around and walked on down the path towards the barn. After a stubborn minute, Sophie walked out the gate and followed her mother.

"It's the same in every species," Anne said with a smile, "the kids want to have their own way. Poor Dream, it will get worse before it gets better."

"You know I've never seen a pair more suited to one another. On the very first day, Ellie was in that stall with that mare. I remember how frightened I was for her. That mare was a wild horse with little or no contact with humans and yet there they were side by side. It was amazing, and now there they go, no bridle, no saddle, just a lead and halter. It's so unusual." He turned to look down at Anne. "I don't think you know what an amazing thing that is. Do you?"

"I don't know anything about horses, except what little I've learned from Ellie. Truthfully, horses scare me. I'm

191

learning a lot living out here in the country. I've been a city girl all my life. I'm finding it liberating and scary out here. I think that I'm going to grow and expand my life here," she looked up at Allen.

The blonde hair had a glow in the gathering darkness of the oncoming storm; Allen thought she was beautiful and vulnerable at the same time. He had an urge to hold her close. That was an interesting thought.

Ellie put Dream and Sophie away. She was thinking again about Sophie's other friend. The person who could communicate with her, as Ellie herself did.

While she was checking their hooves for stones or gravels, she queried Dream. *Is there someone else that can talk to you?*

She's the new person who came with the big horses; Dream was matter of fact about it.

A picture of Rowen came into her mind. She was the woman that had been in the stall the night Sophie was born, who had indicated to Ellie that she could see the unicorn. Now Dream and Sophie were saying they could talk to her. She must talk to her soon. Maybe, this was someone who could help her understand. Maybe she would not be so alone anymore. A feeling of relief was welling up in her and she wiped moisture from her eyes. At last, maybe some answers.

She hurried out of the barn just as the rain started falling heavily. She started running for the house trying to keep from getting drenched. Just as she opened the back door, a bolt of lightning lit up the house like a light bulb. It was so close the thunder came almost immediately. Ellie's hair was standing on end for a moment. Then all the lights in the house went out.

"Mom, Mom, what's going on?" she screamed because at that moment she was deaf and blind. The thunder had been so loud it sounded like an explosion. She still felt the electricity in her body. She could not hear, but Allen and her mother were running toward her. Anne reached out and grabbed her.

"Ellie, Ellie did you get hit?" Anne's mouth was moving but Ellie still could not hear very well, but she understood the question.

"No, I don't think so, but it was extremely close. I felt the hair on my head rise up. At the same time, Dream and Sophie were sending alarms into her mind, *Are you all right?* She drew in a deep breath and let it out. Calm, she must be calm. She would have Dream and Sophie upset as well as her mother and Allen.

Allen was kneeling beside her. She could see the concern in his eyes. "That was a close call it must have just missed you. You're a very lucky girl, very lucky. It probably hit the power line, which is why we don't have any lights. Do you have lanterns," he asked.

Ellie's hearing was coming back, but she was still seeing the world through flashes of bright light. She was breathing okay, but still felt shaky.

Anne and Allen were leading her into the kitchen. The rain was still pounding on the roof. There was another roll of thunder, but it was further away. She sent Dream and Sophie thoughts that all was okay and there was no danger.

Anne went to the closet in the pantry and brought out a large camping lantern. "I hope the batteries are good in this. It's been a while since I changed them."

She turned it on and there was light. "Good," she said. "We won't have to eat in the dark. It's really coming down out there. When we lived in the apartment you couldn't feel or hear the storms like you can in a house." They settled in at the kitchen table to eat the lunch by lantern light. The talk was light. They mostly talked about the party for the next day.

"I'll come early in the afternoon to help you set up. If it doesn't rain the yard will be perfect for a party," Allen said. He was having fun, he realized.

After lunch, the house was still dark, and the lantern was casting shadows around the room. They moved with the lantern into the living room. "I hope that we get lights soon," Anne said. "I don't know how long that lantern will keep working. I need to get some more lights and extra batteries."

"We can run to the store if you want. It sounds like the storm is letting up a bit," Allen was at a window looking out.

"I think we should, I'd hate to be without light tonight. I still can't get used to how dark it is at night out in the country, even with electricity." Anne said, "Do you want to come along, Ellie?"

"No, I think I'll stay here. You won't be very long will you?"

"Not at all, there's a store at the crossroads. They should have batteries and maybe candles and things. You sure you'll be okay alone?" Allen asked.

"Oh sure. You guys go ahead. I'll be fine. I want to work at the piano, no electricity needed there. I'll be fine, and we will need more light if they don't get the lines fixed," Ellie said.

After Anne and Allen left, Ellie sat down at the piano. She put the lantern on top and let herself become immersed in the music she was beginning to think of as the Music of the Spheres. She went back into the dream of being one with the water. Those tones she had written down in her journal. That was the first time she had seen Esophia, through the water. She began to play the music. She would play the notes, and then mark them on the score. Then play them again. Soon she was lost in the music.

She did not notice when the lights came on and was surprised when the door opened and Allen and her mother came in. "Oh, you're back already?"

"Well it's been about an hour. When did the lights come on?" Anne was looking around at the well-lit living room.

"Lights? Oh, they're on. I hadn't noticed," Ellie said.

"You were playing something beautiful. What is it?" Allen asked.

"It doesn't have a name, just something I'm working on. It's elusive and frustrating," Ellie frowned down at the piano.

"You mean this is your music? Not only do you play beautifully, but you write music, too?" Allen asked.

"Ellie has been playing the piano since she was three. I think she's very talented," Anne said.

"I'll say she is."

"Why don't you play something for us, Ellie?" her mother urged.

Anne went to the kitchen poured some iced tea and brought cookies into the living room.

Ellie's fingers hovered over the keys for a moment and then she began a Schumann concerto. Anne remembered it from a performance at the school a year or so ago. Ellie still played beautifully, even though she did not practice as much as she had before Dream, and now Esophia. Anne wondered where all this would lead. She hoped that everything would work out. "*Just be safe,*" she thought, "*please be safe.*"

CHAPTER 29

They woke to a perfect day. The weather was going to cooperate; it was a good omen for the party. The storm had cleared away the dust and the air was crisp and clean. It was going to be a bit warm but a breeze was blowing, and it would be nice under the trees.

Ellie was at the kitchen table eating breakfast. She had already put Dream and Sophie out to graze. Her morning horse chores were done. The phone rang and Anne picked up, "It's for you, Ellie. Mary and Triana are back from Florida. They are coming out for the party."

"Hi, you. Did you have a good time? I missed you. I'll really appreciate you, now that I know how much of the work you did." Ellie laughed into the phone.

"It was amazing. You won't recognize me. I'm brown and lazy. You missed me, did you?" Mary asked.

"I missed you, the ocean, and all the fun you had without me."

"We just picked up the message about the party. What fun. Mom says we can come out about noon to help if you want."

"Let me ask," Ellie said.

"Mom, Mary wants to know if you want them to come out early to help."

"When you're finished with Mary, put Triana on and I'll talk to her. I'm really glad they got home in time to come," Anne said.

The two girls chatted for a couple of minutes and then Ellie gave the phone to her mother. She listened to her mother's side of the conversation.

"I'd love to have you come early, although, most of the work is done. Ellie's been very helpful."

"No, I've got all the food."

"Yes, we're going to grill outside."

"Me? No, not me. I've a new friend —"

"Yes, a man friend."

Ellie, who was listening, glanced up to see her mother fidgeting with the phone cord. Anne was having trouble explaining this man thing to Triana.

"You remember the man at the auction? Where we bought Dream?"

"That's the one. Handsome? Yes, I suppose he is."

"Well, I met him in town the other day. We had an early dinner and he's coming out today and has offered to do the grilling."

There was a long pause, then Anne said, "Yes, he's very nice. Oh by the way, could you bring the ice. About 40 lbs. should do it. That'll save me a trip to the store. I couldn't buy it early. No space —

"Yes, thanks a lot. I'll see you this afternoon."

She sat down with a full coffee cup, took a thoughtful sip. "They're coming about noon. We'll get to hear all about their vacation," Anne said.

Anne and Ellie washed the breakfast dishes and swept the back porch. In the storeroom was a large picnic table and they planned to use it for the party. When they went out to get it, they found it covered in spider webs. Anne looked at it and turned white. "I can't deal with spiders," she shuddered.

"I'll sweep it off, and Allen and I can move it when he gets here. I hope the plastic tablecloth will fit on it. It's pretty long." They had bought a plastic red-checkered tablecloth and red paper napkins, and the huge oak tree would give plenty of shade. Ellie looked out at the view of the yard and the paddocks beyond. The vista was beautiful; there were black wooden fences with horses of all colors grazing inside. In the distance, she could see in each large paddock a small pond reflecting the bright sun back to itself. In the furthest paddock, she could see the calico colored Gypsy Vanner mare and the young stallion. He was showing off by running full gallop around and around the mare. It was going to look very nice with the green lawn and red table. What a good idea it was to have a party.

Later, Ellie went out to Dream and Esophia taking a couple of cut up apples and a grooming box. Dream nuzzled her pockets and took the apple slices out of her hand. Esophia greedily pushed in, grabbed one in her mouth, and ran off with it. She chewed on it, swinging her head about. "You can't really eat them yet, silly girl," Ellie said. After a bit of mushing it around in her mouth, Sophie spit it on the ground. Then she came up to nurse from her mother. She bumped on Dream's flank with her nose, causing Dream to flick her ears back and raise a back hoof.

You'd better be good, Sophie, you're making your mother angry. She'll get after you if you don't watch out. It's hard to be good, you're just full of yourself, you naughty girl. She groomed them both until they were shining. *We're having a lot of company and they will all want to see you. What beauties you both are.* She stood back and admired her work.

When she got back to the house, her mother was dressed in the red short set from the day before. "You should get a shower while you have the time," Anne said. "The phone has been ringing off the hook. Everyone we invited is coming and then a few have asked if they can bring someone else. So far, I've counted twenty! Rowen just called to say she and her friend will be here about 5pm, wondering if there was anything she could bring, and Jackie will be over about then too. She has to see to the barns first. It's going to be fun."

Just then, a horn sounded outside. It was Allen in a sporty bright red convertible with the top down. "I didn't know he had a sports car, too." Ellie said. "That's a cute car."

"It is a fun car, he brought me home in it the other night," Anne said. "He said it was a replacement for the wife who left him."

Allen was full of energy; He seemed as excited about the party as Anne and Ellie. He and Ellie moved the big table out of the storeroom and Ellie washed it with the hose. Then she went in to take the much-needed shower. She dressed in shorts, sandals and a new summer blouse. She had not dressed for a party in a long time. It had been years since they had entertained anyone, since before her father left. Things were changing, that was for sure.

When Triana and Mary arrived with the ice, they brought out a big tin washtub and filled it with drinks. Everything was looking bright and cheery.

Anne introduced Triana and Mary to Allen. "I remember you from the auction. I hear you just got back from Florida, that must have been fun," he said.

"Yes, we were at Disney World. That place is amazing. We were there for five days, and it took all five just to see everything. I wasn't sure when we made plans, but it was wonderful. The weather, the food, the entertainment, and the shore were so much fun. It was nice just to get away and be lazy," Triana said. "We were sorry that Ellie and Anne couldn't come, but they've been so busy with the move, the new foal and all."

"We'll get to go sometime, I'm sure," Anne said.

Soon people were arriving and the party was under way. Allen started the coals in the grill. There was music playing from an old boom box, and guests were wandering around exclaiming about the view, the house, everything.

Ellie and Mary were taking groups of guests out to the paddock to meet Dream and Esophia. They were city people and were just happy being out in country, and getting up close and personal with a real live horse. Yet, a few had ridden horses when they were young. Joanna, a woman about fifty, who worked with Anne, had come from a large ranch in Texas. She was excited about Dream and Sophie. "You know, I should get a horse. I really miss them. Now that my son is off to college, it would give me something to do. I'm not as busy as when he was living at home. I thought I would love being alone, but— well, it's the empty nest syndrome, I guess."

"You could talk to Jackie Long; she's the owner, manager, here. She could give you information and stuff," Ellie told her. "She'll be here about five. She has to take care of the evening chores."

"Thanks, introduce me when she arrives," Joanna said.

"I'll do that. You'll like her, I'm sure," Ellie said.

She and Mary were in the house bringing out some more food, when the phone rang. "I wonder who that can be, maybe someone is lost or something," Ellie said.

"Hello. Oh, hi Dad, how are you," she said. "Is anything wrong?

"No, just need to talk to your mother, can you get her for me? Earl said.

"Yes, she's here, let me go find her."

"Where is she?"

"Out in the yard, we're having a party, and lots of people are here," she paused.

"A party? What for? I mean, why are you having a party? Earl seemed flustered.

"Oh, people from Mom's work, people from the barn, just people," Ellie said.

She could hear the surprise in his voice at that. He said he would hold, and Ellie and Mary went out with bowls. "Hey Mom," Ellie called, "Dad is on the phone. He wants to talk to you."

Anne was talking to a group of people from her work, she looked up, "Tell him, I'm busy and I'll call him back later, please," and continued her conversation.

Ellie went back into the house, "Mom asked me to tell you she'd call you later."

There was an awkward pause, then her father said, "Well yes, I'll be home this evening. She can call me back," but he didn't sound happy. Ellie thought of all the times her mother had gotten that kind of reply from her father. She smiled, turnabout is fair play.

"Was that okay?" Anne asked.

"Yes, he seemed surprised that we were having a party, though," Ellie said.

Anne was helping Allen at the grill. She hardly acknowledged what Ellie had said.

Jackie, Rowen, and Anton, appeared together. They were chatting with each other, and laughing. Anne took them around and introduced them to the others. Everyone was gathering around the grill, with plates. Triana, Mary and Ellie were bringing out potato salad, green salad and the corn. It was time to eat. The steaks were coming off the grill. The talk slowed down as people found places to sit and started eating. Ellie kept her eye on Rowen, and when she sat down at the table with a huge steak and a full plate, she made a point of sitting down next to her. "I've been wanting to talk to you. Do you mind?"

Rowen did not act surprised at being singled out by Ellie. "I would have talked to you sooner, but we have been so busy with the horses and business there has been no time. It looks like it might be coming together now. I think we've got everything sorted out. Just have to stay on top of it all now. My mare looks about ready to foal any time now, so I'll be spending more time here and Anton will be doing the downtown stuff."

Ellie wasn't quite sure how to ask what she wanted to ask, "Dream and Esophia tell me you can talk to them, and I think you saw the unicorn in the stall the night Esophia was born," she blurted out.

Rowen looked at her with a steady gaze, "Yes, I did see the unicorn that night. Magnificent creature, I was startled. I've never seen one before, and yes, I can talk with horses," she paused as if considering how to go on.

"I'm what you might call a horse whisperer. I am Romany. More commonly known as Gypsy. My people have strong ties with horses, and are said to be able to—to have special gifts."

"What kind of special gifts?" Ellie seemed puzzled.

"Well, gifts that are paranormal. Like seeing the future, other things. In fact, my mother is a well-known psychic in New York. She's written several books," she spoke quietly and did not seem upset by any of Ellie's questions.

"You don't know how happy I am to hear that. Most of the time I think I'm losing my mind," Ellie said. There were tears in her eyes. "This has been going on for a long time, and I don't understand any of it."

"I tell you what, Ellie. Let's have lunch at my barn tomorrow. We can really talk then, okay? This is a party. Let's have some fun." Rowen was having a cold beer and started eating with enthusiasm.

Ellie looked at her plate and felt the familiar hunger. She had been eating enormous amounts of food lately, but was still thin. Phellsome probably had something to do with all the energy she was using.

"Okay, then. Tomorrow it is, and thanks so much. I don't think you know how much this means. I can't believe that there's someone else who saw the unicorn and can talk to horses, too."

"Oh, dear, you're not as alone as all that," Rowen said, with her mouth full. "This food is delicious!"

CHAPTER 30

Ellie was very tired as she, her mother and Allen said goodbye to the last of the guests. Mary and Triana had left earlier. They had just gotten home from Florida and pleaded exhaustion. Ellie excused herself and went to her room. She got ready for bed, brushed her teeth, checked in with Dream and Esophia, finding them drowsy in their stall. All was well.

However, once in bed, it was as if her brain had been waiting, and it turned on. She was thinking of many things at once. There would be no sleep, so she got a book and opened it to read. Sometimes this helped calm her and allowed her to get to sleep. After a chapter or two, she put the book on the nightstand, turned off the lamp and again tried to sleep. This time she drifted off right away.

Immediately she was in the stall with Phellsome, Dream, and Sophie. He was explaining something to them, but Ellie was not sure what he was saying. She was watching from a position in the corner of the stall. Again, the sequence played out in front of her. He was there, he shimmered, and then he disappeared. Then, he was back.

This is teleporting; you have to think about where you want to go. Make a good picture of the place and then just go. It's not difficult. Now Sophie, I'm going to touch you and together we are going to go— and they were gone.

Ellie had seen it but she did not understand it. Phellsome had disappeared the night Esophia was born. He had appeared suddenly, and left just as quickly. Now he was teaching Sophie how to do that. She turned cold with the thought. Did this mean that Sophie would be able to just come and go? Would it be possible to take care of her, if she did?

There was a shimmer and there they were back in the stall. Phellsome looked over at her corner and said *Would you like to try*? He looked directly at Ellie.

Ellie took a deep breath, *Where did you go?*

We went to the pasture; Sophie doesn't know many places now, does she? The voice was like a smile in Ellie's head.

Would you like to try? It's not a difficult thing. I'll take you and you can experience it for yourself.

Am I dreaming or am I really here?

Why do you ask that? Do you feel here? If you do, you are here. The mind is a powerful thing. It holds the song that you lost long ago, and it's the song I give you back. Song and magic, the harmony of the whole. Do you want to go?

He had never been this close to Ellie before. Sometimes he was a wisp of something, a ghost. Now he was solid and whole. Did she want to go? Yes, yes she did. At that moment, he touched her with his golden horn, and a place came into her mind, the valley in her dreams, the valley where she had first found Dream and the start of all this. At the same time, she heard a type of music she had never heard before.

It was cold and black for what seemed like a long time, it made her nauseated. She felt like she wanted to throw up. All that food she had eaten at the party began churning in her stomach. Then the blackness was gone, and she was in the middle of the meadow, not far from the stream. The sun was shining and a warm breeze was blowing through her hair. It was as if she were there again with Dream. She thought if she looked, she would see the mare trotting across the meadow to meet her.

How do you feel? Phellsome asked.

I was disoriented for a moment, but now I feel fine. Yet when we left the barn it was night, and now it's bright sunshine. Can time be changed too?

In a way, yes. But that is not important yet. You gave me the picture and here you are. Did you understand how you got here?

No, I certainly do not. It was music but not, maybe a note in a minor key. Something like that. It is music, isn't it?

Yes, music, but something more, something that was lost long ago here. Animals may have some residual memory. He paused, as if trying for something, some words. *A body memory, perhaps a note. A few humans are able to hear it, but most cannot. The music or magic that kept the harmony was lost long ago, before your species was around. Something happened here that damaged the vibrations of the planet, and the music and magic were lost.*

Ellie was looking at him trying to fit it all together. Music and magic, what was he saying to her? She had seen the Seven Spheres in her dreams. Heard music like none she'd ever heard before. Dreams were not real, were they? This was a dream, was it not? Maybe not. She had asked if he could change time. What had he answered? She could not remember. There were theories; she would have to learn more.

They walked around the meadow for a little while. It was as she remembered it, lovely and isolated. Why had Dream been here alone? Horses were herd animals, traveling in small family units in the wild. Yet Dream had been here all alone.

She was trapped here; Phellsome had read her mind.

Ellie was disconcerted; *you read my mind.*

You were broadcasting. You must learn to shield yourself from that. It's very clear if you do not shield. Allow me?

He was asking permission to get into her head again, just as he had done the night of the birth. She remembered what had happened that night, her new power, insight, abilities. She did not know if she wanted any more of his probing.

Ellie, it's important that you accept my help. You are going to need all the power and understanding that I can give you. Believe me, I don't want to hurt you in any way, but you need to be ready for the future. A lot depends on you. You are integral.

Why, why am I a part of anything! I don't want to be! I want to be normal! I didn't even want to be different; it causes too much harm. My mother, my father, what I am causes problems for my family, for me. I never asked for any of this. Special schools, dreams that are real, I never wanted any of it. I wanted my mother and father to stay together, to be happy. I wanted a horse, just a normal horse, just to love and care for it. Sophie is something so unusual. If I thought about what she is for too long, it would terrify me. She looked out over the beautiful little valley. Even with Dream, it could not be just a girl and a horse.

Ellie, I know you think this is unfair, but sometimes a thing is so important, we have to do what's best for the place and our people. I'm in a similar position. What I'm doing is causing great hurt and harm. Yet, I'm doing it. We were both destined, I think, Phellsome said.

She looked at him startled. It had not occurred to her that this being might be just as caught as she was. There he was, beautiful and powerful, a mystical beast from another world, telling her that he was not happy about the situation, either. Maybe there was no happiness? Maybe there was just—she was not sure what. Her mother had told her that life was not always fair, that things happened; timing was important to the life you were born into. War, weather, nature, we knew a lot but we were still creatures subject to laws we do not control or even understand.

Okay, she said with a sigh. *Let's do it.*

It was happening just as it had before, she became confused, a little nauseated, and the pain like lights probing inside her head.

Just relax, breathe.

She tried to do as he asked. Something expanded and there was clarity, a knowing, as if two halves had become a whole. Completely new areas were opening up. Then she felt herself collapsing forward onto the green grass. The last thing she remembered was how wonderful the smell of meadow grass was.

She came awake in the stall with Dream nuzzling her hair. She could sense the concern the mare felt for her. Her eyes opened and there was little Sophie front legs spread wide with her small soft lips caressing her face. *Are you awake? Are you all right?*

I don't' know. Where is Phellsome? What happened? How did I get here? She tried to sit up, but a wave of dizziness kept her on the straw of the stall. Where was he? She took a couple of deep breaths and asked the concerned horse and foal to move back so she could try again to sit up. This time she made it. She leaned herself back against the stall wall. She was getting better, much better.

Where's Phellsome, she was looking around, almost frantically.

You came back but he didn't, Dream said.

I came back? Ellie said.

Well, you're here, Dream said.

Ellie thought that there was a smile in the communication. Could horses have a sense of humor? she wondered.

Right now, she was struggling more and more with what she felt. She remembered the first time she had let Phellsome into her head. After that, she had been able to see people in colors, energy fields, and things had some kind of new definition. She was not sure how to describe her new self. It was as if she had compartments, and could turn on and shut off these new abilities at will. She could communicate with her mind in great clarity, and the shield that she kept around Sophie was effortless.

What was going to happen to her now that she had had another probe from Phellsome? Would she now be able to teleport herself around? Would she be able to do things that she had not done before? What had she done to herself now?

Ellie knew something about human brains; she had studied them, just as others had studied hers. Because she was a prodigy, a very bright, exceptionally gifted, young person, she was an oddity. Prodigies were rare, so neurologists had studied her, physiologists, and others had studied her, trying to learn how her rare brain functioned.

She, in turn, had done her own research, so she had more than common knowledge about the human brain. She knew there were two sides, left and right, and that they communicated with one another through a conduit called the corpus callosum. That conduit was the only connection between them. The left side of the brain controlled the right side of the body, and the right side of the brain controlled the left side of the body.

It was now fashionable to consider that if your left-brain dominated you were more logical and detail oriented. If your right brain dominated, you were more artistic and intuitive. She knew that in her brain, neither side was dominant over the other.

Perhaps Phellsome had increased her brain's ability to communicate with itself. She did not know. She wondered how her next brain scan would look. That would be interesting.

Here we go again, she thought. *I have been changed and I'm not sure what or how.* It was scary to think that just by visualizing a place she could go there. She did not want to try that by herself. She stood up and found that she was not dizzy or nauseated any more. That was good. Ellie took a deep breath. If it were a dream, she was still in bed. If it was not a dream, she'd just think herself back to bed. The dark and disorientation was back, and there she was in bed.

She was now able to teleport. That is, if this was not just a dream. Well if true, it could be useful. She would have to be careful about thinking of places. She hoped she could control this, if it was real.

Phellsome had been more open with her. He had for the first time spoken about himself. He had told her something about the reason he was here. He had said they were destined, but Ellie was not sure what that meant, apart from not letting her be just a normal girl. She was sure there would be more, much more. Tired, so tired. She snuggled into her pillow and fell instantly asleep.

CHAPTER 31

Ellie woke Monday morning full of energy. She took out her journal and wrote down the night's events. Strange as they were, it was important to write down all she could remember about the timeline, her feelings; even her fears were extremely important to her. The pages written in her own hand would keep her sane in this increasingly unusual world.

Phellsome had told her something about himself: *I'm causing harm and strife, too.* He believed they had been destined. Chosen, selected, something like that. The question was what were they being selected for, and there was not yet an answer to that.

Music and magic, intertwined in the universe. Not a new thought, at least the music part, but logical people did not believe in magic. Ellie could not deny that she had gone places without any type of vehicle, just using her brain. It could have been a dream, but she did not think so. There was the possibility that our present science had not advanced enough to understand. Maybe Phellsome knew more than he could tell her. Maybe he-knew things that she was not yet able to understand. Ellie sighed and put the journal back in the nightstand drawer.

Later that morning Ellie was in the kitchen packing a picnic basket with leftover food from the party. She put in a thermos of lemonade and the leftovers from last night. She was always hungry and Rowen was a good eater, too, if she remembered correctly her performance from last night.

Knowing that Rowen could talk with horses had made Ellie feel much better. Last night she had said 'her people'. That meant there were more people who could communicate with horses. Rowen would be able to answer some of her questions and allay some of her fears.

Seeing the Gypsy Vanners would be nice, too. They were quite lovely, but big. Not tall but wide, with heavy manes and tails that would drag on the ground, but she had noticed that they kept the tails braided. It kept them clean and easy to deal with. Rowen's Vanners were all pinto, white with spots of brown, chestnut, or black, and very beautiful.

Ellie was early but she did not care. She walked down the path to the old barn. It was a lovely building from another era, when horses and buggies were the only means of transportation. She noticed how clean the area was. The stalls were deep in sweet smelling bedding and three large heads were staring at her with ears pricked. "I'm in here," came a voice from somewhere near the end of the barn.

Ellie put her basket down on a tack trunk and opened the stall door. A brown and white mare was cross-tied to rings in the walls, and Rowen was busy grooming her. "This mare is holding out on me. If she gets any bigger she is going to explode."

"Oh my, she is really big. Dream wasn't nearly so round. She's going to have a big one," Ellie said eyeing the mare's bulging sides.

"It's a colt, I think," Rowen stood up and patted the mare on the neck. "Her name is Gypsy Rose. Rosy meet Ellie. Ellie this is Rosy." The mare nickered, and stretched her neck forward as much as the ties would let her. Ellie offered her a mint from her jean's pocket. She always kept a good supply there to give as treats.

"Well, you've made a friend for life with those. Rosy loves mints."

"I've got half the leftovers from the party last night in a basket. Interested?"

"Interested, I'm starving, as usual. You saw me eat an entire cow last night, and I can probably do it again today," Rowen said laughing. "Ever since I've moved here, I've been eating everything in sight. But then, I'm working harder than I've ever worked before and that's saying something."

"I guess starting a business is hard," Ellie offered. "Just taking care of two horses is a lot of work. I can't imagine how many do you have?"

"We have twelve Gypsy Vanners. We've bought several more horses, of mixed breeding. I could use about three more, but it's hard to find good driving horses. They have to be very gentle and quiet, since they work in the downtown area with all the traffic, people, and sirens. It's just madness. They have to be very special horses to deal with all that. Vanners are quiet, but it has been a challenge. That's for sure."

"Well, I could help some this summer but I think that Jackie needs me to help with the student load, so you might have to toss a coin for me."

"I couldn't take you away from her; she would throw me out and then what would I do?" Rowen was unsnapping the cross-tie lines and she snapped on a lead line. "Grab the basket, and we'll take these guys out to the field to graze." Rowen led the mare out and then opened two other stall doors. "Brute, Sun, let's go. The two horses came walking out and fell in behind Rowen and Rosie.

A startled Ellie jumped back against the wall. The black and white stallion was big and he was so impressive. He looked huge. Ellie was a little bit intimidated by him, but the stallion walked calmly behind the mare; behind him came what had to

213

be his son, a younger, smaller version. They all ambled along calmly.

They sure are well mannered for stallions," Ellie said. "I've not been around stallions before. I always thought that they were dangerous."

"Oh, Rosie would tear Brute apart if he misbehaved, but he wouldn't. Horses properly handled are usually mannerly, stallions included. I'm a horse trainer and have been around them all my life. We know each other."

They were walking along the path that led to the paddocks. Ellie could see Dream and Sophie grazing. Dream looked up when the three horses went by. She nickered softly, and then dropped her head back to the green grass. Sophie ran to the fence and skidded to a halt with her ears up and neck arched. "You're a little treasure," Rowen said. "She does this every time we come by."

Ellie carried the picnic basket and the procession walked down the lane between the paddocks. The mare went into one of the paddocks by herself and the two stallions went into the other. As soon as the two went in, they bounded away. Ellie could almost feel the earth move with their weight as they ran full out around the large grassy area. Rowen and Ellie snapped the gate latch leaned on the fence and watched the two cavort around, wheeling and turning, rearing up in mock battle. The stallions were large and lovely, all grace and power, yet they seemed to know just what to do with each other and neither was trying to hurt the other.

Ellie could see that the older stallion was using play to teach the younger one about being a horse. Much the same as some of the methods used in her school, the young learn by play that mimics real life. She said as much out loud.

Rowen smiled at her, "Horses can be wonderful teachers if we watch them. The mares with their foals, the way a herd interacts, the wisdom of our fellow creatures can teach us a lot about ourselves."

They walked back and opened the gate to Dream and Sophie's paddock. The tree, a large old oak, was almost in the center and was the perfect place to sit in the cool shade. You could see all the other enclosures and watch horses graze, quiet and peaceful. Ellie and Mary often came here to have lunch and talk.

"Okay, let's see what you brought."

Ellie spread a blanket and opened the basket. There was cold potato salad, fresh berries, some of the grilled corn, removed from the cob, mixed with ripe diced tomatoes and green onion. Ellie had sliced up the cold grilled steak. She opened the thermos and filled two plastic cups with cold lemonade.

Rowen had filled a plate, she said. "This is my idea of Heaven. Shade tree, sweet cold lemonade, and steak. Ah, what fun."

Ellie had filled her own plate. She was always hungry. She believed that her new abilities were using a lot of energy, and that was why she was usually starving. That was just another one of the things that she wanted to talk about. However, first she wanted to talk about Phellsome.

"You said you saw the unicorn in the stall the night that Esophia was born?" she asked.

Rowen looked at her sharply, "Yes, yes I did. He startled me, but I knew what he was."

"Well, of course, you knew. The myth of unicorns is pretty universal," Ellie said. "But you didn't seem scared, or anything. You bowed to him!"

"You have to understand, Ellie, I come from a people that believe in things like unicorns and magic. Some of us can tell the future, some of us can talk to animals; some of us can do things that most people don't believe is possible. The Romany people have strong ties to the paranormal. They hear a sort of music that is magic. In my family, there are people that are very strong in that music. One of our, umm, traditions is the ability to communicate with horses. My uncle trained me as a horse whisperer. My mother, her mother, my aunt, all foretell the future. They read the Tarot. They have dreams, or visions. They do things that most people scoff at or don't believe in.

"When I was very young, they found me curled up in a stall with a Vanner stallion. I was sleeping there. They had been searching for hours. When they woke me up, I wondered why they worried. I thought that everyone could talk to horses.

"My uncle was delighted. Our family had always been horse breeders and trainers. He was quite a well-known horse whisperer. He started teaching me, but my mother didn't like it at all."

Ellie was looking at her in awe. At last, someone who knew was saying that there were others. She was neither alone nor crazy. Rowen had actually said music and magic in the same sentence. Rowan had said that she could communicate with horses, and that there was a whole group of people living on this planet that believed in magic.

"You said magic and music. You hear music. You see unicorns," Ellie was excited.

"Well in truth, the unicorn in your stall is the first one I've ever seen. I don't think anyone has seen one in a long time. There is a story told by our family from time before time. It has been handed down for hundreds of years. A beautiful story that tells us about a unicorn that came to the people. My people. He came and stayed among them for a long time. The unicorn lived among the herds of horses. He was a friend of the Romany people.

"From him, we learned more about the use of the talents that we already had. We had never lost the ability to hear the magic that is music. Some see auras, some could see the future, and some talked to horses. He taught us that all is vibration in balance and harmony. Certain energy fields exist; these can be accessed by music. To us it was magic. Then one day he was gone and he did not return. The myth is that when he returns it

216

Music of the Unicorn

will be to help us save our world. That what had been lost would be found," Rowen said.

"I'm beginning to think that I was sent here to be of help to you. My uncle told me once that our family would be called upon to share our knowledge. This sighting of the unicorn the day Sophie was born may mean that the time is near. I don't know anything other than that."

Ellie was looking at Rowen with her wet eyes. "You just don't know what this means to me. For over two years, I've thought that I was losing my mind. I'm different," she paused, "I'm what they call a prodigy child. Do you know what that is?" she looked at Rowen hopefully.

"Well, I've read about children that can do math, or play an instrument, or understand physics at a very early age. Is that what you mean," Rowen asked.

"Yes that's what I mean. I was playing the piano at three, reading, doing math, all at a very early age. I've gone to special schools all my life and now with the start of the dreams and unicorns—all these new things, I thought I might be losing my mind.

"My mother has always supported me, but it was too much for my father and he left us. I feel that I'm the cause of my mother's divorce. So when I started having these strange dreams and painting ghost horses, well, you can see it was cause for concern," Ellie said.

"Well, if you're losing it, then I'm losing it, too," Rowen said, with a smile.

Rowen continued, "My mother wanted me to become a psychic, and to follow in her footsteps. She's quite well known, and has written several books, but I have always been drawn to horses. I thought that everyone could talk to horses for a long time. I was shocked when I found out that it was a gift, just like my mother's ability. Strange, but true.

"I've done some study about people who talk to horses and there aren't many but they seem to be common enough.

Alexander the Great was probably a horse whisperer. They say he rode Bucephalus when no one else could. Humans have a long association with the horse, maybe as long as we've had association with dogs. I don't know if people talk to dogs, but certainly there are people gifted with the ability to understand them."

Ellie was quiet for quite a long time, "I don't want to be different. I don't want to be special. I want to be normal. I want to go to a normal school, do normal things, and ride my horse like the other girls do. I don't want the responsibility for saving the world, if that's what this is about." The litany of her life, and here she was repeating it to an almost complete stranger.

Rowen watched her with alarm. This young girl was so upset. What could she say to her to make her feel safe? She knew what it was like to be different. She had never been normal. Her people had never been normal, whatever that was.

The Gypsy people were always seen as different. They had paid for that difference by being hated, persecuted, and with no place to call their own. The 'people' as they called themselves were treated as outcasts in almost every country in the world. Yet, the Romany had always had their music, and their magic. In her family the enhancement of those gifts were said to come from the unicorn. He had set them apart. They settled down. They stopped traveling and made a place for themselves in the world. However, they had a dangerous secret. The unicorn had brought them a mixed blessing, no doubt about that.

Ellie was still fighting her emotions, the tears kept coming, "I'm sorry," Rowen said. "Sometimes it's just overwhelming. I am so glad that I'm here. This can't be easy for you. Can it?" she paused.

"Well, I know this. The unicorn is real, you are not crazy, and Dream and Sophie are real. What gifts the unicorn has given you have a purpose. Our planet is in trouble. Humankind has taken a wrong turn somewhere. We are killing our planet with our greed and in the process, we are killing ourselves," Rowen said.

"You will help me?" Ellie asked.

"Well, I certainly will try to help you," Rowen answered. "I'm not sure just how much or what you will need from me."

"Just to know that you saw the unicorn. His name is Phellsome by the way. That you can talk to horses. That I'm not alone. You don't know how lonely I've been. Mary, my friend, understands that I can communicate with Dream, but she has no conception of what is going on. No one has a clue. I'm not sure that I have a clue."

"Sometimes it seems as if we are destined to do something with our life. I think that people who have these—callings, let's say, for lack of a better word, seem not to have a choice in what they are doing," Rowen said. "Like me with the horses, and now you with your life being manipulated by forces you don't understand. But, I think we do often have the ability to make choices. We make choices about how we will develop our gifts and how we will use them. Maybe we didn't overtly order the brain we were born with, but how we use it is ours alone," Rowen sighed and became quiet.

"I've got journals that chronicle the dreams that started all this. I've been writing in journals since the time of the divorce. That was several years ago. My mother and I went to counseling together. Then when the dreams started, I continued to write, describing the dreams as they happened. It also tells about my horse, Dream. I'd like you to read those, if you would. It has all the things the unicorn has shown me how to do. It might give you some insight into what's going on."

"I'd be happy to read whatever you want me to read. Are you sure it's not too personal?" Rowen said.

They finished their lunch and headed back to the barn. "Will you stop by my house, and I'll get the journals for you," Ellie said.

"Of course."

When they arrived at the house, Anne was in her office working. She said hello to Rowen and went back into her room. Ellie led Rowen into her bedroom.

Rowen stood there for a moment and looked around. The bedroom was in the front of the house. It was large and there was lots of light coming in from two big windows. There was an easel set up in the front of to windows. It had the feel of an artist's studio. Paints and brushes were on a table and an unfinished work was in progress. A desk, complete with a computer setup, was on another wall. The rest of the space was filled with bookshelves overflowing with books. The bed was a double size with an Amish quilt of appliqued tulips, in bright primary colors. The windows had no curtains, just shades that pulled down.

Rowen took it all in. This did not look like a young girl's room. There were no posters on the wall, no frills, stuffed animals, nothing to indicate a pre-teen's passions and churning emotions.

Ellie moved over and sat down on the edge of the bed. There a nightstand held a lamp, and underneath on shelves were the blue journals lined neatly in a row.

Ellie picked out about seven of them, "These are the ones that contain the dreams. They are chronological. They start with Dream, Sophie's mother. They will fill you in on what's been going on."

Rowen took the journals, "You're sure about this. You don't want to consult your mother?"

"No, she won't mind. These are mine. As you will see, they mostly pertain to the dreams and what happened, how I found Dream. It also tells about Phellsome and what he has given me, the power I've somehow acquired.

"I hope that you can make some sense out of all this. It's just as I remember it happening, usually written right after it happened, or right after I woke up. It won't be very grammatical and there is no attempt at good punctuation. I hope that it will make sense to you. No one else has ever read these journals, not even my mother."

Rowen was watching Ellie. She could tell that Ellie was nervous, she had a small frown between her eyebrows, and her face was white. Rowen knew how hard this was for her. It showed her how much Ellie needed a confidant. She was taking on a real responsibility here.

Ellie needed someone who can help her relate to the magic. Rowen remembered when she was young and different. She thought about how the other kids had looked at her because she was different. Even with her family's support, she felt isolated. Her teachers treated her a bit different from the others. She turned to horses when that happened, just as Ellie was doing now. Horses were what kept it all in perspective, made it okay, made her feel safe.

"I'll read them, I promise. I'm going to help you if I can. I want to be your friend, Ellie. I understand some of what you are telling me and some of what you are going through."

"You've already helped me. Just talking to someone about this, just knowing that someone knows and still thinks I'm sane. That's help, Rowen. That's real help."

Rowen took a small post-it from Ellie's desk and wrote quickly. "Here is my cell phone number. You can call me anytime day or night. Okay?" She handed her the post-it. We'll talk as soon as I've finished these. Have you seen, what's his name, the unicorn, recently?"

"Oh, Phellsome. Phellsome is his name. I was with him last night. It's written down, the last entry. It may be difficult for you to understand it. I'm not sure if it was a dream or it was real. I wrote it down just as I think it happened, but maybe you will be able to help me figure it out. Sometimes, I have these dreams but they feel so real I can get confused," Ellie said.

"I'm in the city all day tomorrow. Gypsy Rose will foal tomorrow or tomorrow night, I can almost count on it. Keep an eye on her for me, will you?" With a smile, she turned to leave.

At that moment, Anne walked out of her office, stopped and stared at the journals in Rowen's arms. "Oh, I didn't know you were still here. You guys have been quiet."

"Ellie wanted to give me these; she wants me to read them. I hope you don't mind?"

Anne was still staring at the journals; she had turned a bit pale, "Well, if Ellie wants you to have them. Then sure, it's fine with me." She turned and walked back into her office without another word.

CHAPTER 32

Rowen was sitting in her bedroom, by a window, with the journals spread out on one side of her bed in easy reach. They were laid out in chronological order. She wanted to get a sense of how the sequences fitted together. How the dreams and events leading up to Dream and Esophia, had played out. Ellie had done a fine job of recording the dreams. They were concise with visual details that only an artist could convey. Rowen felt she knew the valley and had felt some of the mare's loneliness. The journals chronicled an almost unbelievable story.

Rowen grew up living with people who could read the future in cards with undeniable accuracy, see auras, do magical things, but she had never encountered anything like what she was reading in the journals. Her life had been different, but this was almost beyond her ability to understand.

She was tired and it was late, her clock said 3:00am. That would be 4:00am. in New York. Rowen needed to talk to her mother and it was too late to call, but knowing her mother, she would probably get a call in the morning. Sighing, she let her thoughts turn to sleep. She carefully stacked the journals on the desk, and got into bed, turned out the light and settled herself. She let her mind drift to her horses and the barn. All the horses were either sleeping or nibbling on hay. All was well.

She reached for a sliver chain, dangling from the head of a beautiful creamy horse — no, not a horse, for there was a horn in the middle of her forehead. The head was moving and chain was swinging just out of reach. She was lying down on soft grass looking up at a violet sky. The muted colors swirled around and it seemed the very air was alive with vibrations of music so pure it stung her ears.

"Where am I and who are you, lovey"? She asked but with no sound.

"I am Esophia, of Dream by Phellsome", the almost unicorn replied. Again, with no sound, just the filling of the mind with words.

"Where are we, Esophia, of Dream by Phellsome?"

"We are on the planet of the unicorns. Keepers of the Seven Spheres, is it not lovely?"

Rowen sat up and looked around. "It is indeed," she said. "You have grown up. Only today, you were just a tiny foal, Esophia."

"Time is a relative thing Rowen. Just as distance and matter can be manipulated, so can time. I am as I am."

"You are a dream, Esophia," Rowen said.

"Are you sure?" Esophia replied

Rowen thought about that for a while. "No, not sure, you seem real enough, just in a future time."

Esophia stamped a hoof. "Maybe there is no time, Rowen, and all things just happen at the same time, like a stack of conscious thoughts opening and folding closed again."

"My father says you are of the people, that Ellie will need your support, and that I can trust you. Is that true, Rowen?"

"I don't know about that, Esophia. I hope that Ellie can trust me, but I'm not at all sure what is going to be required of me. There can be no promises of trust."

"I've come to you, as I will be when I'm grown up. That will be a while yet but it is better that you see me now, so that you will believe me. The harmonies that should be balanced in all things, the music or magic if you will, have gone awry. The disharmony is like an illness. It affects our earth and all the lives on it. This illness is affecting the balance of the universe.

Suddenly Rowen's head filled with music, but there was a grating quality about it, something that made her teeth hurt. It was nauseous, making her almost ill.

Then her mind filled with images of the Seven Spheres, pulsing with light, in rainbow colors, but the music flowing in had a dark note. It swelled, and became unbearable. Her head could take no more and she screamed.

The noise changed, became the phone ringing.

Half-awake, she reached over and picked up the phone. "Hello," she said, in a sleepy, muffled voice. "Rowen," the voice was soft, but even half asleep Rowen knew her mother's voice. Her mother was Ginna Martinelli, a psychic, an author, and a TV personality. She was used to having her own way.

Rowen rubbed her eyes, still half in that awful dream, with discordant musical notes still ringing in her ears. She was in no shape to talk to her mother. Conversations with her mother should be after coffee, when she had her wits about her. She was not ready for the talk that would come. "Hey, Mom, can I call you right back. I'm still asleep. It was a late night," she said hopefully.

"Are you okay?"

"Of course, I'm okay."

"No, you are not okay!" said the voice.

"Yes, I'm fine. I just want to make some coffee and wake up, I will call you back in five minutes," Rowen retorted, as she firmly she put down the phone. She had known that her mother would call; she should have set the alarm to be ready for her. Yet that dream would have ruined it anyway. Right now, though, she did not have to time to think about the dream. She felt guilty hanging up on her mother.

Oh, how could her mother make her feel so guilty? Every time she talked to her mother on the phone, she felt like she was ten years old, behind the barn smoking a cigarette with Bradley Elmhurst, and getting caught. That picture made her smile, as she climbed out of bed and made her way into the small kitchen of the apartment. She knew she would have to be quick, so she rushed to make the coffee.

Ten minutes later with a coffee cup in hand, she was sitting by the window in the small living area looking out on the pastures. She could hear faintly the horses below eating their breakfast, which is what she wanted to do. She had not had time to process the dream or nightmare her mother had woken her from. Still, there was no way that she could put off this phone call.

She sighed, took a deep breath and dialed the number engraved in her fingers. The phone did not even ring as her mother picked up.

"What took you so long? I've been sitting here biting my fingernails. What is happening out there? Your face appeared in front of me and you were screaming. You looked scared to death. Tell me what's happening," her mother paused to take another breath.

"Nothing is happening here. All is well. I'm fine, the business is fine, but more work than you'd ever want to know. All the horses are fine, except Rosey is still hanging on to her foal and won't get it over with, which has me anxious, that's all. Why, what did you see?"

"Nothing, nothing much, just your face floating in front of me and you were screaming. That is all I saw. Nothing important," she said with a nervous laugh.

"I was having a dream, maybe a nightmare, but I was going to call you this morning anyway. Something has come up here, Mom, something that is very strange. A young girl lives here on the farm and she gave me some journals that she's been writing." Rowen's voice caught as she said, "She's having dreams in which a unicorn is teaching her about magic. Also, there is a foal, which is the offspring of that unicorn. This has to have serious consequences for the families. Don't you think?" Rowen said.

"What? What did you say?"

Rowen took a deep breath and repeated, "Unicorns, mom. You know those white horse-looking things with a single horn in the middle of their forehead."

"Rowen, are you being funny?"

"Er, no Mom, I'm being serious. I saw one in the barn a while back." Rowen's voice had become quiet and slow. "This girl, Ellie, is being visited and taught by a unicorn, and he has a foal by a mare that the girl, Ellie, owns. He was in the stall when the foal was born. There was magic everywhere. I think that he was shielding the mare and foal from the outside world. He was singing the most beautiful and pure harmonies I've ever heard."

Rowen waited for her mother to respond, but there was only silence. "Mom, you there?"

Then her mother spoke, "You know our history, Rowen. Why have you not told me about this? This has to be about something catastrophic. This may be the prophecy. We could all

227

be in danger. At least the prophecies say that. Yet, I've had no warnings, and I don't think there's been anything at the Institute either. I'll call Maiya and Sean, thought they would surely have called me if they knew about this girl and the unicorn.

"Now tell me about this nightmare that woke you up and scared us both. It has to be significant."

Rowen sighed and started to tell her mother the dream. She wished she had been able to write it down. Things got confused after even a short time. She was glad Ellie had written hers down immediately. "Let me see if I can remember all of it," she said.

When she was finished, there was again only silence on the phone. The only sound was her mother breathing. This dream had done what she had never been able to accomplish on her own. It had silenced her mother.

"Mom, are you there?" she asked.

"Mom, did you hear me?"

"Be quiet, Rowen. Just be quiet. Let me call you back. I—I can't talk right now."

The phone went dead. Rowen held the phone out and looked at it. She wondered what had happened.

She started writing the dream down. *Well, looks like I'm starting a journal, too*, she thought wryly. She was writing steadily when her phone rang again.

"Yes, Mom. What was that all about?" Rowen asked.

"I had a 'seeing,' I was getting information so quickly that I couldn't process it fast enough. I just turned on the tape recorder and recorded what I could. You were asking about unicorns before? Well, I think I saw one, too. There were colors like rainbows and pulsing spheres. There was music, beautiful music, then a feeling of terrible danger. No wonder you woke up screaming. Something very important is happening and this is a warning. I want to know more about that disharmonic music, and how it's affecting our planet."

"Yes, that's what I saw, too. Only, I didn't see a unicorn in my dream, but a grown up version of a foal born on the farm."

"Yes, well, I think I saw a unicorn, white with swirling colors. I heard music unlike any music I've heard before. The unicorn told me that your cousin, Denni is coming from Rome. He'll help us sort this out. Whatever it is, it is prophetic. Let me think about this and I will get back to you. Take care, love, I'll call you just as soon as I can," with that her mother hung up.

Rowen's cousin Denni was coming. She remembered him from the few times that she had been at the Institute in Rome and the one whole summer he had spent in New York City. She had just finished school and he had been a young adolescent, talented in music and magic. He was Maiya and Sean's only child. He had been too young for Rowen to have a lot of contact with. He had come to spend time with her mother. She had been working with his training. He was a wonderful violinist and had actually given a few recitals in New York. She had gone to one. He was brilliant.

She sat for a few minutes trying to organize her day. She had a busy schedule, a meeting and two new drivers to interview. The day would be full. She would have to put this aside and get on with her daily routine. Later tonight, she would be able to read more of Ellie's journals. Maybe then, she could start to understand more about Ellie's experience and now her own.

CHAPTER 33

Rowen finished the last journal and slowly put it down. In Ellie's journals were all of the dreams, and all the experiences that had occurred with Phellsome. Entangled throughout ran the continuing theme of music. Ellie had said at one point, 'I must remember the music'. She had even attempted a score, working on the piece she had heard. Ellie had been extremely articulate and her descriptions were meticulous. No wonder the girl was scared. If these journals were true, she had been experiencing an amazing amount of paranormal events.

Rowen was familiar with the paranormal; her family was steeped in it. Yet, in these journals, she was learning of things that were new to her. She had a lot of sympathy for Ellie. Without any support system, without any prior knowledge, this girl was getting a speedy education in the use of music to produce magic.

Just the events leading up to her acquiring Dream, at of all places, a BLM mustang auction was strange enough, and then there was the birth of Esophia, and a list of new abilities that Ellie claimed Phellsome had given her. Ellie had not told her about the shield she had been holding around the newborn foal. Apparently, she still did that. The entry about Phellsome taking Ellie to the valley indicated some form of teleportation. Ellie had not been sure about the reliability of that. She had wondered if it had all been a dream sequence.

Teleporting was something that Rowen had read about but had no experience of, except in her dream about a grown up Sophia. There was something in that dream about time-space, but she would have to look at her notes in order to sort it out. Her abilities related mostly to horses, communicating with them, training them, that sort of thing. She had other talents, but she had resisted her mother's training in those areas. Now she wished that she had at least learned some of what her mother had wanted to teach her.

Rowen wanted to talk to Ellie, to reassure her, mostly, but also she needed to speak to Anne. She was not sure how she would handle that. Anne had been shocked when she saw the journals in her arms. Maybe that would be a place to start the conversation with Anne. She could not tell Ellie's mother about the magic. She could not even talk to her without Ellie's permission.

She looked at the clock; it was another late night. This thing with Ellie was draining her, making her look at things she thought she had gotten away from. She sighed, closed her eyes and went to sleep with visions of white unicorns in her head.

Just two hours, later she came awake with a start. *The phone. No, it isn't.* Groggily she realized it was the foal monitor. *Ah*, she thought, Rosey, *you rascal you. You're foaling at last.* She jumped up and quickly dressed, went down the hall and knocked on Anton's door. "Anton, Anton, wake up! Rosey is foaling; I'm headed to her stall. Answer me, please, so that I know you're awake and coming."

A muffled voice called, "Okay, I'm awake, with you in a minute."

"Good, hurry, she's down already," Rowen hurried on down the stairs knowing that Anton would be there soon.

When she got to the stall, the big mare was lying on her side with her legs straight out. She was rigid with pain. Rowen knew that she was having a contraction.

She was already talking to the horse in a soft soothing voice. "I'm here. I'm coming in." She kept up the talk as she reached down and removed the foal monitor. The mare was sweating and had begun to strain harder. "Good girl," she crooned. "This is a big one, but you're fine, you're doing fine." Rowen said softly. "Doing fine, dear, I'm here and Anton is coming, luv." She was stroking her, letting her know that she was not alone. New life coming into the world was a magic all its own, as many times as she had seen it happen, in dogs, cats, horses, once even a human baby, it amazed her. Gritty and earthy, with pain and danger, life came.

Anton, her wonderful partner and friend, finally hurried into the stall. He had brought clean towels and a bucket of warm water for hand washing.

"Going quickly, I see. Good. It's in the birth canal."

Mares foaled quickly. If they did not there was trouble, big trouble. Foals were born within a twenty to thirty minute period, longer and she would be on the phone looking for medical assistance. Rosey had done this before, so she was not as nervous as a horse foaling for the first time. She calmly pushed with the contraction, and let both Anton and Rowen pet and talk to her.

Suddenly a white bulbous membrane, looking much like a thick balloon appeared under her tail.

"Here we go," Anton said. Like Rowen, he was awed by the foaling process. You could hear it in his voice.

The mare rested a moment and then gave another push. The foal would present with its tiny hooves, then its small head, then the hardest part, the shoulders, after that, it would slide quickly to the deep yellow straw to start a life of its own.

Rowen did not realize she was holding her breath; she caught herself and started to take deep breaths. When a horse was in trouble, or in this case foaling, she became totally involved, listening to all the signals coming from the distressed animal. That was good, but it was a strain.

Anton was kneeling at the back of the mare; he had taken hold of the membrane and split it open to give the foal air. He was holding the legs and wiping the nostrils free of mucus. "Almost there, little one, almost there, come on, Mom, give us a push here."

As if she had heard him, Rosey gathered herself and strained. Anton was helping free the shoulders through the canal and with a swoosh the baby was in the straw.

"Good job, luv, you've got a wonderful baby here." He took a big white towel and started to rub the wet foal, and remove it from the birth sack. Rowen was at the mare's head, crooning to her softly.

"Filly, Rosey, you've got a girl," Anton sounded delighted.

Rowen gave a sigh of relief, she had thought it was a colt, but she had hoped for a black and white filly. She would have been happy with a colt, but a filly was her preference. "What color is she," she asked.

"Hard to say," Anton answered. "She could be black, but she could be seal brown, either way she's a beauty." He had finished drying her off and stood up. He tidied up the area, removing the messiness of birth. Rowen helped him, and then they started to move out of the stall.

Ellie opened it for them, "Oh," she caught her breath, "Oh, she's so beautiful. Oh, look at you, you little darling you." Her eyes were dancing with excitement. "Rosey, what a nice job you did."

"Did you see the whole thing?" Rowen asked. "How did you know?" Then she realized that Ellie had heard the mare's call and had come to the barn, just as Rowen had. She was not used to others being able to talk to them as she did.

233

Rosey was ignoring them all; she was focused on her new baby. She was sitting up and had turned her head to the foal. She had begun to whicker softly to the foal, and was licking the foal's body. This was her way of saying, *Welcome, I'm your mother and I'll take care of you. You are my little one.* The licks and sounds continued as the three humans stood and watched.

"I never get over the awe of a birth," Rowen said.

"Isn't it amazing," Ellie said in a soft voice.

Even Anton was standing there with a quiet smile on his lips. "Went quickly and went well. She looks okay, no problems. She'll be beautiful like her mother," he said, relieved.

They continued to watch, and then Anton went to make some coffee for himself and Rowen and chocolate for Ellie. They sat down on a couple of straw bales to enjoy their drinks.

They talked about foals they had seen born, and how easy this one was. Ellie had only one experience and it had been different from this one. She and Phellsome had somehow joined for the birth of Sophie. She had not really seen the foaling. In fact, she could not remember much about it. It was probably Phellsome's doing. She was happy to see this one.

"Sophie will have a friend to play with, she'll be so delighted," Ellie said.

"Yes, she will, although this one is already bigger than Sophie and will grow faster," Rowen said.

"I'll bet you Sophie will be the leader, though. She's head strong and bossy to humans and her mother," Ellie laughed.

"No doubt about that," Rowen said.

They sat in companionable silence for a while, reliving the miracle of new life. They needed to stay until the foal was up and nursing, then they could safely leave. Rowen and Anton checked on the mare and foal. They foal was making heroic efforts to stand up. They all watched while the baby learned how to use her long legs. It was comical to see her get her front legs stretched out and try to stand up then fall into the soft straw. Her mother was nuzzling her and whickering to her in encouragement. Finally, she got everything right and was standing on her four-stem like legs. Rowen, Anton, and Ellie encouraged her, as she struggled to stay up. After much searching with her small muzzle, she finally made it to the right place for her first meal.

"Well, the show's over. I think we should all get back to bed," Rowen said.

"Yes," said Ellie. "Although I don't think I'll be able to sleep, it was so wonderful.

Anton yawned, bade them both good night, and disappeared up the stairs.

Rowen looked at her watch, "Oh my, it's 4 o'clock! Not much dark left. You'd better get to bed; don't you have to help Jackie in the morning? Well, this morning now?"

"I've got the morning off, our first students are at one this afternoon. I can sleep in, if I'm able, that is." Ellie zipped her jacket and started for the barn door. "Will you be around today?"

"Yeah, the vet will have to come and make sure that mother and daughter are fine, nothing retained or torn. So, Anton will take the carriage horses in today. Poor guy, we'll both be sleep deprived," but she was saying it with a smile. "Talk to you later, Ellie."

CHAPTER 34

Ellie rushed home and quietly went to her room, hoping not to wake her mother. Dancing in her head was a moving picture of the big mare having that tiny, perfect baby. It was more magic than anything she had experienced with Phellsome. This was life, from the beginning of—well, the beginning. A picture kept forming and she grabbed her sketchpad.

Later when Anne came looking for her to see why she had not come out for breakfast, she found Ellie hard at work. There were sketches tacked up on the wall by the easel and she was working away in the early morning light. Anne smiled it was nice to see Ellie working. The sketches were of Rosie with her new foal, both lying in the straw, the mare nuzzling the tiny foal.

"Is that Rowen's mare?" she asked. "Did she foal?"

"Oh, she did, and I was there. It was wonderful. I've never seen anything so amazing," Ellie said.

"I imagine so. I didn't make it in time to see Sophie's birth, but you must have seen the whole thing."

"Well, yes, I guess. It's strange but the incident seems a long time ago. I guess that I was so involved, I don't remember, but this one was beautiful. Both of them are fine, but the vet will be out to check on them today. You should go over and see them. She's a pinto like her mother and about twice the size of Sophie."

"Well she would be, wouldn't she? Those horses are big. That stallion is enormous," Anne said, adding, "Did you get any sleep? Don't you have to help Jackie this afternoon with the students?"

"Yes, I have to help Jackie this afternoon, and, no, I didn't get any more sleep. I came in and started this painting. It was just awesome to see that birth, I'm trying to capture that moment. It is the most natural, beautiful thing I've ever seen.

"I'm not sure if a painting can show the love and acceptance I saw between the mare and the foal. If I can capture that it will be a good picture," Ellie turned back to her canvas.

As Anne watched her daughter turn away, she felt she was losing this child. Ellie was moving into adulthood, becoming her own person. Anne could watch, she could support, but she could not follow. Ellie must grow and develop on her own. Anne wanted to reach out and grab her child, hold her close and protect her, but from what she did not know.

When breakfast was ready, she called Ellie and they both sat down. Ellie was full of the night's excitement and kept up a steady flow of words, all the while stuffing food in her mouth as if she had not eaten in days. As soon as she finished, she left the table and hurried back to her room, continuing to sketch and mix paints.

She was startled when she heard, *are you going to come and take us out? Sophie is anxious to get out of here and so am I.*

Ellie looked at the clock, *I'm so sorry, I'll be right there!* She quickly covered her paints. She had been so focused on her painting that she had forgotten Dream and Esophia. The painting would have to wait. She had responsibilities. She hurried out to the barn.

We have a new addition to the farm this morning, did you know?

Yes, we do. Sophie is so anxious. We want to go see Rosie's new one.

She is so beautiful and she will be someone that you can play with, Sophie. That should make you happy. She will be much bigger than you though, so you better be nice.

Ellie quickly finished her chores and turned Dream and Sophie out. *You won't get to see them today. The vet is coming. You'll have to wait,* she explained to them.

By then, it was time to go to the barn to help with the lessons. She was still thinking about her painting, but there was no time until after evening chores. *Time, time,* she thought, *always time and not enough of it.*

It was late when Ellie came home, and she was tired. Her mother was out on a date with Allen Edwards, and she wanted to work on her painting. It was not going well. Something was missing. She could not get the image that she had seen, that acceptance and caring. She was having trouble transferring that into painting. Looking at the canvas, she was frustrated. She would try again tomorrow. It would come; at least she hoped it would. This stage of a painting was difficult, trying to capture on the canvas a thought, or idea, the emotion of love from a mother to a newborn child. It involved color, spacing, content and a certainty of form, none of which she had now. The canvas taunted her with its stubborn resistance.

The bed invited her tired body, but her mind refused to quiet, she laid there with images of Rosie and her foal. It took a long time for her to drop into a troubled sleep.

CHAPTER 35

Rowen woke with a start; it was early. She could tell from the light coming through the blinds. She was still not sure why she was so suddenly alert; a noise, a dream, she was not sure. Ah, her mother, then the phone rang. *Trouble,* she thought, *I don't need any trouble right now.* Groaning she picked up the insistent phone.

"Hello, mother, how wonderful to hear from you so early in the morning."

"Rowen, dear, don't be sarcastic. I wouldn't be up myself if I hadn't been awakened, too. I had a late night and an early rising. This unicorn thing is heating up. Denni will be here tomorrow, if he can get a flight." Her mother said.

"Denni? Denni will be here tomorrow?" Rowen was not awake. She was having trouble processing her mother's words. "Why will Denni be coming tomorrow?" What's going on?" Rowen was waking up quickly with this news.

"Maiya and I just got off the phone. They have had a visitation from the unicorn, too. All three of them. Denni, Maiya and Sean. The unicorn told them that Denni was to come to the States, that he was needed here now. So, he's coming. Of course, he's coming."

"Why would Phellsome want Denni, here so quickly? Phellsome, that's the unicorn's name, by the way," Rowen said.

"Nothing here is making sense. I've not talked to Denni but I know he will want to come to your farm. That seems to be where everything is happening. The unicorn, Phellso, phellso, whatever his name is, wants him to meet the girl," Rowen's mother said.

Maiya was also involved; her mother's sister would make it even more convoluted. Her mother and her aunt together were even more formidable. Rowen could hardly believe what she was hearing. This was getting out of hand. Things were happening too fast for her to follow.

"I wanted to tell you that I have booked a flight for Saturday afternoon. We will be flying in to O'Hare, and I've made a reservation at a small bed and breakfast in your area. No need to pick us up as we're renting a car." Ginna said firmly.

"What? You are coming the day after tomorrow? That is such short notice, I've got work tonight and we have a new foal. This is too fast, Mom. This girl is young and very afraid, if we close in on her, she may panic. I don't see how that would help with anything. I'll talk to Ellie. She's the girl. She knows so very little about our family. She's just beginning to trust me. I'm not sure how she will take this invasion of her privacy. This is very new to her. She may not want to meet with you two. Another thing, her mother is very uncomfortable with all that's going on, and your and Denni's interest may frighten her. If Ellie or her mother refuses to see you, then you'll just have to wait."

"Denni is a very talented young man. He will be able to handle the girl. Anyway, the unicorn is involved. He will be in charge here."

Rowen was exasperated, "Well, come if you must. I should be at the farm all day. Anton and I alternate taking the horses in to the city, so that we can get some time to ourselves. I'll leave a message and directions at your bed and breakfast. What's the name?"

"The Crossing, in Morton Grove," she gave Rowen the number and hung up.

Rowen had her own resistance to her mother and Denni coming to the farm. She had tried to turn her back on the teachings of the Institute, but she was a direct descendant of Adrienne, the seer, and that made it hard. Certain things were expected of the women of her line. She had spent a summer in Rome with her aunt Maiya, taking a crash course in the teaching of how music opens the door to magic. Yet, she had resisted the teaching and had been very reluctant to learn. Now, she felt out of her depth, and wished she had been more receptive. What a mess.

Rowen had followed in her uncle's footsteps. He had been resistant to the use of any magic other than what pertained to his beloved horses. He was a renowned horseman and had been charge of the horses and stables that the families still maintained on the continent and in Kentucky. Rowen had loved her uncle; he had been all the teacher she wanted. She had learned from her mother, mostly by association but she had not wanted to be like her. Some of her mothers' abilities frightened her. Horses had always been a safe space for her. Rowen wondered how she was going to tell Ellie about her mother and Denni.

What would Ellie think of this young man coming to see her? Would she think that Rowen had told her mother the content of the journals? She closed her eyes and shuddered. Ellie would think what she would think. Rowen could do nothing about it; her mother was a force of nature. It would be as her mother and Phellsome wanted it to be. In the meantime, she should go see their new addition, and let Rosie and her beautiful, strong, and healthy filly out into the sunshine. Rosey had done herself proud. Rowen could at least have this one beautiful day. This might be the last normal beautiful day in quite a while.

EPILOGUE

Thank you for reading *Music of the Unicorn*. I sincerely hope that you enjoyed meeting Ellie and Dream. I have put the first chapter of Book 2, *Ellie's Music* on the next page. Please read it. If you would like to follow Ellie, Dream and Esophia on this journey, Book 2 will be available in 2018.

To contact me and read updates, please go to www.gloriaconly.com. I would love to hear from you. Also, I would appreciate it so much if you would take time to review the book.

The horse with me in my photo on the website is Annie, a Morgan mare. I've owned her all her life, and her mother before her. Dream is totally based on all the beautiful horses I've been privileged to know in my life.

Thank you,

Gloria Conly

Book 2: Ellie's Music

CHAPTER 1

The darkness was complete. There were no points of reference, and he was afraid. He sensed that his body still lay in his bed, but there was nothing other than the sense of touch to tell him for sure. What was it that had brought him awake? What had made that terrible chill that had his teeth chattering? He was frozen in the position of sleep, but warning bells were going off in his brain.

Then he saw a pinpoint of light at the foot of his bed and slowly it began to get larger and take shape. What was this? He was in his bed inside the Institute. Here strange things could happen. He tried to move but was still held in the vice of what he hoped was sleep. Denni reached out with his mind, and touched another, but it was not a human mind. He had never touched such a mind before. Just then, he was flooded with music, colors and then speech.

Denni, you are awake. Listen carefully. My name is Phellsome. I come from the Spheres. It was my father, Somet, who came to your people a long time ago. He taught them many things. I have come to you because I need you and your people.

Denni was fully awake now, and that pinpoint of light had grown into a unicorn. Denni knew about unicorns, according to his Romany ancestors a unicorn had come and taught them about magic. The unicorn had taught them that magic could be made from the vibrations of musical notes. Seeing the unicorn proved the stories were true. Yet, he had no time to think about any of that. The unicorn was again in his mind. He tried to shield himself but his magic was nothing to what this unicorn could do.

You must go to New York City as soon as possible. I've told your aunt to expect you. I've also informed your parents of this. There is a girl, very special girl, she needs your help. *Your aunt will help you find her. It is time now for the world to experience the music that is magic.* Then he was gone.

By now Denni knew what was going on, or at least he was awake and thinking. A unicorn, named—What? Ah, Phellsome, that's it. Phellsome, son of who? The unicorn of the myth. In his mind he could still see the residue of brilliant color shimmering where the unicorn had been, and hear the lingering sound of music in the air.

Denni was still processing what the unicorn had told him. *The world needs to experience the music that is magic. The world, does that mean that years of secrecy are coming to an end? That's exactly what it sounded like. How would the Institute and the three families deal with that? Exposure would threaten their existence. So many years of learning and teaching the talented to wield the music and make magic. He looked around the room and found that it was unchanged. He was in his bedroom, in the Institute. Nothing was changed, yet nothing could ever be the same again. Centuries of silence, evasion, and secrets, a whole little world of keeping everyone in ignorance, was about to come to an end. How could he be of help with that?*

Denni had been raised and trained along with all the students at the Institute to keep silence on all subjects pertaining to the use of magic. The very deepest secrets of the training were only for a few. It was dangerous to let anyone know about their use. Very dangerous.

Just then his door burst open and both his parents rushed in. Down the hall there was the incessant ringing of a telephone, ringing, ringing. "Well, I guess the news is out." Denni sat up in his bed and greeted both his parents.

"Did he speak to you? What did he say? We just had a visit from a—a unicorn," Denni's father, Sean, was quivering with excitement. His mother, Maiya, was pale and trembling beside him.

"Yes, I had a visit from a unicorn. At first I thought it was a dream, but then I knew that what I was seeing and hearing was indeed a unicorn. The first sighting in centuries. At least that we know of. We should have known after a century of nothing but war, weapons, starving people, genocide. You name it, and we had it last century. The world is in a mess," Denni said.

"Well, what did he say?" demanded his father.

"He said I had to go to New York City. There was a girl there that needed my help. He said that it was time—"

"Time. Time for what?"

"I'm trying to tell you. He said there was a girl who needed my help. Then he said it was time for the world to hear the music that was magic. No, that's not right." Denni frowned, trying to remember the exact phrasing. "Ah, okay, now I've got it. He said it is time for the world to experience the music that is magic. Yes, experience, that was it."

"It's time. It's really time to tell the world about the, the— the Institute! I don't think that's possible. No, no it's not possible," his father said, but Maiya was silent. Sean seeing his wife so quiet, slipped his arm around her, pulling her close.

"He didn't say tell, he said experience, there is a difference, I think," Denni replied.

His father was quiet. He was still holding Maiya close. Denni could see the deep bond between his parents. They were like two halves of a whole. His Irish, redheaded, burly, father and his petite, dark haired, beauty of a mother. He was their meeting point, the place where the two had come together to create a son. He had his father's red hair, but darker, and his mother's black eyes, which could soften with emotion, or shoot black fire when aroused. He was tall, but slim, a refined mix of both his parents. He shook off his musing. He had no time now for this.

He was seeing things with a clarity that he knew was the unicorn's doing. This was the ending of one time and the beginning of another. When there was change, there was uncertainty. The secrecy of the Institute had hidden their true purpose for so long. Now that was going to end. He felt his mother's terror. From the beginning, secrecy had been their salvation. During centuries of religious persecution of anything magical or even different, they had survived behind the guise of music. Now the unicorn was saying, *NO MORE*.

The families would be coming out from behind their curtain of normalcy. They would be exposed for what they really were, workers of magic, manipulators of time and space. The world had not changed. It seemed that all the advances in technology and science, the knowledge of how humans thought and their bodies worked, that we humans had made, we were always returning to a fear of each other, buried so deep within that we seldom were truly aware of it. Denni shook his head to clear it.

Denni became aware of the ringing phone, "Mom, you better answer that, it's your sister, and she won't go away."

His mother was still in her husband's arms, looking smaller than Denni had ever seen her before. At this moment she didn't look like the matriarchal head of the Institute. She looked vulnerable and unsure. It sent chills up his spine. At nineteen, he was not yet ready to see the reality that his parents were not infallible, that they were just human. Denni was facing one of the many insights that would make him an adult.

His mother left to answer the phone that was ringing in the hall. She had not said another word.

"One would think that with all our knowledge and skill, we would be prepared for this," Sean said. "After all, it was the unicorn that started us on this path. The unicorn that persuaded the seer Maria to let him stay and teach them the reality of what their music really was."

"You know, Dad, I had no control, no control at all. It was weird. There was a brilliant beam of white light, and clear musical tones, then the unicorn was just there. The voice just came into my head. I had no control, no shield to keep it out." Denni was now up and looking for a robe. "Was that how you saw him, is that how he appeared to you?"

"I think the music was what woke me up, a piano playing a piece that I didn't know. My mind was trying to identify it, and I came awake. Maiya was sitting on the edge of the bed, with her head down, and there he was, vibrating with the music. She looked around at me, and seeing I was awake said: *We have a visitor, Sean. T*hen he started to speak into my mind. You know the rest," Sean looked over at his son, "This is something that we have been preparing for since Maria and the unicorn Somet first came together. In the lore, Somet tells us that when we see a unicorn again it will be a time of great danger and change," he looked gravely at his son. "Well, we've seen a unicorn again.

My guess is, that it will be just what Somet said, *a time of great danger and change.* At the very least this new unicorn managed to wake up the two most powerful people on the planet, your mother, and her sister, your aunt Ginna," Sean smiled, trying to lighten the mood. "This is going to be an earthquake of surprising proportions. I hope we can survive it. This unicorn, Phellsome, better have the wisdom to keep the structures from crumbling down and burying us," Sean's voice was grave.

There were going to be a lot of changes, for Denni, his family, and the Institute, It seemed that he and Phellsome would be in the middle of it. His life had just taken a turn onto an unknown path and the security he had grown up in was coming to a close. He was on a journey that would be steeped in magic and, maybe, danger.

ABOUT THE AUTHOR

Gloria Conly is a poet and novelist whose writing is heavily influenced by her Native American, Choctaw heritage, residing now in Northern California. Her love of all horses and the Morgan breed in particular is a lifelong passion, and she has been fortunate to have them as her life's work. Her day camps were a learning experience for the students and for herself. Through this work, she became aware of the great benefit that horses can give us in today's complex world. She has always been a writer and lover of the written word. Now she spends her time writing, teaching, riding, and being the slave of two Pomeranians, which brings new meaning to living a dog's life.

74236679R00158